It's the *perfect* season...
for a *little* indiscretion.

GRIFFIN

D1041111

The shock of discovering someone so close when Daisy had thought she was alone caused her heart to skip a beat . . .

"Forgive me," he said in a low voice, "I didn't mean to frighten you."

"Oh, you didn't frighten me," she lied cheerfully, her pulse still off-kilter. "I was just a bit . . . surprised."

"I arrived at the estate a couple of hours ago. They said you were out here walking."

He seemed rather familiar. He was looking at Daisy as if he expected her to know him . . . Daisy regarded him with confusion. She couldn't imagine how she could have forgotten a man this attractive. His features were strong and decisively formed. And his eyes were a rich sky-blue . . .

Suddenly, Daisy realized who he was. Her knees nearly gave way beneath her. "*You*," she whispered, her eyes wide with astonishment as she beheld the face of Matthew Swift.

The man her father demanded she marry.

By Lisa Kleypas

SCANDAL IN SPRING
DEVIL IN WINTER • IT HAPPENED ONE AUTUMN
SECRETS OF A SUMMER NIGHT
AGAIN THE MAGIC • WORTH ANY PRICE
LADY SOPHIA'S LOVER • ONLY IN YOUR ARMS
ONLY WITH YOUR LOVE • WHEN STRANGERS MARRY
SUDDENLY YOU • WHERE DREAMS BEGIN
SOMEONE TO WATCH OVER ME
STRANGER IN MY ARMS • BECAUSE YOU'RE MINE
SOMEWHERE I'LL FIND YOU
PRINCE OF DREAMS • MIDNIGHT ANGEL
DREAMING OF YOU • THEN CAME YOU

And the Anthologies

WHERE'S MY HERO?
THREE WEDDINGS AND A KISS

Lisa KLEYPAS

Scandal in Spring

AVON BOOKS
An Imprint of HarperCollinsPublishers

This is a work of fiction. Names, characters, places, and incidents are products of the author's imagination or are used fictitiously and are not to be construed as real. Any resemblance to actual events, locales, organizations, or persons, living or dead, is entirely coincidental.

AVON BOOKS
An Imprint of HarperCollins*Publishers*
10 East 53rd Street
New York, New York 10022-5299

First Avon Books paperback printing: August 2006

Avon Trademark Reg. U.S. Pat. Off. and in Other Countries, Marca Registrada, Hecho en U.S.A.
HarperCollins® is a registered trademark of HarperCollins Publishers Inc.

Printed in the U.S.A.

10 9 8 7 6 5 4 3 2 1

Prologue

"I have made a decision about Daisy's future," Thomas Bowman announced to his wife and daughter. "Although Bowmans never like to admit defeat, we cannot ignore reality."

"What reality is that, Father?" Daisy asked.

"You are not meant for the British peerage." Frowning, Bowman added, "Or perhaps the peerage isn't meant for you. I have received a poor rate of return on my investment in your husband-seeking. Do you know what that means, Daisy?"

"I'm an underperforming stock?" she guessed.

One would never guess Daisy was a grown woman of twenty-two at this moment. Small, slim, and dark-haired, she still had the agility and exuberance of a child when other women her age had already become sober young matrons. As she sat with her knees drawn up, she looked like an abandoned china doll in the corner of the settee. It annoyed Bowman to see his daughter holding a book in her lap with a finger stuck between its pages to mark her place. Obviously she could hardly wait for him to finish so she could resume reading.

"Put that down," he said.

"Yes, Father." Covertly Daisy opened the book to check the page number and set it aside. The small gesture rankled Bowman. Books, books . . . the mere sight of one had come to represent his daughter's embarrassing failure on the marriage market.

Puffing on a massive cigar, Bowman sat in an overstuffed chair in the parlor of the hotel suite they had occupied for more than two years. His wife Mercedes perched on a spindly cane-backed chair nearby. Bowman was a stout, barrel-shaped man, as bullish in his physical dimensions as he was in his disposition. Although he was bald on top, he possessed a thick broom of a mustache, as if all the energy required for growing the hair on his head had been diverted to his upper lip.

Mercedes had begun marriage as an uncommonly slender girl and had become even thinner through the years, like a cake of soap that had gradually worn to a sliver. Her slick black hair was always severely restrained, her sleeves tightly fitted to wrists so diminutive that Bowman could have snapped them like birch twigs. Even when she sat perfectly still, as she was doing now, Mercedes gave the impression of nervous energy.

Bowman had never regretted choosing Mercedes as a wife—her steely ambition corresponded perfectly with his own. She was a relentless woman, all sharp angles, always pushing to make a place for the Bowmans in society. It was Mercedes who had insisted that since they could not break into the Knickerbocker set in New York, they would bring the girls to England. "We shall simply go over their heads," she had said with determination. And by God, they had succeeded with his older daughter Lillian.

Lillian had somehow managed to catch the greatest prize of all, Lord Westcliff, whose pedigree was pure gold. The earl had been a handsome acquisition for the family. But now Bowman was impatient to return to America. If Daisy were going to land a titled husband she would have done so by now. Time to cut their losses.

Reflecting on his five children, Bowman wondered how it was that they should have so little of him in them. He and Mercedes were both driven, and yet they had produced three sons who were so placid, so accepting of things as they were, so certain that everything they wanted would simply drop into their hands like ripe fruit from a tree. Lillian was the only one who seemed to have inherited a little of Bowman's aggressive spirit . . . but she was a woman and therefore it was a complete waste.

And then there was Daisy. Of all their children, Daisy had always been the one Bowman had understood the least. Even as a child Daisy had never drawn the right conclusions from the stories he told, only asked questions that never seemed relevant to the point he had been trying to make. When he had explained why investors who wanted low risk and moderate returns should put their capital into national debt shares, Daisy had interrupted him by asking, "Father, wouldn't it be wonderful if hummingbirds had tea parties and we were small enough to be invited?"

Throughout the years Bowman's efforts to change Daisy had been met with valiant resistance. She liked herself the way she was and therefore trying to do anything with her was like attempting to herd a swarm of butterflies. Or nailing jelly to a tree.

Since Bowman had been driven half-mad by his daughter's unpredictable nature, he was not at all surprised by the lack of men willing to take her on for a lifetime. What kind of mother would she be, prattling about fairies sliding down rainbows instead of drilling sensible rules into her children's heads.

Mercedes jumped into the conversation, her voice taut with consternation. "Dear Mr. Bowman, the season is far from over. I am of the opinion that Daisy has made excellent progress so far. Lord Westcliff has introduced her to several promising gentlemen, all of whom are exceedingly interested in the prospect of gaining the earl as a brother-in-law."

"I find it telling," Bowman said darkly, "that the lure for these 'promising gentlemen' is to gain Westcliff as a brother-in-law rather than to gain Daisy as a wife." He pinned Daisy with a hard stare. "Are any of these men likely to offer for you?"

"She has no way of knowing—" Mercedes argued.

"Women always know such things. Answer, Daisy—is there a possibility of bringing any of these gentlemen up to scratch?"

His daughter hesitated, a troubled expression appearing in her tip-tilted dark eyes. "No, Father," she finally admitted frankly.

"As I thought." Lacing his thick fingers together over his midriff, Bowman regarded the two quiet women authoritatively. "Your lack of success has become inconvenient, daughter. I mind the unnecessary expense of gowns and fripperies . . . I mind the tedium of carting you from unproductive ball to another. More than that, I mind that this venture has kept me in England when I am needed in New York. Therefore I have decided to choose a husband for you."

Daisy looked at him blankly. "Whom do you have in mind, Father?"

"Matthew Swift."

She stared at him as if he had gone mad.

Mercedes drew a quick breath. "That makes no sense, Mr. Bowman! No earthly sense! There would be no advantage for us or for Daisy in such a match. Mr. Swift is not an aristocrat, nor is he possessed of significant wealth—"

"He is one of the Boston Swifts," Bowman

countered. "Hardly a family one can turn its nose up at. A good name and good blood to go with it. More importantly, Swift is devoted to me. And he has one of the ablest business minds I've ever encountered. I want him as a son-in-law. I want him to inherit my company when the time comes."

"You have three sons who will inherit the company as their birthright!" Mercedes said in outrage.

"None of them gives a damn about the business. They haven't the appetite for it." Thinking of Matthew Swift, who had flourished under his tutelage for almost ten years, Bowman felt a pang of pride. The boy was more a reflection of Bowman than his own offspring. "None of them has the full-blooded ambition and ruthlessness of Swift," Bowman continued. "I will make him the father of my heirs."

"You've taken leave of your senses!" Mercedes cried hotly.

Daisy spoke in a calm tone that neatly undercut her father's bluster. "I should point out that my co-operation is necessary in this matter. Especially now that we've progressed to the subject of begetting heirs. And I assure you, no power on earth would compel me to bear the children of a man I don't even like."

"I should think you'd want to be of some use to someone," Bowman growled. It had always been his nature to quash rebellion with overwhelming force. "I should think you would want a husband and home of your own rather than continue your parasitic existence."

Daisy flinched as if he had slapped her. "I'm not a parasite."

"Oh? Then explain to me how the world has benefitted from your presence in it. What have you ever done for anyone?"

Faced with the task of justifying her existence, Daisy stared at him stonily and remained silent.

"This is my ultimatum," Bowman said. "Find a suitable husband by the end of May, or I will give you to Swift."

Chapter 1

"*I shouldn't tell you about it,*" Daisy railed, pacing back and forth in the Marsden parlor later that evening. "In your condition you shouldn't be distressed. But I can't keep it to myself or I will explode, which you would probably find infinitely more distressing."

Her older sister lifted her head from Lord Westcliff's supportive shoulder. "Tell me," Lillian said, swallowing against another wave of nausea. "I'm distressed only when people keep things from me." She was half-reclining on the long settee, settled in the crook of Westcliff's arm as he spooned some lemon ice into her mouth. She closed her eyes as she swallowed, her dark lashes resting in spiky crescents against her pale cheeks.

"Better?" Westcliff asked gently, swabbing a stray drop near the corner of her lips.

Lillian nodded, her face ghastly white. "Yes, I think it's helping. Ugh. You had better pray for a boy, Westcliff, because this is your only chance at an heir. I'm never going through this again—"

"Open your mouth," he said, and fed her more flavored ice.

Ordinarily Daisy would have been touched by the glimpse into the Westcliffs' private life . . . it was rare that anyone saw Lillian so vulnerable, or Marcus so gentle and concerned. But Daisy was so distracted by her own problems that she barely noticed their interaction as she blurted out, "Father has given me an ultimatum. Tonight he—"

"Wait," Westcliff said quietly, adjusting his hold on Lillian. As he eased his wife to her side, she leaned more heavily on him, one slender white hand coming to rest on the curve of her belly. He murmured something indecipherable into her rumpled ebony hair, and she nodded with a sigh.

Anyone who witnessed Westcliff's tender care of his young wife could not help but take note of the outward changes in the earl, who had always been known as a cold-natured man. He had become far more approachable—he smiled more, laughed more—and his standards for proper behavior had become far less exacting. Which was a good thing if one wished to have Lillian for a wife and Daisy for a sister-in-law.

Westcliff's eyes, so deep a shade of brown they appeared black, narrowed slightly as he focused on Daisy. Although he didn't say a word, Daisy read in his gaze the desire to shield Lillian from anyone and anything that might disturb her peace.

Suddenly Daisy felt ashamed for having rushed over here to recount the injustices dealt by her father. She should have kept her problems to herself and instead she had run to her older sister like a tattling child. But then Lillian's brown eyes opened, and they were warm and smiling, and a thousand childhood memories danced in the air between them like jubilant fireflies. The intimacy of sisters was something not even the most protective husband could disrupt.

"Tell me," Lillian said, nestling against Westcliff's shoulder, "what did the ogre say?"

"That if I don't find someone to marry by the end of May he would choose a husband for me. And guess who that is? Just guess!"

"I can't imagine," Lillian said. "Father doesn't approve of anyone."

"Oh, yes he does," Daisy replied ominously. "There is one person in the world Father approves of *one hundred percent*."

Now even Westcliff was beginning to look interested. "It is someone with whom I am acquainted?"

"You will be soon," Daisy said. "Father sent for him. He'll be arriving at the Hampshire estate next week for the stag-and-hind hunt."

Westcliff riffled through his memory for the names Thomas Bowman had asked him to include on the guest list for the spring hunt. "The American?" he asked. "Mr. Swift?"

"*Yes.*"

Lillian stared at Daisy blankly. Then she turned her face into Westcliff's shoulder with a squeaky gasp. At first Daisy feared she might be crying, but it quickly became apparent that Lillian was giggling helplessly. "No . . . not really . . . how absurd . . . you could never . . ."

"You wouldn't find it so amusing if *you* were supposed to marry him," Daisy said with a scowl.

Westcliff glanced from one sister to the other. "What is wrong with Mr. Swift? From what your father has indicated he seems a respectable enough fellow."

"Everything is wrong with him," Lillian said, giving a last snort of laughter.

"But your father esteems him," Westcliff said.

"Oh," Lillian scoffed, "Father's vanity is flattered by the way Mr. Swift strives to emulate him and hangs onto his every word."

The earl considered her words while he spooned up more lemon ice and pressed it to Lillian's lips. She made a sound of pleasure as the frosty liquid trickled down her throat.

"Is your father incorrect in his claim that Mr. Swift is intelligent?" Westcliff asked Daisy.

"He is intelligent," she admitted. "But one can't have a conversation with him—he asks thousands of questions, and he absorbs everything one says but gives nothing back."

"Perhaps Swift is shy," Westcliff said.

Now Daisy couldn't help laughing. "I assure you, my lord, Mr. Swift is *not* shy. He's—" She paused, finding it difficult to put her thoughts into words.

Matthew Swift's bred-in-the-bone coldness was accompanied by an insufferable air of superiority. One could never tell him anything—he knew it all. Since Daisy had grown up in a family populated with uncompromising natures, she'd had little use for yet one more rigid and argumentative person in her life.

In her opinion it didn't speak well for Swift that he blended in so well with the Bowmans.

Perhaps Swift would have been more tolerable had there been anything charming or attractive about him. But he had been blessed with no softening grace of character or form. No sense of humor, no visible displays of kindness. He was awkwardly formed to boot: tall and disproportionate, and so wiry that his arms and legs seemed to have all the substance of stringbeans. She remembered the way his coat had seemed to hang from his wide shoulders as there was nothing inside it.

"Rather than list all the things I don't like about him," Daisy said finally, "it's far easier to say there is no reason why I *should* like him."

"He's not even attractive," Lillian added. "He's

a bag of bones." She patted Westcliff's muscular chest in silent praise of his powerful physique.

Westcliff looked amused. "Does Swift possess *any* redeeming feature?"

Both sisters considered the question. "He has nice teeth," Daisy finally said grudgingly.

"How would you know?" Lillian asked. "He never smiles!"

"Your assessment of him is severe," Westcliff remarked. "But Mr. Swift may have changed since you last saw him."

"Not so much that I would ever consent to marry him," Daisy said.

"You won't have to marry Swift if you don't wish it," Lillian said vehemently, stirring in her husband's grasp. "Isn't that right, Westcliff?"

"Yes, love," he murmured, smoothing her hair back from her face.

"And you won't let Father take Daisy away from me," Lillian insisted.

"Of course not. Something can always be negotiated."

Lillian subsided against him, having absolute faith in her husband's abilities. "There," she mumbled to Daisy. "No need to worry . . . see? Westcliff has everything . . ." She paused to yawn widely. ". . . well in hand . . ."

Seeing the way her sister's eyelids drooped, Daisy smiled sympathetically. She met Westcliff's gaze over Lillian's head, and motioned that she would leave. He responded with a courteous nod, his attention returning compulsively to Lillian's drowsy face. And Daisy couldn't help but wonder if any man would ever stare at her in such a way, as if the weight of her was precious in his arms.

Daisy was certain that Westcliff would try to help her in any way he could, if only for Lillian's sake. But her faith in the earl's influence was tempered by the knowledge of her own father's inflexible will.

Although she would defy him with every means at her disposal, Daisy had a bad feeling the odds were not in her favor.

She paused at the threshold of the room and looked back at the pair on the settee with a troubled frown. Lillian had fallen fast asleep, her head centered heavily on Westcliff's chest. As the earl met Daisy's unhappy gaze, one of his brows raised in silent inquiry.

"My father . . ." Daisy began, then bit her lip. This man was her father's business partner. It was not appropriate to run to Westcliff with complaints. But the patience in his expression encouraged her to continue. "He called me a parasite," she said, keeping her voice soft to avoid disturbing Lillian. "He asked me to tell him how the world has benefitted from my existence, or what I had ever done for anyone."

"And your reply?" Westcliff asked.

"I . . . couldn't think of anything to say."

Westcliff's coffee-colored eyes were unfathomable. He made a gesture for her to approach the settee, and she obeyed. To her astonishment, he took her hand in his and gripped it warmly. The usually circumspect earl had never done such a thing before.

"Daisy," Westcliff said gently, "most lives are not distinguished by great achievements. They are measured by an infinite number of small ones. Each time you do a kindness for someone or bring a smile to his face, it gives your life meaning. Never doubt your value, little friend. The world would be a dismal place without Daisy Bowman in it."

Few people would argue that Stony Cross Park was one of the most beautiful places in England. The Hampshire estate sustained an infinite variety of terrain from near-impenetrable forests to brilliantly flowered wet meadows and bogs to the stalwart honey-colored stone manor on a bluff overlooking the Itchen river.

Life flourished everywhere, pale shoots springing from the carpet of decayed leaves at the foot of fissured oaks and cedar, stands of bluebells glowing in a darker part of the forest.

Red grasshoppers vaulted through meadows filled with wild primrose and lady's-smock, while translucent blue damselflies hovered over the intricately cut white petals of bog bean flowers. It smelled like spring, the air saturated with the scent of sweet box hedge and tender green lawn.

After a twelve-hour carriage ride that Lillian described as a journey through hell, the Westcliffs,

Bowmans, and assorted guests were gratified to reach Stony Cross Park at last.

The sky was a different color in Hampshire, a softer blue, and the air was filled with blissful quiet. There were no clangs of wheels and hooves on paved streets, or vendors or beggars, or factory whistles, or any of the commotion that constantly assaulted the ears in town. Here there was only the chirping of robins in the hedgerows, the rattle of green woodpeckers among the trees, and the occasional dart of kingfishers from the sheltering river reeds.

Lillian, who had once considered the country deadly dull, was overjoyed to be back at the estate. She thrived in the atmosphere of Stony Cross Park, and after her first night at the manor she looked and felt much better than she had in weeks. Now that Lillian's pregnancy could no longer easily be concealed by high-waisted gowns, she was entering confinement, which meant she could no longer go out in public. On her own estate, however, Lillian would have relative freedom, though she would restrict her interactions with the guests to small groups.

To Daisy's delight she was installed in her favorite bedroom in the manor. The lovely, quaint room had once belonged to Lord Westcliff's sister Lady Aline, who now resided in America with her husband and son. The most charming feature of the bedroom was the tiny attached cabinet room that had been brought over from France and reassembled. It had originally come from a seventeenth-century chateau and had been fitted with a chaise that was perfect for napping or reading.

Curled with one of her books in a corner of the chaise, Daisy felt as if she were hidden from the rest of the world. Oh, if only she could stay here at Stony Cross and live with her sister forever! But even as the thought occurred to her she knew she would never be completely happy that way. She wanted her own life . . . her own husband, her own children.

For the first time in Daisy's memory she and her mother had become allies. They were united in their desire to prevent a marriage with the odious Matthew Swift.

"That wretched young man," Mercedes had exclaimed. "I've no doubt he put the entire blasted notion in your father's head . . . I've always suspected he . . ."

"Suspected what?" Daisy asked, but her mother only clamped her lips together until they formed a bitter hyphen.

As Mercedes pored over the guest list, she informed Daisy that a great number of eligible gentlemen were staying at the manor. "Even if they aren't all directly in line for titles, they are from noble families," Mercedes said. "And one never knows . . . Sometimes disaster occurs . . . fatal illness or large accidents. Several members of the family could be wiped out at once and then your husband could become a peer by default!" Looking hopeful at the thought of a calamity befalling Daisy's future in-laws, Mercedes pored more closely over her list.

Daisy was impatient for Evie and St. Vincent to appear later in the week. She missed Evie dreadfully, especially since Annabelle was occupied with her baby and Lillian was too slow-moving to accompany her on the brisk walks she enjoyed.

On the third day after her arrival in Hampshire, Daisy set out by herself for an afternoon tromp. She took a well-worn path she had traversed on many previous visits. Wearing a pale blue muslin dress printed with flowers, and a pair of sturdy walking boots, she swung a straw bonnet by its ribbons.

Striding along a sunken road past wet meadows brilliant with yellow celandine and red sundew, Daisy considered her problem.

Why was it so hard for her to find a man?

It wasn't as if she didn't want to fall in love with someone. In fact, she was so open to the idea that it seemed monstrously unfair not to have found someone by now. She had tried! But there always was something wrong.

If a gentleman was the right age, he was passive or pompous. If he was kind and interesting, he was either old enough to be her grandfather or he had some off-putting problem such as being perpetually malodorous or spitting in her face when he talked.

Daisy knew she was not a great beauty. She was too small and slight, and although she had been praised for her dark eyes and brown-black hair set against her fair complexion, she had also heard the words "elfin" and "impish" applied to herself far too many times. Elfin women did not attract suitors in anything close to the quantities that statuesque beauties or pocket Venuses did.

It had also been remarked that Daisy spent far too much time with her books, which was probably true. Had she been allowed, Daisy would have spent most of every day reading and dreaming. Any sensible peer would doubtless conclude that she would not be a useful wife in the matters of household management, including those duties that hinged on close attention to detail. And the peer would be correct in this assumption.

Daisy couldn't have cared less about the contents of the larder or how much soap to order for laundry day. She was far more interested in novels and poetry and history, all of which inspired long flights of fancy during which she would stare through a window at nothing . . . while in her imagination she went on exotic adventures, traveled on magic carpets, sailed across foreign oceans, searched for treasure on tropical islands.

And there were thrilling gentlemen in Daisy's dreams, inspired by tales of dashing heroics and noble pursuits. These imaginary men were so much more exciting and interesting than ordinary ones . . . they spoke in beautiful prose, they excelled at sword fights and duels, and they forced swoon-inducing kisses on the women they fancied.

Of course Daisy was not so naive as to think that such men really existed, but she had to admit that with all these romantic images in her head, real-life men did seem terribly . . . well, *dull* in comparison.

Lifting her face to the mild sunshine that shot in bright filaments through the canopy of trees overhead, Daisy sang a lively folk tune called "Old Maid In The Garret":

> *Come rich man, come poor man,*
> *Come fool or come witty,*
> *Come any man at all!*
> *Won't you marry out of pity?*

Soon she reached the object of her mission—a spring-fed well she and the other wallflowers had visited a few times before. A wishing well. According to local tradition, it was inhabited by a spirit who would grant your wish if you threw a pin into it. The only danger was in standing too close, for the well spirit might pull you down with him to live forever as his consort.

On previous occasions Daisy had made wishes on behalf of her friends—and they had always come true. Now she needed some magic for herself.

Setting her bonnet gently on the ground, Daisy approached the sloshing hole and looked into the muddy-looking water. She slipped her hand in the pocket of her walking dress and pulled out a paper rack of pins.

"Well-Spirit," she said conversationally, "since

I've had such bad luck in finding the kind of husband I always thought I wanted, I'm leaving it up to you. No requirements, no conditions. What I wish for is . . . the right man for me. I'm prepared to be open-minded."

She pulled the pins from the paper in twos and threes, tossing them into the well. The slivers of metal sparkled brilliantly in the air before hitting the agitated surface of the water and sliding beneath its murky surface.

"I would like all of these pins to be credited toward the same wish," she told the well. She stood for a long moment with her eyes closed, concentrating. The sound of the water was lightly overlaid by the *hueet* of an olive chiffchaff swooping to catch an insect in midair, and the buzz of a dragonfly.

There was a sudden *snap* behind her, like the crunch of a foot on a twig.

Turning, Daisy saw the dark form of a man coming toward her. He was only a few yards away. The shock of discovering someone so close when she had thought she was alone caused her heart to lurch in a few uncomfortable extra beats.

He was as tall and brawny as her friend Annabelle's husband, though he appeared somewhat younger, perhaps not yet thirty. "Forgive me," he said in a low voice as he saw her expression. "I didn't mean to frighten you."

"Oh, you didn't frighten me," she lied cheerfully, her pulse still off-kilter. "I was just a bit . . . surprised."

He approached her in a relaxed amble, his hands in his pockets. "I arrived at the estate a couple of hours ago," he said. "They said you were out here walking."

He seemed rather familiar. He was looking at Daisy as if he expected her to know him. She felt the rush of pained apology that always attended the circumstance of having forgotten someone she had previously met.

"You're a guest of Lord Westcliff's?" she asked, trying desperately to place him.

He gave her a curious glance and smiled slightly. "Yes, Miss Bowman."

He knew her name. Daisy regarded him with increasing confusion. She couldn't imagine how she could have forgotten a man this attractive. His features were strong and decisively formed, too masculine to be called beautiful, too striking to be ordinary. And his eyes were the rich sky-blue of morning glories, even more intense against the sunglazed color of his skin. There was something extraordinary about him, a kind of barely leashed vitality that nearly caused her to take a step backward, the force of it was so strong.

As he bent his head to look at her a mahogany glitter slid over the shiny dark brown surface of his hair. The thick locks had been clipped much closer to the shape of his head than Europeans preferred. An American style. Come to think of it, he had spoken in an American accent. And that fresh, clean smell she detected . . . if she wasn't mistaken, it was the fragrance of . . . *Bowman's soap?*

Suddenly Daisy realized who he was. Her knees nearly gave way beneath her.

"*You,*" she whispered, her eyes wide with astonishment as she beheld the face of Matthew Swift.

Chapter 2

She must have swayed a little, for he reached out and caught her in a light grasp, his fingers encircling her upper arms.

"Mr. Swift," she choked out, straining backward in instinctive retreat.

"You're going to fall into the well. Come with me."

His grip was gentle but relentless as he drew her several yards away from the bubbling water. Annoyed at being herded like a stray goose from a gaggle, Daisy tensed against his grasp. Some things, she thought darkly, had not changed. Matthew Swift was as domineering as ever.

She couldn't stop staring at him. Good Lord, she had never seen such a transformation in her life. The former "bag of bones," as Lillian had described him, had filled out into a large, prosperous-looking man, radiating health and vigor. He was dressed in an elegant suit of clothes, more loosely tailored than the tight-fitting men's styles of the past. Even so, the easy drape of fabric did not obscure the powerful musculature beneath.

The differences in him were more than physical. Maturity had brought with it an air of blatant self-confidence, the look of a man who knew himself and his abilities. Daisy remembered when he had first come to work for her father . . . he had been a scrawny, cold-eyed opportunist in expensive but ill-fitting garments and dilapidated shoes.

"That's old Boston for you," her father had said indulgently when the ancient shoes had caused comment among the family. "They make a pair of shoes or a coat last forever. Economy is a religion to them no matter how great the family fortune."

Daisy pulled away from Swift's grasp. "You've changed," she said, trying to collect herself.

"You haven't," he replied. It was impossible to tell whether the remark was intended as compliment or criticism. "What were you doing at the well?"

"I was . . . I thought . . ." Daisy searched in vain for a sensible explanation, but could think of nothing. "It's a wishing well."

His expression was solemn, but there was a suspicious flicker in his vivid blue eyes as if he were secretly amused. "You have this on good authority, I take it?"

"Everyone in the local village visits it," Daisy replied testily. "It's a *legendary* wishing well."

He was staring at her the way she had always hated, absorbing everything, no detail escaping his notice. Daisy felt her cheeks turn blood-hot beneath his scrutiny. "What did you wish for?" he asked.

"That's private."

"Knowing you," he said, "it could be anything."

"You don't know me," Daisy shot back. The idea that her father would give her over to a man who was so wrong for her in every way . . . it was madness. Marriage with him would be a business-like exchange of money and obligations. Of disappointment and mutual contempt. And it was certain that he was no more attracted to her than she was to him. He would never marry a girl like her if not for the lure of her father's company.

"Perhaps not," Swift conceded. But the words rang false. He thought he knew exactly who and what she was. Their gazes met, measuring and challenging.

"In light of the well's legendary status," Swift said, "I'd hate to overlook a good opportunity." He reached into a pocket, rummaged briefly and pulled out a large silver coin. It had been forever since Daisy had seen American money.

"You're supposed to throw in a pin," she said.

"I don't have a pin."

"That's a five-dollar piece," Daisy said in disbelief. "You're not going to throw that away, are you?"

"I'm not throwing it away. I'm making an investment. You'd better tell me the proper procedure for making wishes—it's a lot of money to waste."

"You're mocking me."

"I'm in deadly earnest. And since I've never done this before, some advice would be welcome." He waited for her reply, and when it became evident that none was forthcoming, a touch of humor lurked in one corner of his mouth. "I'm going to toss the coin in regardless."

Daisy cursed herself. Even though it was obvious he was mocking her, she could not resist. A wish was not something that should be wasted, especially a five-dollar wish. Drat!

She approached the well and said curtly, "First hold the coin in your palm until it's warm from your hand."

Swift came to stand beside her. "And then?"

"Close your eyes and concentrate on the thing you want most." She let a scornful note enter her voice. "And it has to be a personal wish. It can't be about something like mergers or banking trusts."

"I do think about things other than business affairs."

Daisy gave him a skeptical glance, and he astonished her with a brief smile.

Had she ever seen him smile before? Perhaps once or twice. She had a vague past memory of such an occasion, when his face had been so gaunt that all she had received was an impression of white teeth fixed in a grimace that owed little to any feeling of good cheer. But this smile was just a bit off-center, which made it disarming and tantalizing . . . a flash of warmth that made her wonder exactly what kind of man lurked behind his sober exterior.

Daisy was profoundly relieved when the smile disappeared and he was back to his usual stone-faced self. "Close your eyes," she reminded him. "Put everything out of your mind except the wish."

His heavy lashes fell shut, giving her the chance to stare at him without having him stare back. It was not the sort of face a boy could wear comfortably . . . the features were too strong-boned, the nose too long, the jaw obstinate.

But Swift had finally grown into his looks. The austere angles of his face had been softened by extravagant sweeps of black lashes and a wide mouth that hinted of sensuality.

"What now?" he murmured, his eyes still closed.

Staring at him, Daisy was horrified by the impulse that surged through her . . . to step nearer and explore the tanned skin of his cheeks with her fingertips. "When an image is fixed in your mind," she managed to say, "open your eyes and toss the coin into the well."

His lashes lifted to reveal eyes as bright as fire trapped in blue glass.

Without glancing at the well, he threw the coin right into the center of it.

Daisy realized that her heart had begun to thump

just as it had when she had read the more lurid passages of *The Plight of Penelope,* in which a maiden was captured by an evil villain who locked her in a tower room until she agreed to surrender her virtue.

Daisy had known the novel was silly even as she had read it, but that had not detracted one bit from her enjoyment. And she had been perversely disappointed when Penelope had been rescued from imminent ruin by the bland golden-haired hero Reginald, who was not nearly as interesting as the villain.

Of course the prospect of being locked in a tower room without any books had not sounded at all appealing to Daisy. But the threatening monologues by the villain about Penelope's beauty, and his desire for her, and the debauchery he would force on her, had been quite intriguing.

It was just plain bad luck that Matthew Swift would turn out to look just like the handsome villain of Daisy's imaginings.

"What did you wish for?" she asked.

One corner of his mouth twitched. "That's private."

Daisy scowled as she recognized the echo of her own earlier set-down. Spying her bonnet on the nearby ground, she went to scoop it up. She needed to escape his unnerving presence. "I'm returning to the manor," she said over her shoulder. "Good day, Mr. Swift. Enjoy the rest of your walk."

To her dismay, he reached her in a few long-legged

strides and fell into step beside her. "I'll accompany you."

She refused to look at him. "I'd rather you didn't."

"Why not? We're headed in the same direction."

"Because I prefer to walk in silence."

"I'll be silent, then." His pace did not falter.

Deducing that it was pointless to object when he had obviously made up his mind, Daisy clamped her lips together. The scenery—the meadow, the forest—was just as beautiful as before, but her enjoyment of it had vanished.

She was not surprised Swift had ignored her objections. No doubt he envisioned their marriage in the same light. It would not matter what she wanted, or what she asked. He would brush her wishes aside and insist on having his own way.

He must think she was as malleable as a child. With his ingrained arrogance, perhaps he even thought she would be grateful that he had condescended to marry her. She wondered if he would even bother to propose. Most likely he would toss a ring into her lap and instruct her to put it on.

As the grim walk continued Daisy fought to keep from breaking into a run. Swift's legs were so much longer that he took one step to every two of hers. Resentment rose in a choking knot in Daisy's throat.

It was symbolic of her future, this walk. She could only trudge forward with the knowledge that no matter how far or fast she went, she could not outdistance him.

Finally she could bear the taut silence no longer. "Did you put the idea in my father's head?" she burst out.

"What idea?"

"Oh, don't condescend to me," she said irritably. "You know what I'm referring to."

"No, I don't."

It appeared he would insist on playing games. "The bargain you made with my father," she said. "You want to marry me so you can inherit the company."

Swift stopped with a suddenness that in other circumstances would have made her laugh. It looked like he had slammed into an invisible wall. Daisy stopped as well, folding her arms across her chest as she turned to face him.

His expression was utterly blank. "I . . ." His voice was rusty-sounding and he had to clear his throat before he could speak. "I don't know what the hell you're talking about."

"You don't?" Daisy asked lamely.

So her assumption had been wrong—her father had not yet broached his plan to Swift.

If one could die of mortification, Daisy would have expired on the spot. She had now left herself open to the most withering set-down of her life. All Swift had to do was say he would never have agreed to the prospect of marrying a wallflower.

The rustle of leaves and the twittering of chiff-chaff seemed to be magnified in the silence that followed. Though it was impossible to read Swift's thoughts, Daisy perceived that he was rapidly sorting through possibilities and conclusions.

"My father spoke as if it was all settled," she said. "I thought you had discussed it during his most recent visit to New York."

"He never mentioned anything of the kind to me. The thought of marrying you has never crossed my mind. And I have no ambition to inherit the company."

"You have nothing *but* ambition."

"True," he said, watching her closely. "But I don't need to marry you to secure my future."

"My father seems to think you would jump at the chance to become his son-in-law. That you bear him great personal affection."

"I've learned a great deal from him," came a predictably guarded reply.

"I'm sure you have." Daisy took refuge behind a scornful expression. "He's taught you many lessons that have benefitted you in the business world. But none that will benefit you in the business of life."

"You disapprove of your father's business," Swift said rather than asked.

"Yes, for the way he's given his heart and soul to it and ignored the people who love him."

"It's provided you with many luxuries," he

pointed out. "Including the opportunity to marry a British peer."

"I didn't ask for luxuries! I've never wanted anything but a peaceful life."

"To sit in a library by yourself and read?" Swift suggested a little too pleasantly. "To walk in the garden? To enjoy the companionship of your friends?"

"Yes!"

"Books are expensive. So are nice houses with gardens. Has it occurred to you that someone has to pay for your peaceful life?"

That question was so close to her father's accusation about being a parasite that Daisy flinched.

As Swift saw her reaction, his expression changed. He began to say something else, but Daisy interrupted sharply. "It's none of your concern about how I lead my life or who pays for it. I don't care about your opinions, and you have no right to force them on me."

"I do if my future is being linked to yours."

"It's not!"

"It is in a hypothetical sense."

Oh, Daisy hated people who mired every point in semantics when they argued. "Our marriage will never be anything but hypothetical," she told him. "My father has given me until the end of May to find someone else to marry—and I will."

Swift stared at her with alert interest. "I can guess what kind of man you've been looking for.

Fair-haired, aristocratic, sensitive, with a cheerful disposition and ample leisure time for gentlemanly pursuits—"

"Yes," Daisy interrupted, wondering how he managed to make the description seem fatuous.

"I thought so." The smugness in his voice set her nerves on edge. "The only possible reason a girl with your looks could have gone for three seasons without a betrothal is that you've set impossibly high standards. You want nothing less than the perfect man. Which is why your father is forcing the issue."

She was momentarily distracted by the words "a girl with your looks," as if she were a great beauty. Deciding the comment could only have been made in a vein of deepest sarcasm, Daisy felt her temperature escalate. "I do not aspire to marry the perfect man," she said through gritted teeth. Unlike her older sister, who cursed with spectacular fluency, she found it difficult to speak when she was angry. "I am well aware there is no such thing."

"Then why haven't you found someone when even your sister has managed to catch a husband?"

"What do you mean, 'even my sister'?"

" 'Marry Lillian, you'll get a million.' " The insulting phrase had caused much snide amusement in the upper circles of Manhattanville society. "Why do you think no one in New York ever offered for your sister in spite of her huge dowry? She is every man's worst nightmare."

That did it.

"My sister is a *jewel* and Westcliff has the good taste to recognize it. He could have married anyone, but she was the one he wanted. I dare you to repeat your opinion of her to the earl!" Daisy whirled around and stormed along the path, walking as fast as her abbreviated legs would allow.

Swift kept up with her easily, his hands shoved to a nonchalant depth in his pockets. "The end of May . . ." he mused, not the slightest bit out of breath despite their pace. "That's just a bit shy of two months. How are you going to find a suitor in that length of time?"

"I'll stand on a street corner wearing a placard if I have to."

"My sincere wishes for your success, Miss Bowman. In any event, I'm not certain I'll be willing to put myself forth as the winner by default."

"You will not be the winner by default! Rest assured, Mr. Swift, nothing in the world would ever make me consent to be your wife. I feel sorry for the poor woman who ends up with you—I can't think of anyone who would deserve to have such a cold, self-righteous prig for a husband—"

"Wait." His tone had softened in what might have been the beginnings of conciliation. "Daisy . . ."

"Don't speak my name!"

"You're right. That was improper. I beg your pardon. What I meant to say, Miss Bowman, is that there is no need for hostility. We're facing an issue that has great consequence for both of us. I expect we can manage to be civil long enough to find an acceptable solution."

"There is only one solution," Daisy said grimly, "and that is for you to tell my father you categorically refuse to marry me under any circumstances. Promise me that and I'll try to be civil to you."

Swift stopped on the path, which forced Daisy to stop as well. Turning to face him, she raised her brows expectantly. God knew it would not be a difficult promise for him to make in light of his earlier statements. But he was giving her a long, unfathomable glance, his hands still buried in his pockets, his body tensed in stillness. It seemed as if he were listening for something.

His gaze slid over her in open evaluation, and there was a strange gleam in his eyes that drew a shiver from the marrow of her bones. He was staring at her, she thought, like a tiger in wait. She stared back at him, trying desperately to discern the clever workings of his mind, managing to decipher shadows of amusement and bewildering hunger. But hunger for *what?* Not for her, certainly.

"No," he said softly, as if to himself.

Daisy shook her head in bewilderment. Her lips were dry, and she had to dampen them with the tip of her tongue before she could speak. It unnerved her that his gaze followed the tiny movement. "Was that a 'no' as in . . . 'No, I won't marry you?' " she asked.

"That was a 'no,' " he replied, "as in . . . 'No, I won't promise *not* to.' "

And with that, Swift passed by her and continued toward the manor, leaving her to stumble after him.

"He's trying to torture you," Lillian said in disgust as Daisy related the entire story later in the day. They sat in the private upstairs parlor of the country manor with their two closest friends, Annabelle Hunt and Evie, Lady St. Vincent. They had all met two years earlier, a quartet of wallflowers who for various reasons had not been able to bring any eligible gentlemen up to scratch.

It was a popular belief in Victorian society that women, with their mercurial natures and lesser brains, could not have the same quality of friendship that men did. Only men could be loyal to each other, and only men could have truly honest and high-minded relationships.

Daisy thought that was rubbish. She and the other wallflowers . . . well, former wallflowers . . . shared a bond of deep, caring trust. They helped each other, encouraged each other with no hint of competition or jealousy. Daisy loved Annabelle and Evie nearly as much as she did Lillian. She could easily envision them all in their later years, prattling about their grandchildren over tea and biscuits, traveling together as a silver-haired horde of tart-tongued old ladies.

"I don't believe for one second that Mr. Swift

knew nothing about it," Lillian continued. "He's a liar and he's in league with Father. Of course he wants to inherit the company."

Lillian and Evie sat in brocade-upholstered chairs by the windows, while Daisy and Annabelle lounged on the floor amid the colorful heaped masses of their skirts. A plump baby girl with a mass of dark ringlets crawled back and forth between them, occasionally pausing with frowning concentration to tweeze something from the carpet with her miniature fingers.

The infant, Isabelle, had been born to Annabelle and Simon Hunt approximately ten months earlier. Surely no baby had ever been doted on more, by every one in the household including her father.

Contrary to all expectations the virile and masculine Mr. Hunt had not been at all disappointed that his firstborn was a girl. He adored the child, showing no compunction about holding her in public, cooing to her in a way that fathers seldom dared. Hunt had even instructed Annabelle to produce more daughters in the future, claiming roguishly that it had always been his ambition to be loved by many women.

As might have been expected, the baby was exceptionally beautiful—it would be a physical impossibility for Annabelle to produce a less than spectacular offspring.

Picking up Isabelle's sturdy, wriggling body, Daisy nuzzled into her silky neck before setting her on the carpet again. "You should have heard him," Daisy said. "The arrogance was incredible. Swift has decided that it is my own fault that I am still unmarried. He said I must have set my standards too high. And he lectured me on the cost of my books and said that someone has to pay for my expensive lifestyle."

"He didn't dare," Lillian exclaimed, her face turning scarlet with sudden rage.

Daisy immediately regretted telling her. The family physician had advised that Lillian must not be upset as she approached the last month of her pregnancy. She had become pregnant the previous year and had miscarried early on. The loss had been difficult for Lillian, not to mention surprising given her hardy constitution.

In spite of the doctor's assurances that she was not to blame for the miscarriage, Lillian had been melancholy for weeks afterward. But with Westcliff's steadfast comfort and the loving support of her friends, Lillian had gradually returned to her usual high-spirited self.

Now that Lillian had conceived again she was far less cavalier about the pregnancy, mindful of the possibility of another miscarriage. Unfortunately she was not one of those women who bloomed during confinement. She was splotchy, nauseous, and often ill-tempered, chafing at the restrictions her condition imposed.

"I won't stand for this," Lillian exclaimed. "You're not going to marry Matthew Swift, and

I'll send Father to the devil if he tries to take you away from England!"

Still seated on the floor, Daisy reached up and settled a calming hand on her older sister's knee. She forced her lips into a reassuring smile as she stared into Lillian's distraught face.

"Everything will be fine," she said. "We'll think of something. We'll have to." They had been too close for too many years. In the absence of their parents' affection Lillian and Daisy had been each other's sole source of love and support for as long as they could remember.

Evie, the least talkative of the four friends, spoke with a slight stammer that appeared whenever she was nervous or moved by strong emotion. When they had all met two years earlier, Evie's stammer had been so severe as to make conversation an exercise in frustration. But since leaving her abusive family and marrying Lord St. Vincent, Evie had gained far greater confidence.

"W-would Mr. Swift really agree to take a bride not of his own choosing?" Evie pushed back a gleaming red curl that had slipped over her forehead. "If what he said was true—that his financial situation is already s-secure—there is no reason for him to marry Daisy."

"There is more to it than money," Lillian replied, squirming in her chair to find a more comfortable position. Her hands rested on the ample curve of her belly. "Father has made Swift into a substitute son, since none of our brothers turned out the way he wanted."

"The way he wanted?" Annabelle asked in puzzlement. She flopped over to kiss the baby's tiny wiggling toes, eliciting a gurgling chuckle from the infant.

"Devoted to the company," Lillian clarified. "Efficient and callous and unscrupulous. A man who will put business interests ahead of everything else in his life. It's a language they speak together, Father and Mr. Swift. Our brother Ransom has tried to make a place for himself in the company, but Father always pits him against Mr. Swift."

"And Mr. Swift always wins," Daisy said. "Poor Ransom."

"Our other two brothers don't even bother trying," Lillian said.

"But wh-what of Mr. Swift's own father?" Evie asked. "Does he have no objection to his son becoming someone else's de facto son?"

"Well, that's always been the odd part," Daisy replied. "Mr. Swift comes from a well-known New England family. They settled in Plymouth and some of them ended up in Boston by the early seventeen hundreds. Swifts are known for their distinguished ancestry, but only a few of them have managed to retain their money. As Father always says, it takes one generation to make it, the second to spend it, and the third is left with only the name. Of course, when it's Old Boston one is talking about, the process takes ten generations instead of three—they're so much slower about everything—"

"You're drifting, dear," Lillian interrupted. "Back to the point."

"Sorry." Daisy grinned briefly before resuming. "Well, we suspect there was some kind of falling-out between Mr. Swift and his relations because he hardly ever speaks of them. And he rarely travels to Massachusetts to visit. So even if Mr. Swift's father does object to his son inserting himself into someone else's family, we would never know about it."

The four women were quiet for a moment as they considered the situation.

"We'll find someone for Daisy," Evie said. "Now that we are able to look beyond the peerage, it will be much easier. There are many acceptable gentlemen of good blood who do not h-happen to possess titles."

"Mr. Hunt has many unmarried acquaintances," Annabelle said. "He could make any number of introductions."

"I appreciate that," Daisy said, "but I don't like the idea of marrying a professional man. I could never be happy with a soulless industrialist." Pausing, she said apologetically, "No offense to Mr. Hunt, of course."

Annabelle laughed. "I wouldn't characterize all professional men as soulless industrialists. Mr. Hunt can be quite sensitive and emotional at times."

The others regarded her dubiously, none of them able to picture Annabelle's big, bold-featured husband as being sensitive in any way. Mr. Hunt was clever and charming, but he seemed as impervious to emotion as an elephant would be to the buzzing of a gnat.

"We'll take your word for that," Lillian said. "Back to the matter at hand—Evie, will you ask Lord St. Vincent if he knows of any suitable gentlemen for Daisy? Now that we've expanded our definition of 'suitable,' he ought to be able to find a decent specimen. Heaven knows he possesses information about every man in England who has two shillings to rub together."

"I will ask him," Evie said decisively. "I am certain we can come up with some presentable candidates."

As the owner of Jenner's, the exclusive gaming club that Evie's father had established long ago, Lord St. Vincent was rapidly bringing the business to a height of success it had never reached before. St. Vincent ran the club in an exacting manner, keeping meticulous files on the personal lives and financial balances of every one of its members.

"Thank you," Daisy replied sincerely. Her mind lingered on thoughts of the club. "I wonder . . . do you think Lord St. Vincent could find out more about Mr. Rohan's mysterious past? Perhaps he's a long-lost Irish lord or something of the sort."

A brief silence sifted through the room like a flurry of tiny snowflakes. Daisy was aware of significant glances being exchanged between her sister and friends. She was abruptly annoyed with them, and even more with herself for mentioning the man who helped manage the gaming club.

Rohan was a young half-gypsy with dark hair and bright hazel eyes. They had only met once, when Rohan had stolen a kiss from her. Three kisses, if one wished to be factual, and it had been by far the most erotic experience of her entire life. Also the only erotic experience of her entire life.

Rohan had kissed her as if she were a grown woman instead of someone's younger sister, with a coaxing sensuality that had hinted of all the forbidden things kisses led to. Daisy should have slapped his face. Instead she had dreamed about those kisses at least a hundred thousand times.

"I don't think so, dear," Evie said very gently, and Daisy smiled too brightly, as if she had made a joke.

"Oh, of course he isn't! But you know how my imagination is . . . it wants to plunge into every little mystery."

"We must remain focused on what is important, Daisy," Lillian said sternly. "No fantasies or stories . . . and no more thoughts of Rohan. He's only a distraction."

Daisy's initial impulse was to utter some biting reply as she always had when Lillian became bossy. However, as she stared into her sister's brown eyes, the same spiced-gingerbread color of her own, she saw the flicker of panic in them and she felt a rush of protective love.

"You're right," she said, forcing a smile. "You

needn't worry, you know. I'm going to do whatever it takes to stay here with you. Even marry a man I don't love."

Another silence, and then Evie spoke. "We'll find a man whom you could love, Daisy. And hope that mutual affection will grow in time." A wry little smile quirked her full lips. "Sometimes it happens that way."

Chapter 3

"The bargain you made with my father . . ."

The echo of Daisy's voice lingered in Matthew's mind long after they had parted company. He was going to take Thomas Bowman aside at the first opportunity and ask him what the hell was going on. But in the bustle of arriving guests that moment would not likely come until this evening.

Matthew wondered if old Bowman had really taken it into his head to pair him off with Daisy. *Jesus.* Through the years Matthew had entertained many thoughts concerning Daisy Bowman, but none of them had involved marriage. That had always been so far out of the realm of possibility it was not even worth considering. So Matthew had never kissed her, had never danced with her or even walked with her, knowing full well the results would be disastrous.

The secrets of his past haunted his present and endangered his future. Matthew was never without the awareness that the identity he had created for himself could be blown to bits at any moment. All it would take was for one person to put two and two together . . . one person to recognize him for what and who he really was. Daisy deserved a husband who was honest and whole, not one who had built his life on lies.

But that didn't stop Matthew from wanting her. He had always wanted Daisy, with an intensity that seemed to radiate from the pores of his skin. She was sweet, kind, inventive, excessively reasonable yet absurdly romantic, her dark sparkling eyes filled with dreams. She had occasional moments of clumsiness when her mind was too occupied with her thoughts to focus on what she was doing. She was often late to supper because she had gotten too involved in her reading. She frequently lost thimbles and slippers and pencil stubs. And she loved to stargaze. The never-forgotten sight of Daisy leaning wistfully on a balcony railing one night, her pert profile lifted to the night sky, had charged Matthew with the most blistering desire to stride over to her and kiss her senseless.

Matthew had imagined being in bed with her far more often than he should have. If such a thing could ever have occurred, he would have been so gentle . . . he would have worshipped her. Anything and everything to please her. He longed for the intimacy of her hair in his hands, the soft jut of her hipbones beneath his palms, the smoothness of her shoulders against his lips. The sleeping weight of her in his arms. He wanted all of that, and so much more.

It amazed Matthew that no one had ever guessed at his feelings. Daisy should have been able to see it every time she looked at him. Fortunately for Matthew she never had. She had always dismissed him as another cog in the machine of her father's company, and Matthew had been grateful for that.

Something had changed, however. He thought of the way Daisy had stared at him earlier in the day, the startled wonder in her expression. Was his appearance that different from before?

Absently Matthew shoved his hands deep in his pockets and walked through the interior of Stony Cross Manor. He had never given a thought to his looks other than to make certain his hair was cut and his face was clean. A stern New England upbringing had extinguished any flicker of vanity, as Bostonians abhorred conceit and did everything possible to avoid the new and fashionable.

However, in the past couple of years Thomas Bowman had insisted that Matthew go to his Park Avenue tailor, and visit a hair-dresser instead of a barber, and have his nails manicured once in a while as befitted a gentleman of his position. Also at Bowman's insistence, Matthew had hired a cookmaid and a housekeeper, which meant he had been eating better of late. That, along with losing the last vestiges of young adulthood, had given him a new look of maturity. He wondered if that appealed to Daisy, and immediately cursed himself for caring.

But the way she had looked at him today . . . as if she were seeing him, really noticing him, for the first time . . .

She had never given him such a glance on any of the occasions he had visited her family's Fifth Avenue house. His mind ventured back to the first time he had met Daisy, at a private supper with just the family attending.

The grandly appointed dining-room had glittered in the effusively scattered light from a crystal chandelier, the walls covered in thick gilded paper and gold-painted molding. One entire wall was lined with a succession of four massive looking glasses, larger than any others he'd ever seen.

Two of the sons had been present, both of them sturdy young men who were easily twice Matthew's weight. Mercedes and Thomas had been seated at opposite ends of the table. The two daughters, Lillian and Daisy, had sat on one side, surreptitiously nudging their plates and chairs closer together.

Thomas Bowman had a contentious relationship with both his daughters, alternately ignoring them and subjecting them to harsh criticisms. The older daughter Lillian responded to Bowman with surly impudence.

But Daisy, the fifteen year-old, regarded her father in a speculative, rather cheerful way that seemed to annoy him beyond his ability to bear. She had made Matthew want to smile. With her luminous skin, her exotic cinnamon-colored eyes and quicksilver expressions, Daisy Bowman seemed to have come from an enchanted forest populated with mythical creatures.

It had immediately become apparent to Matthew that any conversation Daisy took part in was apt to veer into unexpected and charming directions. He had been secretly amused when Thomas Bowman had chastised Daisy in front of everyone for her latest mischief. It seemed that the Bowman household had lately become overrun with mice because all the traps they set had failed.

One of the servants had reported that Daisy had been sneaking around the house at night, deliberately tripping all the traps to keep the mice from being killed.

"Is this true, daughter?" Thomas Bowman had rumbled, his gaze filled with ire as he stared at Daisy.

"It could be," she had allowed. "But there is another explanation."

"And what is that?" Bowman had asked sourly.

Her tone turned congratulatory. "I think we are hosting the most intelligent mice in New York!"

From that moment on Matthew had never refused an invitation to the Bowman mansion, not just because it pleased the old man but because it gave him the chance to see Daisy. He had collected as many stolen glances as possible, knowing it was all he would ever have of her. And the moments he had spent in her company, regardless of her cool politeness, had been the only times in his life he had come close to happiness.

Hiding his troubled thoughts, Matthew wandered farther into the manor. He had never been abroad before but this was exactly what he had imagined England would look like, the manicured gardens and the green hills beyond, and the rustic village at the feet of the grand estate.

The house and its furniture were ancient and comfortably worn at the edges, but it seemed that in every corner there was some priceless vase or statue or painting he had seen featured in art history books. Perhaps a bit drafty in the winter, but with the plenitude of hearths and thick carpets and velvet curtains, one could hardly say that living here would be suffering.

When Thomas Bowman, or rather his secretary, had written with the news that Matthew would be required to oversee the establishment of a division of the soap company in England, Matthew's initial impulse had been to refuse. He would have relished the challenge and the responsibility. But being in the proximity of Daisy Bowman—even in the same country—would have been too much for Matthew to withstand. Her presence pierced him like arrows, promising a future of endless unsatisfied wanting.

It was the secretary's last few lines, reporting on

the Bowman family's welfare, that had seized Matthew's attention.

There is private doubt, the secretary had written, *that the younger Miss Bowman will have any success at finding a suitable gentleman to wed. Therefore Mr. Bowman has decided to bring her back to New York if she is still not betrothed by the end of spring . . .*

This had left Matthew in a quandary. If Daisy was returning to New York, Matthew was damned well going to England. He would hedge his bets by accepting the position in Bristol, and waiting to see if Daisy managed to catch a husband. If she did, Matthew would find a replacement for himself and head back to New York.

As long as there was an ocean between them, everything would be fine.

As Matthew crossed through the main entrance hall he caught sight of Lord Westcliff. The earl was in the company of a big, black-haired man who possessed a somewhat piratical appearance despite his elegant attire. Matthew guessed that he was Simon Hunt, Westcliff's business partner and reportedly his closest friend. For all Hunt's financial success—which by all reports was remarkable—he had been born a butcher's son, with no blood ties to the aristocracy.

"Mr. Swift," Westcliff said easily, as they met near the bottom of the grand staircase. "It seems you've returned early from your walk. I hope the views were pleasing?"

"The views were magnificent, my lord," Matthew replied. "I look forward to many such walks around the estate. I came back early because I happened to meet with Miss Bowman along the way."

"Ah." Westcliff's face was impassive. "No doubt that was a surprise for Miss Bowman."

And not a welcome one was the unspoken subtext. Matthew met the earl's gaze without blinking. One of his more useful skills was that of being able to read the minute alterations in expression and posture that gave people's thoughts away. But Westcliff was an unusually self-controlled man. Matthew admired that.

"I think it's safe to say it was one of many surprises Miss Bowman has received recently," Matthew replied. It was a deliberate attempt to find out if Westcliff knew anything about the possible arranged marriage with Daisy.

The earl responded only with an infinitesimal lift of his brows, as if he found the remark interesting but not worthy of a response. *Damn,* Matthew thought with increasing admiration.

Westcliff turned to the black-haired man beside him. "Hunt, I would like to introduce Matthew Swift—the American I mentioned to you earlier. Swift, this is Mr. Simon Hunt."

They shook hands firmly. Hunt was five to ten years older than Matthew and looked as if he could be mean as hell in a fight. A bold, confident man who reputedly loved to skewer pretensions and upper-class affectations.

"I've heard of your accomplishments with Consolidated Locomotive Works," Matthew told Hunt. "There is a great deal of interest in New York regarding your merging of British craftsmanship with American manufacturing methods."

Hunt smiled sardonically. "Much as I would like to take all the credit, modesty compels me to reveal that Westcliff had something to do with it. He and his brother-in-law are my business partners."

"Obviously the combination is highly successful," Matthew replied.

Hunt turned to Westcliff. "He has a talent for flattery," he remarked. "Can we hire him?"

Westcliff's mouth twitched with amusement. "I'm afraid my father-in-law would object. Mr. Swift's talents are needed to built a factory and start a company office in Bristol."

Matthew decided to nudge the conversation in a different direction. "I've read of the recent movement in Parliament for nationalization of the British railroad industry," he said to Westcliff. "I would be interested in hearing your thoughts on the matter, my lord."

"Good God, don't get him started on that," Hunt said.

The subject caused a scowl to appear on Westcliff's brow. "The last thing the public needs is for government to take control of the industry. God save us from yet more interference from politicians.

The government would run the railroads as ineffi-
ciently as they do everything else. And the mono-
poly would stifle the industry's ability to compete,
resulting in higher taxes, not to mention—"

"Not to mention," Hunt interrupted slyly, "the
fact that Westcliff and I don't want the government
cutting into our future profits."

Westcliff gave him a stern glance. "I happen to
have the public's best interest in mind."

"How fortunate," Hunt commented, "that in
this case what is best for the public also happens to
be best for you."

Matthew bit back a smile.

Rolling his eyes, Westcliff told Matthew, "As
you can see, Mr. Hunt overlooks no opportunity
to mock me."

"I mock everyone," Hunt said. "You just happen
to be the most readily available target."

Westcliff turned to Matthew and said, "Hunt
and I are going out to the back terrace for a cigar.
Will you join us?"

Matthew shook his head. "I'm afraid I don't
smoke."

"Neither do I," Westcliff said ruefully. "It has
always been my habit to enjoy a cigar every now
and again, but unfortunately the scent of tobacco
is not welcomed by the countess in her condition."

It took a moment for Matthew to recall that
"the countess" was Lillian Bowman. How odd that

funny, feisty, furious Lillian was now Lady West-cliff.

"You and I will converse while Hunt has a cigar," Westcliff informed him. "Come with us."

The "invitation" didn't seem to allow the possibility of a refusal, but Matthew tried nonetheless. "Thank you, my lord, but there is a certain matter I wish to discuss with someone, and I—"

"That someone would be Mr. Bowman, I expect."

Hell, Matthew thought. *He knows.* Even if it hadn't been for those words, he could tell by the way Westcliff was looking at him. Westcliff knew about Bowman's intention of marrying him off to Daisy . . . and not surprisingly, Westcliff had an opinion about it.

"You will discuss the matter with me first," the earl continued.

Matthew glanced warily at Simon Hunt, who gave him a bland look in return. "I'm certain," Matthew said, "that Mr. Hunt doesn't want to be bored by a discussion of someone else's personal affairs—"

"Not at all," Hunt said cheerfully. "I love hearing about other people's affairs. Particularly when they're personal."

The three of them went to the back terrace, which overlooked acres of manicured gardens separated by graveled paths and carefully sculpted hedges. An orchard of ancient pear trees was visible in the lush green distance. The breeze that swept across the gardens was thick with the perfume of flowers. The turgid rush of the nearby river underlaid the rustle of the wind in the trees.

Sitting at an outside table, Matthew forced himself to relax back in his chair. He and Westcliff watched Simon Hunt clip the end off a cigar with a pocket knife. Matthew remained silent, patiently waiting for Westcliff to speak first.

"How long," Westcliff asked abruptly, "have you known about Bowman's plan for you and Daisy to marry?"

Matthew replied without hesitation. "Approximately an hour and fifteen minutes."

"It wasn't your idea, then?"

"Not at all," Matthew assured him.

Settling back, the earl laced his fingers over the lean surface of his midriff, and surveyed him through narrowed eyes. "You have a great deal to gain by such an arrangement."

"My lord," Matthew said prosaically, "if I have one talent in life, it's making money. I don't need to marry into it."

"I'm glad to hear it," the earl replied. "I have one more question to ask, but first I will make my position clear. I have great affection for my sister-in-law, and I consider her under my protection. Being well acquainted with the Bowmans, you undoubtedly know about the close relationship between the countess and her sister. If anything were to make Daisy unhappy, my wife would suffer as a result . . . and I will not allow that."

"Understood," Matthew said tersely. There was biting irony in the fact that he was being warned away from Daisy when he had already resolved to do everything in his power to avoid marrying her. He was tempted to tell Westcliff to go to hell. Instead he kept his mouth shut and remained outwardly composed.

"Daisy has a unique spirit," Westcliff said. "A warm and romantic nature. If she is forced into a loveless marriage, she will be devastated. She deserves a husband who will cherish her for everything she is, and who will protect her from the harsher realities of the world. A husband who will allow her to dream."

It was surprising to hear such sentiment from Westcliff, who was universally known as a pragmatic and level-headed man. "What is your question, my lord?" Matthew asked.

"Will you give me your word that you will not marry my sister-in-law?"

Matthew held the earl's cold black gaze. It would not be wise to cross a man like Westcliff, who was not accustomed to being denied. But Matthew had endured years of Thomas Bowman's thunder and bluster, standing up to him when other men would flee in fear of his wrath.

Although Bowman could be a ruthless, sarcastic bully there was nothing he respected more than a man who was willing to go toe-to-toe with him. And so it had quickly become Matthew's lot in the company to be the bearer of bad tidings and deliver the hard truths that everyone else was afraid to give him.

That had been Matthew's training, which was why Westcliff's attempt at domination had no effect on him.

"I'm afraid not, my lord," Matthew said politely.

Simon Hunt dropped his cigar.

"You won't give me your word?" Westcliff asked in disbelief.

"No." Matthew bent swiftly to retrieve the fallen cigar and returned it to Hunt, who regarded him with a glint of warning in his eyes as if he were silently trying to prevent him from jumping off a cliff.

"Why not?" Westcliff demanded. "Because you don't want to lose your position with Bowman?"

"No, he can't afford to lose me right now." Matthew smiled slightly in an attempt to rob the words of arrogance. "I know more about production, administration, and marketing than anyone else at Bowman's . . . and I've earned the old man's trust. So I won't be dismissed even if I refuse to marry his daughter."

"Then it will be quite simple for you to put the entire matter to rest," the earl said. "I want your word, Swift. *Now.*"

A lesser man would have been intimidated by Westcliff's authoritative demand. "I might consider it," Matthew countered coolly, "if you offered the right incentive. For example, if you promise to endorse me as the head of the entire division and guarantee the position for at least, say . . . three years."

Westcliff gave him an incredulous glance.

The tense silence was broken as Simon Hunt roared with laughter. "By God, he has brass ballocks," he exclaimed. "Mark my words, Westcliff, I'm going to hire him for Consolidated."

"I'm not cheap," Matthew said, which caused Hunt to laugh so hard that he nearly dropped his cigar again.

Even Westcliff smiled, albeit reluctantly. "Damn it," he muttered. "I'm not going to endorse you so readily—not with so much at stake. Not until I am convinced you're the right man for the position."

"Then it seems we're at an impasse." Matthew made his expression friendly. "For now."

The two older men exchanged a glance, tacitly agreeing to discuss the situation later, outside his hearing. That caused Matthew a twinge of sharp curiosity, but he mentally shrugged, knowing there was only so much he could control. At least he had made it clear that he could not be bullied, and he was leaving his options open.

Besides . . . he could hardly give his word on the matter when Bowman hadn't yet mentioned it to him.

Chapter 4

"*Obviously Daisy is the runt of the* litter," Thomas Bowman said later that night, pacing back and forth across the small private receiving area attached to his room. He and Matthew had agreed to meet after supper while the other guests congregated downstairs. "She is undersized and frivolous. 'Give her a solid, practical name,' I told my wife when the child was born. Jane or Constance or something of the sort. Instead she chose Marguerite . . . *French,* mind you! . . . after a cousin on her maternal side. And then it degenerated further when Lillian, who was only four at the time, learned that Marguerite was the French word for a damned insignificant flower. But from then on Lillian called her Daisy, and it stuck . . ."

As Bowman continued to ramble, Matthew

thought of how perfect the name was, the small white-petaled flower that appeared so delicate and yet was remarkably hardy. It said something that in a family of overpowering personalities that Daisy had always remained stubbornly true to her own nature.

". . . obviously I would have to sugarcoat the deal," Thomas Bowman was saying. "I know you well enough to be certain that you would choose a very different sort of woman for yourself, one with more practical uses than a flighty slip of a girl like Daisy. Therefore—"

"No sugarcoating would be necessary," Matthew interrupted calmly. "Daisy . . . that is, Miss Bowman, is entirely—" *Beautiful. Desirable. Bewitching.* "—acceptable. Marrying a woman like Miss Bowman would be a reward in itself."

"Good," Bowman grunted, clearly unconvinced. "Very gentlemanly of you to say so. Still, I will offer you fair recompense in the form of a generous dowry, more shares in the company and so forth. You will be quite satisfied, I assure you. Now as to the wedding arrangements—"

"I didn't say yes," Matthew interrupted.

Bowman stopped pacing and sent him a questioning stare.

"To start with," Matthew continued carefully, "it is possible Miss Bowman will find a suitor within the next two months."

"She will find no suitors of your caliber," Bowman said smugly.

Matthew replied gravely despite his amusement. "Thank you. But I don't believe Miss Bowman shares your high opinion."

The older man made a dismissive gesture. "Bah. Women's minds are as changeable as English weather. You can persuade her to like you. Give her a posy of flowers, throw a few compliments in her direction . . . better yet, quote something from one of those blasted poetry books she reads. Seducing a woman is easily accomplished, Swift. All you have to do is—"

"Mr. Bowman," Matthew interrupted with a sudden touch of alarm. God in heaven, all he needed was an explanation of courtship techniques from his employer. "I believe I could manage that without any advice. That's not the issue."

"Then what . . . *ah*." Bowman gave him a man-of-the-world smile. "I understand."

"You understand what?" Matthew asked apprehensively.

"Obviously you fear my reaction if you should decide later on that my daughter is not adequate to your needs. But as long as you behave with discretion, I won't say a word."

Matthew sighed and rubbed his eyes, suddenly feeling weary. This was a bit much to face so soon after his ship had landed in Bristol. "You're saying you'll look the other way if I stray from my wife," he said rather than asked.

"We men face temptations. Sometimes we stray. It is the way of the world."

"It's not my way," Matthew said flatly. "I stand by my word, both in business and in my personal life. If or when I promise to be faithful to a woman, I would be. No matter what."

Bowman's heavy mustache twitched with amusement. "You're still young enough to afford scruples."

"The old can't afford them?" Matthew asked with a touch of affectionate mockery.

"Some scruples have a way of becoming overpriced. You'll discover that someday."

"God, I hope not." Matthew sank into a chair and buried his head in his hands, his fingers tunneling through the heavy locks of his hair.

After a long moment Bowman ventured, "Would it really be so terrible having Daisy for a wife? You'll have to marry sometime. And she comes with benefits. The company, for example. You will be given controlling interest in it upon my death."

"You'll outlive us all," Matthew muttered.

Bowman let out a pleased laugh. "I want you to have the company," he insisted. It was the first time he had ever spoken this frankly on the subject. "You're more like me than any of my sons. The company will be far better off in your hands than anyone else's. You have a gift . . . an ability to enter a room and take it over . . . you fear no one, and they all know it, and they esteem you for it. Marry my daughter, Swift, and build my factory. By the time you come home, I'll give you New York."

"Could you throw in Rhode Island? It's not very large."

Bowman ignored the sardonic question. "I have ambitions for you beyond the company. I am connected with powerful men, and you have not escaped their notice. I will help you achieve anything your mind can conceive . . . and the price is a small one. Take Daisy and sire my grandchildren. That's all I ask."

"That's all," Matthew repeated dazedly.

When Matthew had begun to work for Bowman ten years ago, he had never expected the man would come to be a surrogate father to him. Bowman was like a barrel of explosives, short, round and so quick-tempered you could predict one of his infamous tirades by watching the top of his bald head turn fiery red. But Bowman was clever with numbers, and when it came to managing people he was incredibly shrewd and calculating. He was also generous to those who pleased him, and he was a man who kept his promises and fulfilled his obligations.

Matthew had learned a great deal from Thomas Bowman, how to sniff out an opponent's weakness and turn it to his advantage, when to push and when to hold back . . . and he had learned, too, that it was all right to unleash his aggressiveness in business as long as he never crossed the line into outright rudeness. New York businessmen—the real ones, not the upper-class dilettantes—did not respect you unless you displayed a certain amount of contentiousness.

At the same time Matthew had learned to temper his vigor with diplomacy after learning that winning an argument didn't necessarily mean he would get his way. Charm had not come easily to him, with his guarded nature. But he had painstakingly acquired it as a necessary instrument to do his job well.

Thomas Bowman had backed Matthew every step of the way and had steered him through a couple of precarious deals. Matthew had been grateful for his guidance. And he couldn't help but like his prickly employer despite his faults—because there was some truth in Bowman's claim that they were alike.

How a man like Bowman had produced a daughter like Daisy was one of life's great mysteries.

"I need some time to consider this," Matthew said.

"What is there to consider?" Bowman protested. "I've already said—" He stopped as he saw Matthew's expression. "All right. All right. I suppose there is no need for an immediate answer. We'll discuss it later."

"Did you speak to Mr. Swift?" Lillian demanded as Marcus entered their bedroom. She had dozed off while trying to wait up for him, and was struggling to a sitting position in the bed.

"Oh, I spoke to him," Marcus replied ruefully, shrugging out of his coat. He laid the well-tailored garment across the arms of a Louis XIV chair.

"I was right, wasn't I? He's abominable. Detestable. Tell me what he said."

Marcus stared at his pregnant wife, who was so beautiful with her long hair unbound and her eyes still heavy-lidded from sleep that it made his heart skip a beat. "Not yet," he murmured, half-sitting on the bed. "First I want to stare at you for a while."

Lillian smiled and scrubbed her hands through her wild dark mane. "I look a fright."

"No." He moved closer, his voice lowering. "Every part of you is lovely." His hands slid gently over the abundant curves of her body, soothing rather than arousing. "What can I do for you?" he whispered.

She continued to smile. "One glance at me will reveal that you've done quite enough already, my lord." Encircling him with her slender arms, she let him rest his head against her breasts. "Westcliff," she said against his hair, "I could never have anyone's child but yours."

"That is reassuring."

"I feel so overtaken . . . and bloody uncomfortable. Is it wrong to say I don't like being pregnant?"

"Of course not," Marcus returned, his voice muffled in her cleavage. "I wouldn't like it either."

That drew a grin from her. Releasing him, she settled back against the pillows. "I want to hear about Mr. Swift. Tell me what was said between you and that odious walking scarecrow."

"I wouldn't describe him as a scarecrow, precisely. It appears he has changed since you saw him last."

"Hmm." Lillian was obviously displeased by the revelation. "He is ill-favored, nonetheless."

"Since I rarely dwell on thoughts of male attractiveness," Marcus said dryly, "I do not qualify as a competent judge. But I think hardly anyone would describe Mr. Swift as being ill-favored."

"Are you saying he's attractive?"

"I believe many would claim so, yes."

Lillian thrust a hand in front of his face. "How many fingers am I holding up?"

"Three," Marcus said, amused. "My love, what are you doing?"

"Checking your eyesight. I think your vision is failing. Here, follow the movement of my finger—"

"Why don't you follow the movement of mine?" he suggested, reaching for her bodice.

She grabbed his hand and stared into his sparkling eyes. "Marcus, do be serious. Daisy's future is at stake!"

Marcus settled back obligingly. "Very well."

"Tell me what was said," she prompted.

"I informed Mr. Swift quite sternly that I will not allow anyone to make Daisy unhappy. And I demanded that he give me his word not to marry her."

"Oh, thank God," Lillian said with a sigh of relief.

"He refused."

"He what?" Her mouth fell open in astonishment. "But no one refuses you."

"Apparently Mr. Swift wasn't told about that," he said.

"Marcus, you're going to do something, aren't you? You won't let Daisy be browbeaten and harassed into marrying Swift—"

"Hush, love. I promise, Daisy will not be forced to marry anyone against her will. However . . ." Marcus hesitated, wondering exactly how much of the truth he should admit. "My opinion of Matthew Swift is somewhat different than yours."

Her brows lowered. "My opinion is more accurate. I've known him longer."

"You knew him years ago," Marcus said evenly. "People change, Lillian. And I think much of what your father has claimed about Swift is true."

"*Et tu*, Marcus?"

He grinned at Lillian's theatrical grimace and reached beneath the covers. Fishing out one of her bare feet, he pulled it into his lap and began to knead her aching arch with deep strokes of his thumbs. She sighed and relaxed against the pillows.

Marcus considered what he had learned about Swift so far. He was an intelligent young man, deft and well-mannered. The kind who thought before he spoke. Marcus had always felt comfortable around such men.

On the surface, the pairing of Matthew Swift with Daisy Bowman was wildly incongruous. But Marcus did not entirely agree with Lillian's belief that Daisy should marry a man who possessed the same romantic and sensitive nature. There would be no equilibrium in such a union. After all, every swift-sailing ship needed an anchor.

"We must send Daisy to London as soon as possible," Lillian fretted. "It's the height of the season, and she's buried in Hampshire away from all the balls and soirées—"

"It was her choice to come here," Marcus reminded her, reaching for her other foot. "She would never forgive herself if she missed the baby's birth."

"Oh, bother that. I would rather Daisy miss the birth and meet eligible men instead of having to wait here with me until her time runs out and she has to marry Matthew Swift and move with him to New York and then I'll never see her again—"

"I've already thought of that," Marcus said. "Which is why I undertook to invite a number of eligible men to Stony Cross Park for the stag-and-hind hunt."

"You did?" Her head lifted from the pillow.

"St. Vincent and I came up with a list and debated the merits of each candidate at length. We settled on an even dozen. Any one of them would do for your sister."

"Oh, Marcus, you are the most clever, most wonderful—"

He waved away the praise and shook his head with a grin, remembering the lively arguments. "St. Vincent is damned finicky, let me tell you. If he were a woman, no man would be good enough for him."

"They never are," Lillian told him impudently. "Which is why we women have a saying . . . 'Aim high, then settle.' "

He snorted. "Is that what you did?"

A smile curved her lips. "No, my lord. I aimed high and got far more than I'd bargained for." And she giggled as he crawled over her prone body and kissed her soundly.

The sun had not yet risen by the time a group of guests bent on trout fishing had partaken of a hasty breakfast on the back terrace and had gone out dressed in tweed and rough twill and waxed linen. Sleepy-eyed servants followed the gentlemen to the trout stream, carrying rods, creels, and wooden cases containing flies and tools. The men would be gone for a good part of the morning while the ladies slept.

All the ladies except Daisy. She loved fishing, but she knew without asking that she would not be welcome in the all-male group. And while she and Lillian had often gone by themselves in the past, her older sister was certainly in no condition to do so now.

Daisy had done her best to persuade Evie or Annabelle to come with her to the artificial lake that Westcliff kept generously stocked with trout, but neither of them had seemed enthusiastic about the prospect.

"You'll have a smashing time," Daisy had wheedled. "I'll teach you how to cast—it's quite easy, really. Don't say you're going to stay inside on a beautiful spring morning!"

As it turned out, Annabelle thought that sleeping late was a fine idea. And since Evie's husband St. Vincent had decided not to go fishing, Evie said she would rather remain in bed with him.

"You would have much more fun fishing with me," Daisy had told her.

"No," Evie had said decisively, "I wouldn't."

Feeling cross and just a little bit lonely, Daisy breakfasted by herself and set out to the lake, carrying her favorite lancewood rod with the whalebone top and the clamp-foot reel.

It was a glorious morning, the air soft and alive. Overwintering salvia sprang in bright blue and purple spikes alongside the blackthorn hedgerows. Daisy crossed a mown green field toward ground that was blanketed with buttercups, yarrow, and the bright pink petals of ragged robin.

As she rounded a mulberry tree Daisy saw a disturbance at the water's edge . . . two young boys, with something between them, some kind of animal or bird . . . a goose? The creature was protesting with angry honks, flapping its wings violently at the giggling lads.

"Here, now," Daisy called out. "What is this? What's going on?"

Seeing the intruder, the boys yelped and broke

into a full bore run, their legs a blur as they headed away from the lake.

Daisy quickened her pace and approached the indignant goose. It was a huge domestic Greylag, a breed known for its gray plumage, muscular neck and sharp orange beak.

"Poor fellow," Daisy said as she saw that its leg was tied with something. As she drew closer, the hostile goose darted forward as if to attack her. It was abruptly caught up on whatever it was that tethered his leg. Pausing, Daisy set down her fishing gear. "I'm going to try to help you," she informed the aggressive bird. "But an attitude like that is rather off-putting. If you could manage to control your temper . . ." Inching toward the goose, Daisy investigated the source of the problem. "Oh, dear," she said. "Those little scamps . . . they were making you fish for them, weren't they?"

The goose screeched in agreement.

A length of fishing line had been knotted around the goose's leg, leading to a tin spoon with a hole punched through the bowl. A fishhook had been attached to the hole. Were it not for her sympathy for the ill-used goose, Daisy would have laughed.

It was ingenious. As the goose was tossed out into the water and had to swim its way back, the tin spoon would flash like a minnow. If a trout was attracted by the lure it would be caught on the hook, and the goose would tow it in. But the hook had caught on some bramble, effectively imprison-ing the goose.

Daisy kept her voice soft and her movements slow as she crept toward the bramble. The bird froze and peered at her with one bright black eye.

"There's a nice fellow," Daisy soothed, carefully reaching for the line. "My goodness, you're large. If you'll just be patient a moment longer, I'll—ouch!" Suddenly the goose had rushed forward and struck her forearm with a hammer-blow of its beak.

Scampering back, Daisy glanced down at the little dent on her skin, which was beginning to bruise. She scowled at the belligerent goose. "You ungrateful creature! Just for that I ought to leave you here like this."

Rubbing the sore spot on her arm, Daisy won-dered if she might be able to use her fishing rod to unhook the line from the bramble . . . but that still didn't solve the problem of removing the spoon from the goose's leg. She would have to walk back to the manor and find someone to help.

As she bent to pick up her fishing gear, she heard an unexpected noise. Someone whistling an oddly familiar tune. Daisy listened intently, remembering the melody. It was a song that had been popular in New York just before she had left, called "The End Of A Perfect Day."

Someone was walking toward her from the direction of the river. A man dressed in sodden clothes, carrying a fishing creel and wearing an ancient low-brimmed hat. He was wearing a sportsman's tweed coat and rough trousers, and it was impossible not to notice the way the layers of his clothing clung wetly to the lean contours of his body. Her senses leaped with recognition, galvanizing her pulse to a new pace.

The man stopped in mid-whistle as he saw her. His eyes were bluer than the water or the sky, startling in his tanned face. As he removed his hat in deference, the sun brought out rich mahogany glints in the heavy dark locks of his hair.

"Blast," Daisy said to herself. Not just because he was the last person she wanted to see at the moment, but also because she had to admit that Matthew Swift was extraordinarily good-looking. She didn't want to find him so physically appealing. Nor did she want to feel such curiosity about him, the desire to steal inside his privacy and discover his secrets and pleasures and fears. Why had she never taken an interest in him before? Perhaps she had been too immature. Perhaps it wasn't he who had changed, but she.

Swift approached her cautiously. "Miss Bowman."

"Good morning, Mr. Swift. Why aren't you fishing with the others?"

"My creel is full. And I was outfishing them to the extent that it was going to embarrass them all if I continued."

"How modest you are," Daisy said wryly. "Where's your rod?"

"Westcliff took it."

"Why?"

Setting down his creel, Swift replaced his hat. "I brought it with me from America. It's a jointed hickory rod with a flexible ash tip and a Kentucky multiplying reel with a balanced crank handle."

"Multiplying reels don't work," Daisy said.

"British multipliers don't," Swift corrected. "But in the states we've made a few improvements. As soon as Westcliff realized I was able to cast directly from the spool, he practically ripped the thing from my hands. He's fishing with it as we speak."

Knowing her brother-in-law's love of technological devices, Daisy smiled ruefully. She felt Swift's gaze on her, and she didn't want to look back at him, but she found herself staring anyway.

It was jarring to reconcile her memories of the odious young man she had known with this robust specimen of manhood. He was like a new-minted copper penny, bright and shiny and perfect. The morning light slid over his skin and caught in the glittering length of his lashes and the tiny fans of lines radiating from the outward corners of his eyes. She wanted to touch his face, to make him smile and feel the curve of his lips beneath her fingers.

The silence lengthened, becoming strained and awkward until it was broken by the goose's imperious honk.

Swift glanced at the massive bird. "You have a

companion, I see." When Daisy explained what the two boys had been doing with the goose, Swift grinned. "Clever lads."

The remark did not strike Daisy as being especially compassionate. "I want to help him," she said. "But when I tried to get near, he pecked me. I expected a domestic breed would have been a bit more receptive to my approach."

"Greylags are not known for their mild temperaments," Swift informed her. "Particularly males. He was probably trying to show you who was boss."

"He proved his point," Daisy said, rubbing her arm.

Swift frowned as he saw the growing bruise on her arm. "Is that where he pecked you? Let me see."

"No, it's all right—" she began, but he had already come forward. His long fingers encircled her wrist, the thumb of his other hand passing gently near the dark purple mark.

"You bruise easily," he murmured, his dark head bent over her arm.

Daisy's heart dispensed a series of hard thumps before settling into a fast rhythm. He smelled like the outdoors—sun, water, grassy-sweet. And deeper in the fragrance lingered the tantalizing incense of warm, sweaty male. She fought the instinct to move into his arms, against his body . . . to pull his hand to her breast. The mute craving shocked her.

Glancing up at his downturned face, Daisy found his blue eyes staring right into hers. "I . . ." Nervously she pulled away from him. "What are we to do?"

"About the goose?" His broad shoulders hitched in a shrug. "We could wring his neck and take him home for dinner."

The suggestion caused Daisy and the Greylag to stare at him in shared outrage.

"That was a very poor joke, Mr. Swift."

"I wasn't joking."

Daisy placed herself squarely between Swift and the goose. "I will deal with the situation on my own. You may leave now."

"I wouldn't advise making a pet of him. You'll eventually find him on your plate if you stay at Stony Cross Park long enough."

"I don't care if it makes me a hypocrite," she said. "I would rather not eat a goose I'm acquainted with."

Though Swift did not crack a smile, Daisy sensed he was amused by her remark.

"Philosophical questions aside," he said, "there's the practical matter of how you intend to free his leg. You'll get beaten black and blue for your pains."

"If you would hold him still, I could reach for the spoon and—"

"Not," Swift said firmly, "for all the tea in China."

"That expression has never made sense to me,"

she told him. "In terms of total world production, India grows far more tea than China."

Swift's lips twitched as he considered the point. "Since China is the leading international producer of hemp," he said, "I suppose one could say 'Not for all the hemp in China' . . . but it doesn't have the same ring. However you care to phrase it, I'm not going to help the goose." He bent to pick up his creel.

"Please," Daisy said.

Swift gave her a long-suffering look.

"Please," she repeated.

No gentleman could refuse a lady who had used the word twice.

Muttering something indecipherable beneath his breath, Swift set the creel back down.

A self-satisfied smile curved Daisy's lips. "Thank you."

Her smile faded, however, when he warned, "You'll owe me for this."

"Naturally," Daisy replied. "I would never expect you to do something for nothing."

"And when I call in the favor, you're not even going to think of refusing, no matter what it is."

"Within reason. I'm not going to agree to marry you just because you rescued a poor trapped goose."

"Believe me," Swift said darkly, "marriage won't be any part of it." He began to remove his coat, having difficulty stripping the damp olive-colored tweed from his broad shoulders.

"Wh-what are you doing?" Daisy's eyes widened.

His mouth held an exasperated slant. "I'm not going to let that blasted bird ruin my coat."

"There's no need to make a fuss over getting a few feathers on your coat."

"It's not feathers I'm worried about," he said curtly.

"Oh." Daisy fought to hold back a sudden smile.

She watched him take off his coat and his vest. His creased white shirt adhered to his broad chest, becoming wetter and almost transparent as it stuck to the muscle-banded surface of his abdomen and disappeared beneath the sodden band of his trousers. A pair of white braces stretched over his shoulders and crossed the powerful surface of his back. He laid his discarded garments carefully over his creel to keep them from becoming muddy. A breeze played with the clipped layers of his hair, briefly lifting a lock on his forehead.

The strangeness of the situation . . . the baleful goose, Matthew Swift waterlogged and dressed in his shirtsleeves . . . caused an irrepressible giggle to rise to Daisy's lips. Hastily she clapped her hand over her mouth, but it came out anyway.

He shook his head, while an answering smile broke out on his face. Daisy noticed that his smiles never lasted for long, they vanished as quickly as they appeared. It was like catching sight of some rare natural phenomenon, like a shooting star, brief and striking.

"If you tell anyone about this, you little imp . . . you'll pay." The words were threatening, but something in his tone . . . an erotic softness . . . sent a hot-and-cold chill down her spine.

"I'm not going to tell anyone," Daisy said breathlessly. "The situation would reflect as badly on me as it would on you."

Swift reached into his discarded coat, extracted a small penknife and handed it to her. Was it her imagination, or had his fingers lingered an extra second on the surface of her palm?

"What's this for?" she asked uneasily.

"To cut the string from the bird's leg. Be careful—it's very sharp. I'd hate for you to accidentally slice open an artery."

"Don't worry, I won't hurt him."

"I was referring to myself, not the goose." He slid an assessing glance over the impatient fowl. "If you make this difficult," he said to the goose, "you'll be paté by suppertime."

The bird raised its wings threateningly to make itself appear as large as possible.

Moving forward in a deliberate step, Swift placed one foot on the line, shortening the goose's range of movement. The creature flapped and hissed, pausing for a moment before making the decision to hurl itself forward. Swift seized the goose, cursing as he tried to avoid the driving beak. A flurry of feathers rose around the pair.

"Don't choke him," Daisy cried, seeing that Swift had gotten hold of the goose's neck.

It was perhaps fortunate that Swift's reply was lost in the explosion of movement and honking and goose-battling. Somehow Swift managed to restrain the bird until it was a writhing, spitting mass in his arms. Disheveled and blanketed with feathers and down, he glared at Daisy, "Get over here and cut the line," he snapped.

Hastily she obeyed, dropping to her knees beside the grappling pair. Gingerly she reached for the goose's muddy webbed foot, and it squawked and jerked its leg away.

"For God's sake, don't be timid," she heard Swift say impatiently. "Just grab hold of the thing and get to work."

Had there not been thirty pounds of furious goose caught between them, Daisy would have glared at Matthew Swift. Instead she seized the goose's tethered foot in a firm grip and carefully slid the tip of the knife beneath the line. Swift had been right—the blade was wickedly sharp. With one nick it cut the line cleanly in two.

"It's done," she said triumphantly, closing the knife. "You may release our feathered friend, Mr. Swift."

"Thank you," came his sardonic reply.

But as Swift opened his arms and freed the bird, it reacted unexpectedly. Bent on vengeance, blaming its captor for all its woes, the creature twisted to aim a jab at his face.

"*Ow!*" Swift fell back to a half-sitting position,

clutching a hand to his eye while the goose sped away with a triumphant honk.

"Mr. Swift!" Daisy crawled over him in concern, straddling his lap. She tugged at his hand. "Let me see."

"I'm all right," he said, rubbing his eye.

"Let me see," she repeated, grasping his head in her hands.

"I'm going to *demand* goose hash for dinner," he muttered, letting her turn his face to the side.

"You will do no such thing." Daisy gently inspected the tiny wound at the edge of his dark eyebrow and used her sleeve to blot a drop of blood. "It's bad form to eat someone after you've saved them." A tremor of laughter ran through her voice. "Fortunately the goose had bad aim. I don't think your eye will turn black."

"I'm glad you find this amusing," he muttered. "You're covered with feathers, you know."

"So are you." Tiny bits of fluff and spars of gray and white were caught in his shiny brown hair. More laughter escaped her, like bubbles rising to the surface of a pond. She began to pick feathers and down from his hair, the thick locks tickling-soft against her fingers.

Levering himself upward, Swift reached for her hair, which had begun to fall from its pins. His fingers were gentle as he pulled feathers from the glinting black strands.

For a silent minute or two they worked on each

other. Daisy was so intent on the task that the impropriety of her position didn't occur to her at first. For the first time she was close enough to notice the variegated blue of his eyes, ringed with cobalt at the outer edge of the irises. And the texture of his skin, satiny and sun-hued, with the shadow of close-shaven stubble on his jaw.

She realized that Swift was deliberately avoiding her gaze, concentrating on finding every tiny piece of down in her hair. Suddenly she became aware of a simmering communication between their bodies, the solid strength of him beneath her, the incendiary drift of his breath against her cheek. His clothes were damp, the heat of his skin burning through wherever it pressed against hers.

They both went still at the same moment, caught together in a half-embrace while every cell of Daisy's skin seemed to fill with liquid fire. Fascinated, disoriented, she let herself relax into it, feeling the throb of her pulse in every extremity. There were no more feathers, but Daisy found herself gently lacing her fingers through the dark waves of his hair.

It would be so easy for him to roll her beneath him, his weight pressing her into the damp earth. The hardness of their knees pressed together through layers of fabric, triggering a primitive instinct for her to open to him, to let him move her limbs as he would.

She heard Swift's breath catch. He clamped his hands around her upper arms and unceremoniously removed her from his lap.

Landing on the grass beside him with a decisive thump, Daisy tried to gather her wits. Silently she found the pen-knife on the ground and handed it back to him.

After slipping the knife back into his pocket, he made a project of brushing feathers and dirt from his calves.

Wondering why he was sitting in such an oddly cramped posture, Daisy struggled to her feet. "Well," she said uncertainly, "I suppose I'll have to sneak back into the manor through the servants' entrance. If Mother sees me, she'll have conniptions."

"I'm going back to the river," Swift said, his voice hoarse. "To find out how Westcliff is faring with the reel. And maybe I'll fish some more."

Daisy frowned as she realized he was deliberately avoiding her.

"I should think you'd had enough of standing up to your waist in cold water today," she said.

"Apparently not," Swift muttered, keeping his back to her as he reached for his vest and coat.

Chapter 5

Perplexed and annoyed, Daisy strode away from the artificial lake.

She wasn't going to tell anyone about what had just happened, even though she would have loved to amuse Lillian with the story of the goose encounter. But she did not want to reveal that she had seen a different side of Matthew Swift, and that she had briefly allowed herself to flirt with a dangerous attraction to him. It had meant nothing, really.

Although Daisy was still an innocent, she understood enough of sexual matters to be aware that one's body could respond to a man without any involvement of the heart. As she had once responded to Cam Rohan. It disconcerted her to realize she was drawn to Matthew Swift in that same way. Such different men, one romantic, one reserved. One a handsome young gypsy who had stirred her imagination with exotic possibilities . . . one a man of business, hard-eyed and ambitious and pragmatic.

Daisy had seen an endless parade of power-seeking men during the Fifth Avenue years. They wanted perfection, a wife who could be the best hostess and give the best suppers and soirees, and wear the best gowns, and produce the best children who would play quietly upstairs in the nursery while their fathers were negotiating business deals downstairs in the study.

And Matthew Swift, with his enormous drive, the one her father had singled out for his talent and brilliant mind, would be the most exacting husband imaginable. He would want a wife who formed her entire life around his goals, and he would judge her severely when she failed to please him. There could be no future with a man like that.

But there was one thing in Matthew Swift's favor: He *had* helped the goose.

By the time Daisy had stolen into the manor, washed and dressed in a fresh day-gown, her friends and sister had gathered in the morning room for tea and toast. They sat at one of the round tables by a window, looking up as Daisy entered the room.

Annabelle held Isabelle against her shoulder,

rubbing her tiny back in soothing circles. A few of the other tables were occupied, mostly by women, although there were about a half-dozen men present, including Lord St. Vincent.

"Good morning," Daisy said brightly, going to her sister. "How was your sleep, dear?"

"Splendid." Lillian looked lovely, her eyes clear, her black hair pulled back from her face and caught in a pink silk net at the nape of her neck. "I slept with the windows open, and the breeze coming from the lake was so refreshing. Did you go fishing this morning?"

"No." Daisy tried to sound offhand. "I just walked."

Evie leaned toward Annabelle to take the baby. "Let me hold her," she said. The baby was chewing frantically on a small fist and drooling copiously. Taking the restless child, Evie explained to Daisy, "She's teething, poor thing."

"She's been fretful all morning," Annabelle said. Daisy saw that her luminous blue eyes looked a little tired, the eyes of a young mother. The touch of weariness only enhanced Annabelle's beauty, softening the goddess-like perfection of her features.

"Isn't it rather soon for the baby to be teething?" Daisy asked.

"She's a Hunt," Annabelle said dryly. "And Hunts are an unusually hardy lot. According to my husband, everyone in his family is practically born with teeth." She regarded the baby with concern. "I think I should take her from the room."

A score of disapproving glances were cast in their direction. It was not the done thing for children, especially infants, to be brought into adult company. Unless it was strictly for show, with the child dressed in white ruffles and ribbons and briefly exhibited for general approval, and then carted quickly back up to the nursery.

"Nonsense," Lillian said at once, not bothering to lower her voice. "Isabelle is hardly screaming or carrying on. She's just a bit agitated. I think everyone can manage to have a little tolerance."

"Let's try the spoon again," Annabelle murmured, her cultured voice touched with anxiety. She pulled a chilled silver spoon from a little bowl of crushed ice, and told Daisy, "My mother suggested giving her this—she said it always worked with my brother Jeremy."

Daisy sat beside Evie, watching as the baby bit down on the bowl of the spoon. Isabelle's round little face was flushed and a few tears had tracked from her eyes. As she whimpered, the tender, inflamed part of her gums was visible, and Daisy winced in sympathy.

"She needs a nap," Annabelle said. "But she's in too much pain to sleep."

"Poor darling."

As Evie tried to soothe the baby there was a minor stir at the other side of the room. Someone's entrance had caused a ripple of interest. Turning in her chair, Daisy saw the tall, striking form of Matthew Swift.

So he hadn't gone back to the river. He must have waited until Daisy had gone sufficiently far ahead, then walked to the manor without having to escort her.

Like her father, Swift found little in her that was worthy of interest. Daisy told herself that she shouldn't care, but the knowledge stung.

He had changed into a perfectly pressed suit of clothes, dark gray with a dove-colored vest, his black necktie crisp and conservatively knotted. Although it had become fashionable in Europe for men to grow their side whiskers longer and wear their hair in loose waves, it appeared the style had not yet reached America. Matthew Swift was completely clean-shaven, and his gleaming brown hair had been shaped close to the sides of his head and neck, giving him an appealing touch of boyishness.

Daisy watched covertly as introductions were made. She saw the pleasure on the faces of the older gentlemen as they spoke to him, and the jealousy of the younger gentlemen. And the flirtatious interest of the women.

"Good heavens," Annabelle murmured, "who is that?"

Lillian replied grumpily. "That is Mr. Swift."

Both Annabelle's and Evie's eyes widened.

"The same Mr. Swift you described as a bag of b-bones?" Evie asked.

"The one you said was about as exciting as a dish of wilted spinach?" Annabelle added.

Lillian's frown deepened into an outright scowl. Ripping her attention from Swift, she dropped a lump of sugar in her tea. "I suppose he may not be quite as hideous as I described," she allowed. "But don't let his appearance deceive you. Once you are acquainted with the inner man, it will change your impression of the outer one."

"I th-think there are quite a few ladies who would like to become acquainted with any part of him," Evie observed, causing Annabelle to snicker into her teacup.

Daisy threw a quick glance over her shoulder and saw it was true. Ladies were fluttering, giggling, extending soft white hands to be taken and pressed.

"All this fuss just because he's American and therefore a novelty," Lillian muttered. "If any of my brothers were here, those ladies would forget all about Mr. Swift."

Although Daisy would have liked to agree, she was fairly certain that their brothers would not have the same effect as Mr. Swift. For all that they were heirs to a great fortune, the Bowman brothers did not have Swift's carefully cultivated social finesse.

"He's looking over here," Annabelle reported.

Anxiety lent subtle tension to her posture. "He's frowning, along with everyone else. The baby is making too much of a fuss. I'll take her outside and—"

"Do not take her anywhere," Lillian commanded. "This is *my* home, and you're *my* friend, and anyone who doesn't care for the baby's noise is welcome to leave at once."

"He's coming this way," Evie whispered. *"Hush."*

Daisy stared steadily into her tea, tension coiling in her muscles.

Swift came to the table and bowed politely. "My lady," he said to Lillian, "what a pleasure it is to see you again. May I offer my renewed congratulations on your marriage to Lord Westcliff, and . . ." He hesitated, for although Lillian was obviously pregnant, it would be impolite to refer to her condition. ". . . you are looking quite well," he finished.

"I'm the size of a barn," Lillian said flatly, puncturing his attempt at diplomacy.

Swift's mouth firmed as if he was fighting to suppress a grin. "Not at all," he said mildly, and glanced at Annabelle and Evie. They all waited for Lillian to make the introductions.

Lillian complied grudgingly. "This is Mr. Swift," she muttered, waving her hand in his direction. "Mrs. Simon Hunt and Lady St. Vincent."

Swift bent deftly over Annabelle's hand. He would have done the same for Evie except she was holding the baby. Isabelle's grunts and whimpers were escalating and would soon become a full-out wail unless something was done about it.

"That is my daughter Isabelle," Annabelle said apologetically. "She's teething."

That should get rid of him quickly, Daisy thought. Men were terrified of crying babies.

"Ah." Swift reached into his coat and rummaged through a rattling collection of articles. What on earth did he have in there? She watched as he pulled out his pen-knife, a bit of fishing line and a clean white handkerchief.

"Mr. Swift, what are you doing?" Evie asked with a quizzical smile.

"Improvising something." He spooned some crushed ice into the center of the handkerchief, gathered the fabric tightly around it, and tied it off with fishing line. After replacing the knife in his pocket, he reached for the baby without one trace of self-consciusness.

Wide-eyed, Evie surrendered the infant. The four women watched in astonishment as Swift took Isabelle against his shoulder with practiced ease. He gave the baby the ice-filled handkerchief, which she proceeded to gnaw madly even as she continued to cry.

Seeming oblivious to the fascinated stares of everyone in the room, Swift wandered to the window and murmured softly to the baby. It appeared he was telling her a story of some kind. After a minute or two the child quieted.

When Swift returned to the table Isabelle was half-drowsing and sighing, her mouth clamped firmly on the makeshift ice pouch.

"Oh, Mr. Swift," Annabelle said gratefully, taking the baby back in her arms, "how clever of you! Thank you."

"What were you saying to her?" Lillian demanded.

He glanced at her and replied blandly, "I thought I would distract her long enough for the ice to numb her gums. So I gave her a detailed explanation of the Buttonwood agreement of 1792."

Daisy spoke to him for the first time. "What was that?"

Swift glanced at her then, his face smooth and polite, and for a second Daisy half-believed that she had dreamed the events of that morning. But her skin and nerves still retained the sensation of him, the hard imprint of his body.

"The Buttonwood agreement led to the formation of the New York Stock and Exchange Board," Swift said. "I thought I was quite informative, but it seemed Miss Isabelle lost interest when I started on the fee-structuring compromise."

"I see," Daisy said. "You bored the poor baby to sleep."

"You should hear my account of the imbalance of market forces leading to the crash of '37," Swift said. "I've been told it's better than laudanum."

Staring into his glinting blue eyes, Daisy chuckled reluctantly, and he gave her another one of those brief, dazzling smiles. Her face turned unaccountably warm.

Swift's attention remained on her for a moment too long, as if he were fascinated by something he saw in her eyes. Abruptly he tore his gaze from hers and bowed to the table again. "I will leave your to enjoy your tea. A pleasure, ladies." Glancing at Annabelle, he added gravely, "You have a lovely daughter, madam. I will overlook her lack of appreciation for my business lecture."

"That is very kind of you, sir," Annabelle replied, her eyes dancing.

Swift returned to the other side of the room while the young women all busied themselves, stirring unnecessary spoonfuls of sugar into their tea, smoothing their napkins on their laps.

Evie was the first to speak. "You were right," she said to Lillian. "He's absolutely horrid."

"Yes," Annabelle agreed emphatically. "When one looks at him, the first words that come to mind are 'wilted spinach.' "

"Shut up, the both of you," Lillian said in response to their sarcasm, and sank her teeth into a piece of toast.

Lillian insisted on dragging Daisy out to the east lawn in the afternoon, where most of the young people were playing bowls. Ordinarily Daisy wouldn't have minded, but she had just reached a riveting part in a new novel about a governess named Honoria who had just encountered a ghost in the attic. "*Who are you?*" Honoria had quavered, staring at the ghost who looked remarkably like her old love, Lord Clayworth. The ghost had been about to answer when Lillian had decisively torn the book from Daisy's hands and pulled her from the library.

"Blast," Daisy complained. "Blast, *blast* . . . Lillian, I had just gotten to the best part!"

"As we speak there are at least a half-dozen eligible men who are lawn-bowling outside," her sister said crisply. "And playing games with them is far more productive than reading by yourself."

"I don't know anything about bowls."

"Good. Ask them to teach you. If there's one thing every man loves to do, it's telling a woman how to do something."

They approached the bowling lawn, where chairs and tables had been set out for onlookers. A group of players were busy rolling large round wooden balls along the green, laughing as one player's ball, or bowl, dropped into the narrow ditch dug at the side of the green.

"Hmm," Lillian said, observing the gathering. "We have competition." Daisy recognized the three women her sister was referring to: Miss Cassandra Leighton, Lady Miranda Dowden, and Elspeth Higginson. "I would have preferred not to invite any unmarried women to Hampshire," Lillian said, "but Westcliff said that would be too obvious. Fortunately you're prettier than all of them. Even if you are short."

"I'm not short," Daisy protested.

"Petite, then."

"I don't like that word any better. It makes me sound trivial."

"It's better than stunted," Lillian said, "which is the only other word I can come up with to describe your lack of stature." She grinned at Daisy's scowl. "Don't make faces, dear. I'm taking you to a buffet of bachelors and you can pick any—oh, *hell*."

"What? What?"

"*He's* playing."

There was no need to ask who *he* was . . . the annoyance in Lillian's voice made his identity perfectly clear.

Surveying the group, Daisy saw Matthew Swift standing at the end of the lane with a few other young men, watching as the distances between the bowls were being measured. Like the others he was dressed in light-colored trousers, a white shirt, and a sleeveless waistcoat. He was lean and fit, his relaxed posture imbued with physical confidence.

His gaze caught everything. He appeared to be taking the game seriously. Matthew Swift was a man who could never do less than his best, even in a casual lawn game.

Daisy was fairly certain that he competed for something every day of his life. And that didn't quite fit with her experience of the privileged young men of Old Boston, or Old New York, the pampered scions who were always aware that they didn't have to work if they didn't wish to. She wondered if Swift ever did something just for the enjoyment of it.

"They're trying to determine who's lying the shot," Lillian said. "That means who managed to roll their bowls closest to the white ball at the end."

"How do you know so much about the game?" Daisy asked.

Lillian smiled wryly. "Westcliff taught me to play. He's so good at bowls that he usually sits out because no one else ever wins when he plays."

They approached the group of chairs, where Westcliff was sitting with Evie and Lord St. Vincent, and the Craddocks, a retired major general and his wife. Daisy headed toward an extra chair, but Lillian pushed her toward the bowling green.

"Go," Lillian commanded in the same tone one would have used to send a dog to fetch a stick.

Sighing, Daisy cast a longing thought to her unfinished novel and trudged forward. She had met at least three of the gentlemen on previous occasions. Not bad prospects, actually. There was Mr. Hollingberry, a pleasant-looking man in his thirties, round-cheeked and a bit pudgy but attractive nonetheless. And Mr. Mardling, with his athletic build and thick blond curls and green eyes.

There were two men she had not seen at Stony Cross before, Mr. Alan Rickett, who was rather scholarly looking with his spectacles and slightly rumpled coat . . . and Lord Llandrindon, a handsome dark-haired gentleman of medium height.

Llandrindon approached Daisy immediately,

volunteering to explain the rules of the game. Daisy tried not to look over his shoulder at Mr. Swift, who was surrounded by the other women. They were giggling and flirting, asking his advice on how to hold the bowl properly and how many steps one should take before releasing the bowl onto the green.

Swift appeared to take no notice of Daisy. But as she turned to pick up a wooden bowl from a pile on the ground, she felt a tingling at the back of her neck. She knew he was looking at her.

Daisy sorely regretted having asked him to help her with the trapped goose. The episode had set off something that was beyond her control, some troubling awareness she couldn't seem to banish. *Stop being ridiculous,* Daisy told herself. *Start bowling.* And she forced herself to listen attentively to Lord Llandrindon's advice on bowls strategy.

Observing the action on the green, Westcliff commented softly, "She's getting on well with Llandrindon, from the looks of it. And he's one of the most promising possibilities. He's the right age, well-educated, and possessed of a pleasant disposition."

Lillian regarded Llandrindon's distant form speculatively. He was even the right height, not too tall for Daisy, who disliked it when people towered over her. "He has an odd name," Lillian mused aloud. "I wonder where he's from?"

"Thurso," replied Lord St. Vincent, who was sitting on the other side of Evie.

An uneasy truce had come to exist between

Lillian and St. Vincent after a great deal of past conflict. Although she would never truly like him, Lillian had prosaically decided that St. Vincent would have to be tolerated, since he had been friends with Westcliff for years.

Lillian knew if she asked her husband to end the friendship he would do so for her sake, but she loved him too much to make such a demand. And St. Vincent was good for Marcus. With his wit and perceptiveness, he helped to bring a measure of balance to Marcus's overburdened life. Marcus, as one of the most powerful men in England, was in dire need of people who didn't take him too seriously.

The other point in St. Vincent's favor was that he appeared to be a good husband to Evie. He seemed to worship her, actually. One would never have thought of putting them together—Evie the shy wallflower, St. Vincent the heartless rake—and yet they had developed a singular attachment to each other.

St. Vincent was self-assured and sophisticated, possessing a male beauty so dazzling that people sometimes caught their breath when they glanced at him. But all it took was one word from Evie to make him come running. Even though their relationship was quieter, less outwardly demonstrative than those of the Hunts or Westcliffs, a mysterious and passionate intensity existed between the two.

And as long as Evie was happy, Lillian would be cordial to St. Vincent.

"Thurso," Lillian repeated suspiciously, glancing from St. Vincent to her husband. "That doesn't sound English to me."

The two men exchanged a glance, and Marcus replied evenly. "It's located in Scotland, actually."

Lillian's eyes narrowed. "Llandrindon is Scottish? But he doesn't have an accent."

"He spent most of his formative years at English boarding schools and then Oxford," St. Vincent said.

"Hmm." Lillian's knowledge of Scottish geography was scant, but she had never even heard of Thurso. "And where is Thurso precisely? Is it just past the border?"

Westcliff didn't quite meet her gaze. "Somewhat more north than that. Near the Orkney islands."

"The *northern edge of the continent?*" Lillian couldn't believe her ears. It took a great deal of effort to keep her voice to a furious whisper. "Why don't we just save ourselves some time and banish Daisy to Siberia? It would probably be warmer! Good God, how can the two of you have agreed on Llandrindon as a candidate?"

"I had to throw him in," St. Vincent protested. "He owns three estates and an entire string of thoroughbreds. And every time he comes to the club my nightly profits go up at least five thousand pounds."

"He's a spendthrift, then," Lillian said darkly.

"That makes him even more eligible for Daisy,"

St. Vincent said. "Someday he'll need your family's money."

"I don't care how eligible he is, the object is to keep my sister in *this* country. How often will I get to see Daisy if she's in bloody Scotland?"

"It's still closer than North America," Westcliff pointed out in a matter-of-fact tone.

Lillian turned to Evie in hopes of enlisting her as an ally. "Evie, say something!"

"It doesn't matter where Lord Llandrindon is from." Evie reached over to gently untangle a strand of dark hair that had caught in Lillian's ear-bob. "Daisy's not going to marry him."

"Why do you think so?" Lillian asked warily.

Evie smiled at her. "Oh . . . just a feeling."

In her desire to finish the game and return to her novel, Daisy had picked up the knack of lawn-bowling rather quickly. The first player rolled the white ball, called the jack, to the end of the lane of grass without going over the edge. The object was to roll three wooden balls, called bowls, until they ended up as close as possible to the jack.

The only difficult part was that the wooden bowls were deliberately less rounded on one side, so they never quite rolled in a straight line. Daisy soon learned to compensate for the bowls' asymmetry by casting a little to the right or left, as needed. It was a fast green with short grass and hard-packed soil, which was a good thing since Daisy was in a hurry to be done and return to Honoria and the ghost.

Since there was an equal number of women and men, the players were divided into teams of two. Daisy was paired with Llandrindon, who was a proficient player.

"You're quite good, Miss Bowman," Lord Llandrindon exclaimed. "Are you sure you've never played before?"

"Never," Daisy replied cheerfully. Picking up a wooden sphere, she turned the flat side to the right. "It must be your able instructions, my lord." Taking two steps forward to the edge of the delivery line, she drew back and released the bowl in a deftly spun roll. It knocked one of the opposing players' bowls smartly out of the way and ended up exactly two inches from the jack. They had won the round.

"Well done," said Mr. Rickett, pausing to polish his spectacles. Replacing them, he smiled at Daisy and added, "You move with such grace, Miss Bowman. It is a delight to witness your skill."

"It has nothing to do with skill," Daisy said modestly. "Beginner's luck, I'm afraid."

Lady Miranda, a slender blond girl with a porcelain complexion, was examining her delicate hands with concern. "I believe I've broken a fingernail," she announced.

"Let me help you to a chair," Rickett said in instant concern, as if she had broken an arm rather than a fingernail, and the two made their way off the green.

Daisy reflected ruefully that she should have

deliberately lost the game, and then she wouldn't have to play another round. But it was unfair to one's teammate to lose a game on purpose. And Lord Llandrindon seemed positively delighted by their success.

"Now," Llandrindon said, "let's see who we are to face in the final round."

They watched the two remaining teams compete, Mr. Swift and Miss Leighton against Mr. Mardling and Miss Higginson. Mr. Mardling was an uneven player, following brilliant shots with awkward ones, whereas Miss Higginson was far more consistent. Cassandra Leighton was hopelessly bad and highly amused by the fact, giggling and tittering uncontrollably during the entire match. It was profoundly annoying, that continuous laughter, but it didn't seem to bother Matthew Swift.

Swift was an aggressive and tactical player, considering each shot carefully, displaying an easy economy of motion as he bowled. Daisy noticed that he showed no compunction about knocking the other players' bowls out of the way, or moving the jack to their disadvantage.

"A formidable player," Lord Llandrindon commented softly to Daisy, his eyes twinkling. "Do you think we can best him?"

Suddenly Daisy forgot all about the novel that awaited her inside the manor. The prospect of playing against Matthew Swift filled her with anticipation. "Doubtful. But we can give it a good try, can't we?"

Llandrindon laughed appreciatively. "We certainly can."

Swift and Miss Leighton won the game, and the others left the green with good-natured exclamations.

The four remaining players gathered up the bowls and the jack, and returned to the delivery line. Each team would get four bowls total, two shots for each player.

As Daisy turned to face Matthew Swift, he looked at her for the first time since she had arrived. His gaze, direct and challenging, caused her heart to thump hard in her chest, sending blood hurtling through her veins. His tousled hair fell over his forehead, and his sun-warmed complexion glowed with a subtle sheen of perspiration.

"We'll toss a coin to see who goes first," Lord Llandrindon suggested.

Swift nodded, his gaze dropping away from Daisy.

Cassandra Leighton squealed with delight as she and Swift won the coin toss. Skillfully Swift rolled the jack out to the head of the green in a perfect position.

Miss Leighton picked up a bowl, holding it close to her bosom in what Daisy suspected was a deliberate ploy to call attention to her generous endowments. "You must advise me, Mr. Swift," she said, sliding him a helpless glance from beneath curly lashes. "Should I throw it with the flat side of the ball on the right or the left?"

Swift moved closer to her, repositioning the ball in her hands. Miss Leighton radiated delight at the attention he paid her. He murmured some advice, pointing out the best path for the bowl while Miss Leighton leaned closer until their heads were nearly touching. Annoyance spiraled upward from Daisy's chest, tightening her throat muscles like a corkscrew.

Finally Swift stepped back. Miss Leighton moved forward with a few graceful steps, letting the bowl fly. But the drive was weak, and the bowl wobbled and rolled to a halt right in the middle of the grass lane. The rest of the game would be far more difficult with that bowl in the way unless someone cared to waste one of their shots to knock it aside.

"Hang it all," Daisy muttered beneath her breath.

Miss Leighton nearly collapsed with more loud giggles. "Dear me, I've fouled things up awfully, haven't I?"

"Not at all," Swift said easily. "It's no fun if it's not a challenge."

Irritably Daisy wondered why he was being so nice to Miss Leighton. She wouldn't have thought he was the kind of man who was attracted to silly women.

"Your turn," Lord Llandrindon urged, handing a bowl to Daisy.

She curved her fingers around the scarred wooden surface of the sphere and turned it until it felt right in her hands. Staring at the distant white shape of the jack, she envisioned the path she wanted her bowl to go in. Three steps, a back swing of her arm and a fast forward drive. The bowl shot down the side of the green, neatly avoiding Miss Leighton's, then curving at the last second to land precisely in front of the jack.

"Brilliant!" Llandrindon exclaimed, while the onlookers cheered and applauded.

Daisy stole a quick glance at Matthew Swift. He was watching with a faint smile, subjecting her to a survey that seemed to penetrate to her bones. Time stopped as if it had been tacked down with diamond pins. It was seldom, if ever, that a man ever looked at Daisy this way.

"Did you do that on purpose?" Swift asked softly. "Or was it a stroke of luck?"

"On purpose," Daisy replied.

"I doubt that."

Daisy bristled. "Why?"

"Because no rank novice could plan and carry out a shot like that."

"Are you questioning my honesty, Mr. Swift?" Without waiting for his reply, Daisy called to her sister, who was watching them from the cluster of chairs. "Lillian, to your knowledge have I ever played bowls before?"

"Certainly not," came Lillian's emphatic reply.

Turning back to Swift, Daisy gave him a challenging stare.

"To make that shot," Swift said, "you would have to calculate the green speed, the required angle to offset the bowl bias, and the point of deceleration at which the bowl's path would turn. While also taking into consideration the possibility of a cross wind. And you'd have to have the experience to pull it off."

"Is that how you play?" Daisy asked breezily. "I just envision how I want the bowl to go, and then I roll it."

"Luck and intuition?" He gave her a superior glance. "You can't win a game that way."

For answer Daisy stood back and folded her arms. "Your turn," she said.

Swift reached down and picked up a bowl in one hand. As he adjusted his fingers around the object, he walked to the delivery line and contemplated the green. Even vexed as she was, Daisy felt a tug of pleasure inside her abdomen as she watched him. Examining the sensation, she wondered how it was that he had acquired such a mortifying physical influence on her. The sight of him, the way he moved, filled her with an embarrassing thrill of awareness.

Swift released the bowl in a strong drive. It sped obediently down the green, perfectly reproducing Daisy's shot, though with more calculated momentum. Hitting Daisy's bowl cleanly off the grass, it took her place right in front of the jack.

"He knocked my bowl into the ditch," Daisy protested. "Is that legal?"

"Oh, yes," Lord Llandrindon said. "A bit ruthless,

but perfectly legal. Now it is properly referred to as a 'dead bowl.' "

"My bowl is dead?" Daisy asked indignantly.

Swift returned her scowl with an implacable glance. "Never do an enemy a small injury."

"Only you would quote Machiavelli during *lawn bowling,*" Daisy said through gritted teeth.

"Pardon," Lord Llandrindon said politely, "but I believe it's my turn." Seeing that neither of them were paying attention, he shrugged and went to the delivery line. His bowl careened down the green and ended just beyond the jack.

"I always play to win," Swift said to Daisy.

"Good God," Daisy said in exasperation, "you sound exactly like my father. Have you ever considered the possibility that some people play just for the fun of it? As a pleasant activity to pass the time? Or must everything be brought down to life-and-death conflict?"

"If you're not out to win, the game is pointless."

Seeing that she had completely slipped from Swift's notice, Cassandra Leighton sought to intervene. "I fancy it's my shot now, Mr. Swift. Would you please be so kind as to retrieve a bowl for me?"

Swift complied with barely a glance at her, his attention riveted on Daisy's small, tense face. "Here," he said brusquely, thrusting the bowl into Miss Leighton's hands.

"Perhaps you could advise me . . ." Miss Leighton began, but her voice faded as Swift and Daisy continued to bicker.

"All right, Mr. Swift," Daisy said coolly. "If you can't enjoy a simple game of bowls without making it into a war, you'll have a war. We'll play for points." She wasn't quite certain if she had moved forward or if he had, but suddenly they were standing very close, his head bent over hers.

"You can't beat me," Swift said in a low voice. "You're a novice, and a woman besides. It wouldn't be fair unless I was assigned a handicap."

"Your teammate is Miss Leighton," she whispered sharply. "In my opinion, that's enough of a handicap. And are you implying that women can't bowl as well as men?"

"No. I'm saying straight out they can't."

Daisy felt a rush of outrage, augmented by a fiery desire to pound him into the ground. *"War,"* she repeated, stalking back to her side of the green.

Years later it would still be called the most bloodthirsty game of lawn bowling ever witnessed in Stony Cross. The game was extended to thirty points, and then fifty, and then Daisy lost count. They fought over every inch of ground and every rule of play. They mulled over each shot as if fates of nations depended on it. And most of all they devoted themselves to knocking each other's bowls into the ditch.

"Dead bowl!" Daisy crowed after executing a

perfect shot that sent Swift's tumbling off the green.

"Perhaps you should be reminded, Miss Bowman," Swift said, "the object of the game is not to keep me off the field. You're supposed to land your bowl as close as possible to the jack."

"That's not bloody likely when you keep whacking them out of the way!" Daisy heard Miss Leighton gasp at her language. This really wasn't like her—she never swore—it was just that current circumstances made it impossible to keep a cool head.

"I'll stop whacking your bowls," Swift offered, "if you'll stop whacking mine."

Daisy considered the proposition for a half-second. But the unfortunate fact was, it was much, much too enjoyable to send his bowls into the ditch. "Not for all the hemp in China, Mr. Swift."

"Very well." Picking up a battered bowl, Swift rolled it in a mighty drive, which made such violent contact with her bowl that an earsplitting *crack* shot through the air.

Daisy's mouth fell open as she saw the separate halves of her bowl wobbling into the ditch. "You broke it!" she exclaimed, rounding on him with clenched fists. "And you bowled out of turn! Miss Leighton was supposed to go next, you ruthless fiend!"

"Oh no," Miss Leighton said uneasily, "I am perfectly content to let Mr. Swift bowl in my stead . . . his skill being so much greater than . . ."

Her voice faded as she realized no one was listening to her.

"Your turn," Swift said to Lord Llandrindon, who looked taken aback by the game's new level of ferocity.

"Oh, no it isn't!" Daisy plucked the ball from Llandrindon's hands. "He's too much of a gentleman to whack your bowl. But I'm not."

"No," Swift agreed, "you are definitely not a gentleman."

Striding to the delivery line, Daisy drew back and released the bowl with all her might. It sped down the green and knocked Swift's bowl to the edge of the green, where it teetered uncertainly before plonking into the ditch. She shot Swift a vengeful glance, and he responded with a mocking congratulatory nod.

"I say," Llandrindon remarked, "your performance at bowls is exceptional, Miss Bowman. I've never seen a beginner do so well. How do you manage to deliver it perfectly every time?"

"Where the willingness is great, the difficulties cannot be," she replied, and saw the line of Swift's cheek tighten with a sudden grin as he recognized the Machiavelli quote.

The game went on. And on. Afternoon ripened into early evening. Daisy gradually became aware that they had lost Lord Llandrindon, Miss Leighton and most of the onlookers. It was clear that Lord Westcliff would have liked to go inside as well, but Daisy and Swift kept summoning him to arbitrate or to take a measurement as his judgement was the only one they both trusted.

An hour passed, and another, the game too absorbing for either player to give a thought to hunger, thirst, or weariness. At some point, Daisy wasn't exactly certain when, their competitiveness changed to grudging appreciation of each other's skill. When Swift complimented her on a particularly masterful shot or when she found herself enjoying the sight of his silent calculations, the way his eyes narrowed and his head tilted a little to the side . . . she was enthralled. There had been few occasions when Daisy's real life had been infinitely more entertaining than her fantasy life. But this was one of them.

"Children." Westcliff's sardonic voice caused them both to look at him blankly. He was standing from his chair and stretching underused muscles. "I'm afraid this has gone on long enough for me. You are welcome to continue playing, but I beg to take leave."

"But who will arbitrate?" Daisy protested.

"Since no one has been keeping score for at least a half hour," the earl said dryly, "there is no further need for my judgement."

"Yes we have," Daisy argued, and turned to Swift. "What is the score?"

"I don't know."

As their gazes held, Daisy could hardly restrain a snicker of sudden embarrassment.

Amusement glittered in Swift's eyes. "I think you won," he said.

"Oh, don't condescend to me," Daisy said. "You're ahead. I can take a loss. It's part of the game."

"I'm not being condescending. It's been point-for-point for at least . . ." Swift fumbled in the pocket of his waistcoat and pulled out a watch. ". . . two hours."

"Which means that in all likelihood you preserved your early lead."

"But you chipped away at it after the third round—"

"Oh, hell's bells!" came Lillian's voice from the sidelines. She sounded thoroughly aggravated, having gone into the manor for a nap and come out to find them still at the bowling green. "You've quarreled all afternoon like a pair of ferrets, and now you're fighting over who won. If someone doesn't put a stop to it, you'll be squabbling out here 'til midnight. Daisy, you're covered with dust and your hair is a bird's nest. Come inside and put yourself to rights. *Now.*"

"There's no need to shout," Daisy replied mildly, following her sister's retreating figure. She glanced over her shoulder at Matthew Swift . . . a friendlier glance than she had ever given him before, then turned and quickened her pace.

Swift began to pick up the wooden bowls.

"Leave them," Westcliff said. "The servants will put things in order. Your time is better spent preparing yourself for supper, which will commence in approximately one hour."

Obligingly Matthew dropped the bowls and went toward the house with Westcliff. He watched Daisy's small, sylphlike form until she disappeared from sight.

Westcliff did not miss Matthew's fascinated gaze. "You have a unique approach to courtship," he commented. "I wouldn't have thought beating Daisy at lawn games would catch her interest, but it seems to have done the trick."

Matthew contemplated the ground before his feet, schooling his tone into calm unconcern. "I'm not courting Miss Bowman."

"Then it seems I misinterpreted your apparent passion for bowls."

Matthew shot him a defensive glance. "I'll admit, I find her entertaining. But that doesn't mean I want to marry her."

"The Bowman sisters are rather dangerous that way. When one of them first attracts your interest, all you know is she's the most provoking creature you've ever encountered. But then you discover that as maddening as she is, you can scarcely wait until the next time you see her. Like the progression of an incurable disease, it spreads from one organ to the next. The craving begins. All other women begin to seem colorless and dull in comparison. You want her until you think you'll go mad from it. You can't stop thinking—"

"I have no idea what you're talking about," Matthew interrupted, turning pale. He was *not* about to succumb to an incurable disease. A man had choices in life. And no matter what Westcliff believed, this was nothing more than a physical urge. An unholy powerful, gut-wrenching, insanity-producing physical urge . . . but it could be conquered by sheer force of will.

"If you say so," Westcliff said, sounding unconvinced.

Chapter 6

Staring in the looking glass poised atop the cherrywood dresser, Matthew carefully knotted his formal starched white evening cravat with deft twists and pulls. He was hungry, but the thought of going down to the long formal supper in the dining hall filled him with unease. He felt as if he were walking on a narrow plank suspended high in the air, and a misstep would send him hurtling to his doom.

He should never have allowed himself to accept Daisy's challenge, should never have stayed and played that bloody game for hours.

It was just that Daisy had been so adorable, and while they played her attention had been focused entirely on him, and that had been too much temptation to withstand. She was the most provoking, beguiling woman he had ever met. Thunderstorms and rainbows wrapped together in a convenient pocket-sized parcel.

Bloody hell, how he wanted to bed her. Matthew was amazed Llandrindon or any other man there had been able to function rationally in her presence.

It was time to take control of the situation. He was going to do whatever was necessary to shove her together with Llandrindon. Compared to the other bachelors present, the Scottish lord was the pick of the lot. Llandrindon and Daisy would have a calm, well-ordered life, and although Llandrindon might stray occasionally, as most men of leisure did, Daisy would be too busy with her family and her books to notice. Or if she did, she would learn to turn a blind eye to his indiscretions and take refuge in her daydreams.

And Llandrindon would never appreciate the unimaginable gift of having Daisy in his life.

Moodily Matthew went downstairs and joined the elegant throng that had gathered in anticipation of the dining hall procession. The women were dressed in colorful gowns that had been embroidered and beaded and trimmed with lace. The men were clad in sober black and brilliant white, the plainness of their attire meant to serve as a suitable backdrop for the display of the women.

"Swift," came Thomas Bowman's hearty welcome. "Come here—I want you to quote the latest production estimates to these fellows." In Bowman's view there was never an inappropriate time to discuss business. Obediently Matthew joined the group of a half-dozen men who stood in the corner, and recited the numbers his employer wanted.

One of Matthew's more convenient skills was the ability to store long lists of figures in his head. He loved numbers, their patterns and secrets, the way something complex could be reduced to something simple. In mathematics, unlike life, there was always a solution, a definite answer.

But as Matthew was speaking he caught sight of Daisy and her friends standing with Lillian, and half his brain promptly shut down.

Daisy was wearing a butter-yellow gown that wrapped tightly around her slender waist and pushed the small, pretty shapes of her breasts upward into a low-cut bodice of gleaming, ruched satin. Yellow satin ribbons had been braided into artful ropes that held the bodice in place. Her black hair had been pulled to the top of her head with a few spiraling curls falling to her neck and shoulders. She looked delicate and perfect, like one of the artful sugared garnishes on the dessert tray that one was never supposed to eat.

Matthew wanted to tug her bodice down until her arms were confined by those satin ropes. He wanted to drag his mouth across her tender pale skin, finding the tips of her breasts, making her writhe—

"But do you really think," came Mr. Mardling's voice, "there is any room for the market to expand? After all, we are discussing the lower classes. No matter what their nationality, it is a known fact that they do not prefer to bathe often."

Matthew dragged his attention to the tall, well-groomed gentleman, whose blond hair shone brightly beneath the light of the chandeliers. Before he replied, he reminded himself that there was probably no malice intended behind the question. Those of the privileged classes often had genuine misconceptions about the poor, if they bothered to consider them at all.

"Actually," Matthew said mildly, "the available figures indicate that as soon as soap is mass-produced at an affordable price, the market will increase approximately ten percent a year. People of all classes want to be clean, Mr. Mardling. The problem is that good quality soap has always been a luxury item and therefore difficult to obtain."

"Mass production," Mardling mulled aloud, his lean face furrowed with thought. "There is something objectionable about the phrase . . . it seems to be a way of enabling the lower classes to imitate their betters."

Matthew glanced at the circle of men, noting that the top of Bowman's head was turning red—never a good sign—and that Westcliff was holding his silence, his black eyes unreadable.

"That's exactly what it is, Mr. Mardling," Matthew said gravely. "Mass production of items such as clothing and soap will give the poor a chance to live with the same standards of health and dignity as the rest of us."

"But how will one sort out who is who?" Mardling protested.

Matthew shot him a questioning glance. "I'm afraid I don't follow."

Llandrindon joined in the discussion. "I believe what Mardling is asking," he said, "is how one will be able to tell the difference between a shop-girl and a well-to-do woman if they are both clean and similarly dressed. And if a gentleman is not able to tell what they are by their appearance, how is he to know how to treat them?"

Stunned by the snobbery of the question, Matthew considered his reply carefully. "I've always thought all women should be treated with respect no matter what their station."

"Well said," Westcliff said gruffly, as Llandrindon opened his mouth to argue.

No one wished to contradict the earl, but Mardling pressed, "Westcliff, do you see nothing harmful in encouraging the poor to rise above their stations? In allowing them to pretend there is no difference between them and ourselves?"

"The only harm I see," Westcliff said quietly, "is in discouraging people who want to better themselves, out of fear that we will lose our perceived superiority."

The statement caused Matthew to like the earl even more than he had previously.

Preoccupied with the question of the hypothetical shopgirl, Llandrindon spoke to Mr. Mardling. "Never fear, Mardling—no matter how a woman is attired, a gentleman can always detect the clues that betray her true status. A lady always has a soft, well-modulated voice, whereas a shopgirl speaks with a strident tone and a vulgar accent."

"Of course," Mardling said with relief. He affected a slight shiver as he added, "A shopgirl dressed in finery, speaking in cockney . . . it's like fingernails on slate."

"Yes," Llandrindon said with a laugh. "Or like seeing a common daisy stuck in a bouquet of roses."

The comment was unthinking, of course. There was a sudden silence as Llandrindon realized he had just inadvertently insulted Bowman's daughter, or rather the name of his daughter.

"A versatile flower, the daisy," Matthew commented, breaking the silence. "Lovely in its freshness and simplicity. I've always thought it went well in any kind of arrangement."

The entire group rumbled in immediate agreement—"Indeed," and "Quite so".

Lord Westcliff gave Matthew an approving glance.

A short time later, whether by previous planning or a last-minute shuffling of places, Matthew discovered he had been seated at Westcliff's left at the main dining table. There was patent surprise on the faces of many guests as they registered that a place of honor had been given to a young man of undistinguished position.

Covering up his own surprise, Matthew saw that Thomas Bowman was beaming at him with fatherly pride . . . and Lillian was giving her husband a discreet glare that would have struck terror in the hearts of lesser men.

After an uneventful supper the guests dispersed in various groups. Some men desired port and cigars on the back terrace, some women wanted tea, while others headed to the parlor for games and conversation.

As Matthew went toward the terrace, he felt a tap on his shoulder. He looked down into Cassandra Leighton's mischievous eyes. She was a high-spirited creature whose primary skill seemed to be the ability to draw attention to herself.

"Mr. Swift," she said, "I insist that you join us in the parlor. I will not allow you to refuse. Lady Miranda and I have planned some games that I think you will find *quite* entertaining." She lowered one eyelid in a sly wink. "We've been scheming, you see."

"Scheming," Matthew repeated warily.

"Oh yes." She giggled. "We've decided to be a bit wicked this evening."

Matthew had never liked parlor games, which required a personal frivolity he had never been able to muster. Moreover it was generally known that in the permissive atmosphere of British society, the forfeits of these games often consisted of tricks and potentially scandalous behavior. Matthew had an innate and very sensible aversion to scandal. And if he was ever entangled in one, it would have to be for a very good reason. *Not* as the result of some imbecilic parlor game.

Before he replied, however, Matthew noticed something on the periphery of his vision . . . a flash of yellow. It was Daisy, her hand lightly resting on Lord Llandrindon's arm as they proceeded to the hallway that led to the parlor.

The logical part of Matthew's brain pointed out that if Daisy was going to indulge in scandalous behavior with Llandrindon, it was her own affair. But a deeper, more primitive part of his mind reacted with a possessiveness that caused his feet to start moving.

"Oh, lovely," Cassandra Leighton trilled, tucking her hand in the crook of his arm. "We'll have such fun."

This was a new and unwelcome discovery, that a primal urge could abruptly seize control of the rest of Matthew's body. Frowning, he went along with Miss Leighton, while she spouted a stream of nonsense.

A group of young men and women had assembled in the parlor, laughing and chattering. Anticipation was thick in the air. And there was a sense of roguery, as if a few of the participants had been warned they were about to take part in something naughty.

Matthew stood near the threshold, his gaze instantly finding Daisy. She was seated near the hearth with Llandrindon half-leaning on the arm of her chair.

"The first game," Lady Miranda said with a grin, "will be a round of 'Animals.' " She waited for a ripple of chuckles to die down before continuing. "For those of you unfamiliar with the rules, they are quite simple. Each lady will select a male partner for herself, and each gentleman will be assigned a particular animal to imitate—dog, pig, donkey and so forth. The ladies will be sent from the room and blindfolded, and when they return, they will attempt to locate their partners. The gentlemen will assist the ladies by making the correct animal sound. The last lady to find her partner will have to pay a forfeit."

Matthew groaned inwardly. He *hated* games that served no purpose other than to make fools out of the participants. As a man who did not enjoy being embarrassed, voluntarily or otherwise, this was the kind of situation he would have done anything to avoid.

Glancing at Daisy, he saw that she was not giggling as the other women were. Instead she looked resolute. This was her attempt to be one of the crowd, to behave like the empty-headed women around her. Bloody hell. No wonder she had been a wallflower, if this was what was expected of marriage-minded young women.

"You shall be my partner, Mr. Swift," cried Miss Leighton.

"A privilege," Matthew returned politely, and she giggled as if he had said something vastly amusing. Matthew had never met a woman who giggled so incessantly. He was half-afraid she might cause herself seizures if she didn't stop.

A hat filled with slips of paper was passed around, and Matthew plucked one out and read it.

"Cow," he informed Miss Leighton stonily, and she tittered.

Feeling like an idiot, Matthew stood aside while Miss Leighton and all the other ladies left the room.

Men positioned themselves strategically, chortling as they anticipated the fun of being bumped into and groped by various blindfolded women.

A few practice calls from around the parlor—

"*Squawk!*"

"*Meow!*"

"*Ribbit!*"

Rumbles of laughter ensued. As the blindfolded ladies paraded into the room, the place erupted in animal cries. It sounded like a rabid zoo. The ladies set out to find their partners, bumping into braying, cheeping, snorting men.

Matthew hoped to God that Westcliff, Hunt, or God forbid, Bowman, wouldn't chance to come into the room and see him like this. He would never live it down.

His dignity was dealt a mortal blow as he heard Cassandra Leighton's voice—"Where is Mr. Cow?"

Matthew heaved a sigh. "Moo," he said grimly. Miss Leighton's giggle sailed through the air. She gradually came into view, her hands groping every male form in proximity. A few unplanned *squeaks* and *squawks* were emitted as she made her way through the crowd.

"Oh, Mr. Co-ow," Miss Leighton called. "I need more assistance from you!"

Matthew scowled. "Moo."

"Once more," she trilled.

It was lucky for Cassandra Leighton that her blindfold shielded her from Matthew's murderous glare. *"Moo."*

Giggle. Giggle. Giggle. Miss Leighton approached, arms outstretched, fingers opening and closing on empty air. She reached him, her hands fumbling at his waist and sliding downward. Matthew seized her wrists and tugged them firmly upward.

"Have I found Mr. Cow?" she asked disingenuously, leaning into him.

He pushed her back with a firm nudge. "Yes."

"Hurrah for me!" she cried, removing her blindfold.

Other couples had also been reunited, the animals quieting one by one as they were claimed.

Finally only one sound was left . . . an awkward attempt at some kind of insect vibration. A katydid? A cricket?

Matthew craned his neck to see who was making the noise, and whom his unfortunate partner turned out to be. There was an exclamation, and ripples of friendly laughter. The crowd parted to reveal Daisy Bowman removing her blindfold, while Lord Llandrindon shrugged apologetically. "That is *not* the noise a cricket makes," Daisy protested, flushed and laughing. "You sound as if you're clearing your throat!"

"It was the best I could do," Llandrindon said helplessly.

Oh, God. Matthew closed his eyes briefly. It *would* be Daisy.

Cassandra Leighton seemed inordinately pleased. "Too bad," she said.

"No quarreling," Lady Miranda said gaily, coming to stand between Daisy and Llandrindon. "It befalls you to pay the forfeit, my dear!"

Daisy's smile faltered. "What is the forfeit?"

"It's called 'play the wallflower,' " Lady Miranda explained. "You must stand against the wall and draw one of the gentlemen's names from a hat. If he refuses to kiss you, you will remain against the wall and continue drawing names until someone consents to your offer."

Daisy's smile held fast, although her face turned white, leaving two red flags of color at the crests of her cheeks.

Damn it, Matthew thought savagely.

This was a serious dilemma. The incident would start rumors that could easily produce a scandal. He couldn't allow it. For her family's sake, and her own. And his . . . but that was something he didn't want to think about.

Automatically he started forward, but Miss Leighton grabbed his arm. Her long nails bit into the fabric of his coat sleeve. "No interfering," she warned. "Everyone who plays must be willing to accept the forfeit!" She was smiling, but there was a hardness in her eyes that Matthew didn't like. She intended to relish every second of Daisy's downfall.

Dangerous creatures, women.

Glancing around the room, Matthew saw the anticipation on the gentlemen's faces. Not one man there was going to turn away an opportunity to kiss Daisy Bowman. Matthew longed to crash heads together and yank Daisy out of the room. Instead he could only watch as the hat was brought to her and she reached inside with unsteady fingers.

Withdrawing a slip of paper, Daisy read it silently, her fine dark brows knitting together. A hush fell over the room, a few breaths caught in hope . . . and then Daisy said the name without looking up.

"Mr. Swift." She thrust the slip back into the hat before it could be confirmed.

Matthew felt his heart catch violently in his chest.

He wasn't certain if the situation had just improved drastically or become exponentially worse.

"That's impossible," Miss Leighton hissed. "It couldn't have been you."

Matthew glanced down at her almost absently. "Why not?"

"Because I didn't put your name into the hat!"

He made his face unreadable. "Obviously someone did," he said, and jerked his arm from her clutches.

A nervous hush fell over the room as Matthew approached Daisy, and then excited titters scattered through the group. Daisy controlled her expression admirably, but there was a frantic riot of color on her face. Her slender body was as tense as a bowstring. She forced a careless smile on her lips. Matthew could see the violent pulse in her throat. He wanted to put his mouth on that visible throb and stroke it with his tongue.

Stopping in front of her, he held her gaze, trying to read her thoughts.

Just who held the upper hand in this situation?

Ostensibly he did . . . but Daisy was the one who had called his name.

She had chosen him. *Why?*

"I heard you during the game," Daisy said, so softly that no one else could make out the words. "You sounded like a cow with digestive problems."

"Judging from the results, my cow was better than Llandrindon's cricket," Matthew pointed out.

"He didn't sound at all like a cricket. He sounded as if he were clearing phlegm from his throat."

Matthew sternly choked back a sudden laugh. She looked so annoyed and adorable that it was all he could do not to snatch her against him. Instead he said, "Let's get this over with, shall we?"

He wished Daisy wouldn't blush so hard. Her fair coloring made it even more apparent, her cheeks like scarlet poppies.

There was a collective intake of breath from the group as Matthew stepped closer until their bodies were nearly touching. Daisy's head fell back, her eyes closing, her lips slightly pursed. Reaching for her hand, Matthew lifted it to his lips and pressed a chaste kiss to the backs of her fingers.

Daisy's eyes snapped open. She looked stunned.

More laughter from the group, and a few playfully chiding cries.

After trading a few good-natured quips with some of the gentlemen, Matthew turned to Daisy and said in a pleasant but decisive tone, "You had mentioned earlier, Miss Bowman, that you wanted to look in on your sister at this time. May I escort you to her?"

"But you can't leave!" Cassandra Leighton exclaimed from the back of the room. "We've only just begun!"

"No, thank you," Daisy told Matthew. "I'm certain my sister can wait a bit longer while I enjoy myself here."

Matthew gave her a hard, penetrating glance.

He saw from the sudden change in her expression that she understood.

He was calling in the favor.

Leave with me now, his gaze commanded, *and no arguing.*

He saw also that Daisy wanted badly to refuse him, but her own sense of honor would not allow that. A debt was a debt.

Daisy swallowed hard. "On the other hand . . ." She nearly choked on the words. ". . . I did promise to sit with my sister while she had her tea."

Matthew presented his arm to her. "At your service, Miss Bowman."

There were a few protests, but by the time they had crossed the threshold, the group was busy organizing another game. God knew what minor scandals were brewing in the parlor. As long as neither himself nor Daisy was involved, Matthew didn't give a damn.

Daisy snatched her hand away from his arm as soon as they entered the hallway. They proceeded several yards and came to the open doorway of the library. Seeing that it was empty, Daisy charged into the room without a word.

Matthew went in after her and closed the door for privacy. It wasn't proper, but neither was brawling in the hallway.

"Why did you do that?" Daisy demanded, rounding on him immediately.

"Take you away from the games?" Disconcerted,

Matthew adopted a censorious tone. "You shouldn't have been there, and you know it."

Daisy was so furious that her dark eyes seemed to be shooting sparks. "Where should I have been, Mr. Swift? Reading alone in the library?"

"That would have been preferable to causing a scandal."

"No it wouldn't have. I was exactly where I belonged, doing exactly what everyone else was doing, and everything was just fine until you ruined it!"

"I?" Matthew couldn't believe his ears. "*I* ruined the evening for you?"

"Yes."

"*How?*"

She glared at him accusingly. "You didn't kiss me."

"I . . ." Caught off-guard, Matthew stared at her in bewilderment. "I did kiss you."

"On the hand," Daisy said scornfully, "which means absolutely nothing."

Matthew wasn't certain how he had been so abruptly derailed from self-righteous superiority to affronted protest. "You should be grateful."

"For what?"

"Isn't it obvious? I saved your reputation."

"If you had kissed me," Daisy retorted, "it could only have improved my reputation. But you rejected me publicly, which means Llandrindon and Mardling and all the rest know there is something wrong with me."

"I didn't reject you."

"It certainly felt like rejection, you cad!"

"I am not a cad. If I had kissed you in public, *then* I would be a cad." Matthew paused before adding in baffled irritation, "And there is nothing wrong with you. Why the devil would you say that?"

"I'm a wallflower. No one ever wants to kiss me."

This was too much. Daisy Bowman was furious because he hadn't done the thing he had craved and dreamed of for years of his life. He had behaved *honorably,* damn it all, and instead of being appreciative she was angry.

". . . am I that undesirable?" Daisy was ranting. "Would it have been *so* disagreeable?"

He wanted her for so long. He had reminded himself a thousand times of all the reasons he could never have her. And it had been a hell of a lot easier to bear knowing she detested him and there was no reason to hope. But the possibility that her feelings might have changed, that she might want him in return, filled him with a dizzying thrill.

Another minute of this and he would become unhinged.

". . . don't know how to do whatever it is women are supposed to do to attract men," Daisy was saying irately. "And when I finally had a chance to gain a little experience, you—" She broke off and frowned as she saw his face. "Why do you look like that?"

"Like what?"

"As if you're in pain."

Pain. Yes. The kind of pain a man felt when he had lusted after a certain woman for years and found himself alone with this woman and then had to endure her complaints that he hadn't kissed her when all he wanted was to tear her clothes off and have her right there on the floor.

She wanted experience? Matthew was ready to give her the experience of a lifetime. His body had become so unbearably hard that the brush of his trouser fabric was enough to make him wince. Struggling to control himself, he concentrated on breathing. Breathing. But there was only more arousal, until red mist had gathered at the edges of his vision.

He wasn't aware of reaching for her but suddenly his hands were on her, hooked just beneath her arms where the yellow satin was permeated with the warmth of her body. She was light and supple, like a cat . . . he could lift her so easily, pin her against the wall . . .

Daisy's dark eyes were wide and startled. "What are you doing?"

"I want the answer to one question," Matthew managed to say. "Why did you call my name in there?"

Emotions crossed her face in rapid succession . . .

surprise, guilt, embarrassment. Every inch of exposed skin turned pink. "I don't know what you mean. Your name was on the paper. I had no choice but to—"

"You're lying," Matthew said tersely. His heart stopped as she refused to reply. She wasn't going to deny it. Her flush deepened to crimson. "My name wasn't on that paper," he continued with great effort. "But you said it anyway. *Why?*"

They both knew there could only be one reason. Matthew closed his eyes briefly. His pulse was so hot and fast that its reckless momentum stung the insides of his veins.

He heard Daisy's hesitant voice. "I just wanted to know what you . . . how you . . . I just wanted . . ."

This was temptation at its most brutal. Matthew tried to make himself let go of her, but his hands would not release the slim curves encased in yellow satin. It felt too good to hold her. He stared at her exquisite mouth, the subtle but delicious indentation in the center of her lower lip. *One kiss,* he thought desperately. Surely he could have at least that. But once he started . . . he wasn't certain he could stop.

"Daisy . . ." He tried to find words to defuse the situation, but it was difficult to speak coherently. "I'm going to tell your father . . . at the first opportunity . . . I can't marry you under any circumstances."

She still wouldn't look at him. "Why didn't you tell him so right away?"

Because he had wanted to make her notice him.

Because he had wanted to pretend, just for a little while, that the thing he had never dared to dream about was just within reach.

"I wanted to annoy you," he said.

"Well, you did!"

"But I never considered it seriously. I could never marry you."

"Because I'm a wallflower," she said sullenly.

"No. That's not—"

"I'm undesirable."

"Daisy, would you stop—"

"Not even worth a single kiss."

"*All right,*" Matthew snapped, finally losing the grip on his sanity. "Damn it, you win. I'll kiss you."

"Why?"

"Because if I don't you'll never stop complaining about it."

"It's too late now! You should have kissed me back there in the parlor but you didn't, and now that you've doomed any chance I'll ever have of being kissed by anyone else, I'm not going to settle for some half-rate consolation prize."

"*Half-rate?*"

That had been a mistake. Matthew could see that Daisy realized it the instant she had said it.

She had just sealed her fate.

"I-I meant to say half-*hearted,*" she said breathlessly, trying to wriggle away from him. "It's obvious you don't want to kiss me and therefore—"

"You said half-*rate*." He jerked her hard against him. "Which means now I have something to prove."

"No you don't," she said quickly. "Really. You don't—" She gave a little cry as he clamped one hand behind her neck, and all sound was muffled as he tugged her head to his.

Chapter 7

Matthew knew it was wrong the instant their lips met. Because nothing would ever equal the perfection of Daisy in his arms. He was ruined for life. God help him, he didn't care.

Her mouth was soft and hot, like sunshine, like the white blaze of a heartwood fire. She gasped as he touched her lower lip with the tip of his tongue. Slowly her hands came to his shoulders, and then he felt her fingers at the back of his head, sliding into his hair to keep him from pulling away. There wasn't a chance in hell of that happening. Nothing could have made him stop.

A tremor shook his fingers as he bracketed the exquisite line of her jaw in the open framework of his hand, gently angling her face upward. The flavor of her mouth, sweet and elusive, fueled a hunger that threatened to rage out of control . . . he searched the damp silk beyond her lips, deeper, harder, until she began to breathe in long sighs, her body molding against his.

He let her feel how much stronger he was, how much heavier, one muscular arm clamped along her back, his feet spread to hold her between the powerful length of his thighs. Her upper half was bound in a laced and padded corset. He was almost overcome by a savage desire to tear away the stays and quilting and find the tender flesh beneath.

Instead he sank his fingers into her pinned-up hair and tugged it backward until the weight of her head was cradled in his hand, and her pale throat was exposed. He searched for the pulse he had seen earlier, his lips dragging softly along the secret pathway of nerves beneath her skin. When he reached a senstive spot, he felt the vibration of her suppressed moan against his mouth.

This was what it would be like to make love to her, he thought dazedly . . . the sweet shivering of her flesh as he entered her, the delicate chaos of her breath, the helpless sounds that rustled in her throat. Her skin, warm and female, scented like tea and talcum and a trace of salt. He found her mouth again, opened it, delving into wet silk, heat, and an intimate flavor that drove him mad.

She should have struggled, but there was only yielding and more softness, driving him past all limits. He began to ravish her mouth with deep, twisting kisses, bringing her body rhythmically against his. He felt her legs part beneath her gown, his thigh fitting neatly between them. She squirmed with innocent desire, her face blooming with the color of late summer poppies. Had she understood exactly what he wanted from her, she would have done more than blush. She would have fainted on the spot.

Lifting his mouth from hers, Matthew pressed his jaw against the side of her head. "I think," he said raggedly, "this puts to rest any question of whether I find you desirable or not."

Daisy gathered the strength to twist around in his grasp until she faced away from him, staring blindly at the rows of leather-bound books before her. Her small hands braced on the mahogany shelf as she fought to control the turbulent pace of her breathing.

Matthew stood behind her, reaching around to cover her hands with his. The narrow framework of her shoulders went rigid against his chest as he searched for the tender ridge of her ear.

"Don't," she said thickly, straining away from him.

Matthew couldn't stop. Following the movement of her head, he nuzzled the downy curve of her neck. He released one of her hands to settle his palm on the exposed skin over her bodice, just above the rise of her breasts. Daisy's free hand came up to press his fingers harder against her chest, as if their combined efforts were necessary to restrain the pounding of her reckless heart.

Matthew tightened all his muscles against the overpowering urge to snatch her up and carry her to the nearby settee. He wanted to make love to her, to bury himself inside her until bitter memories had dissolved in her sweetness. But that chance had been stolen from him long before they had ever met.

He had nothing to offer her. His life, his name, his identity . . . it was all an illusion. He was not the man she thought he was. And it was only a matter of time until she found out.

To his chagrin he realized he had unconsciously clenched a hand in her skirts as if in preparation to hike them up. The satin spilled in gleaming drifts between his fingers. He thought of her body wrapped up in all these garments and lacing, and the ungodly pleasure it would be to strip her naked. To map her body with his mouth and fingertips, learning every curve and hollow, every hidden place.

Watching his hand as if it belonged to someone else, Matthew uncurled his fingers one by one until the yellow satin dropped. He turned her to face him, staring into the rich brown depths of her eyes.

"Matthew," she said thickly.

It was the first time she had ever used his first name. He struggled to conceal the strength of his response. "Yes?"

"The way you phrased yourself earlier . . . you didn't say you *won't* marry me under any circumstances . . . you said you *can't*. Why?"

"Since it's not going to happen," he said, "the reasons are irrelevant."

Daisy frowned, her lips pursing in a way that made him long to kiss them.

He moved aside to let her go.

Obeying the silent signal, Daisy began to brush by him.

But as Daisy's arm bumped against his, Matthew caught her wrist in his fingers, and suddenly she was in his arms again. He couldn't stop himself from taking her mouth with his, kissing her as if she belonged to him, as if he were inside her.

This is what I feel for you, he told her with fierce, consuming kisses. *This is what I want*. He felt the new tension in her limbs, tasted her arousal, and realized he could bring her to climax here and now, if he reached beneath her dress and—

No, he told himself savagely. This had already gone too far. Realizing how close he was to losing all self-control, Matthew ripped his mouth from hers with a quiet groan and thrust Daisy away from him.

She fled the library immediately. The hem of the yellow gown trailed after her, curling around the edge of the doorjamb before disappearing like the last ray of the sun slipping over the horizon.

And Matthew wondered bleakly how he was going to interact with her in a normal manner ever again.

* * *

It was a time-honored tradition for the mistress of a country estate to act as Lady Bountiful to the tenants and local villagers. This meant giving assistance and advice, and donating necessary items such as food and clothing to those who needed it most. Lillian had performed the duties willingly until now, but her condition had made it impossible.

There was no question of asking Mercedes to substitute for her—Mercedes was too abrasive and impatient for such an undertaking. She did not like to be around sick people. She made the elderly uneasy, and something in her tone inevitably caused babies to cry.

Therefore Daisy was the logical choice. Daisy didn't mind visiting day at all. She liked taking the pony cart out by herself, to deliver parcels and jars, read to those with bad vision, and collect news from the villagers. Even better, the informal nature of the errands meant she didn't have to dress fashionably or worry about etiquette.

There was yet another reason Daisy was glad to go to the village . . . it kept her busy and away from the manor, so she could focus her thoughts on something other than Matthew Swift.

It had been three days since that dreadful parlor game and its consequences—namely, being kissed out of her wits by Matthew. Now he was behaving toward her as he always had, cool and courteous.

Daisy could almost believe it had been a dream except that whenever she was near Swift, her nerves began throwing off sparks, and her stomach swooped up and down like a drunken sparrow.

She wanted to discuss it with someone but that would have been too mortifying, and somehow it would have felt like a betrayal, though of whom she wasn't certain. All she knew was that nothing felt right. She wasn't sleeping well, and as a result she was clumsy and distracted in the daytime.

Thinking she might be ill, Daisy had gone to the housekeeper with a description of her condition and had been dosed with a nasty spoonful of castor oil. It hadn't helped in the least. Worst of all, she couldn't keep her mind on her books. She had read the same pages over and over again, and they had no power to interest her.

Daisy had no idea how to put herself to rights again. But she thought it would be a good thing to stop thinking about herself and do something for someone else.

She set out mid-morning in the big open ponycart drawn by a sturdy brown pony named Hubert. The cart was laden with china jars filled with food, bolts of flannel, wheels of cheese, parcels of turnip-fed mutton, bacon and tea, and bottles of port.

The visits were generally quite pleasant, the villagers seeming to enjoy Daisy's cheerful presence. Some of them made her laugh as they slyly described how it had been in the old days when Lord Westcliff's mother had come to call.

The dowager countess had dispensed her gifts

grudgingly, expecting a great show of gratitude. If the women hadn't curtseyed deeply enough, the dowager countess had asked sourly if their knees were stiff. She had also expected to be consulted about what names they should call their children, and she had instructed them on what their views on religion and hygiene should be. More aggravating still, the countess had brought food that had been mixed in an unappetizing jumble, meats and vegetables and sweets all crammed together in the same tin.

"Gracious," Daisy exclaimed, setting out jars and fabric bolts on the table. "What a wicked old witch she was! Just like the fairy tales . . ." And she regaled the children with a dramatic recitation of Hansel and Gretel that sent them giggling and screeching beneath the table, peering out at her with delight.

By the end of visiting day, Daisy had filled a little book with notes . . . would it be possible to locate a specialist to look at old Mr. Hearnsley's failing eyes and might the Blunts be given another bottle of the housekeeper's tonic for Mr. Blunt's digestive complaints?

Promising that she would convey all questions directly to Lord and Lady Westcliff, Daisy climbed back into the now-empty pony cart and headed back to Stony Cross Park.

It was almost twilight, long shadows of oaks and chestnuts crossing the unpaved road leading away from the village. This part of England had not yet been deforested to feed the fleets and factories that had sprung up in the major cities. The woodlands were still pristine and other-worldly, scored with small cartways half-buried by overhanging branches thick with leaves. In the gathering shade the trees were wreathed in vapor and mystery, like sentinels for a world of druids and warlocks and unicorns. A brown owl glided over the lane, mothlike in the darkening sky.

The lane was quiet except for the rattle of cart wheels and the clop-clop of Hubert's iron-shod hooves. Daisy kept a firm grip on the ribbons as the pony quickened his pace. Hubert seemed nervous, his head tossing from side to side.

"Easy, boy," Daisy soothed, forcibly slowing his pace as the cart's axle rattled over a rough patch. "You don't like the forest, do you? No need to worry—we'll reach open ground soon."

The pony's fidgeting continued until the vegetation had thinned and the overhead foliage had disappeared. They passed into a dry sunken lane that was girdled by a forest on one side and a meadow on the other. "There, nervous Nellie," Daisy said brightly. "Nothing to worry about, you see?"

As it turned out, her confidence was premature.

She heard a few heavy cracks coming from the forest, twigs and branches snapped underfoot. Hubert nickered apprehensively, swinging his head toward the noise. A loud animal grunt caused the hairs to rise on the back of Daisy's neck.

Good Lord, what was *that*?

With startling suddenness a huge, bulky shape charged toward the cart from the forest cover.

Everything happened too fast for Daisy to comprehend. She gripped the ribbons as Hubert jerked forward with a panicked whinny, the cart rattling and bouncing as if it were a child's toy.

Daisy tried in vain to keep her seat, but as the cart hit a deep rut she was thrown clear of the vehicle. Hubert continued racing pell-mell down the lane while Daisy landed on the hard-packed earth with stunning force.

The breath was knocked from her, and she choked and wheezed. She had the impression of a massive creature, a monster rushing toward her, but the sound of a gunshot rent the air and caused her ears to ring.

A bone-chilling animal squeal . . . then nothing.

Daisy tried to sit up, then flopped weakly on her stomach as her lungs spasmed. Her chest felt as if it had been caught in a vise. There was a good chance she was going to cast up her crumpets, but the thought of how much *that* would hurt was enough to keep her gorge down.

In a moment the thundering of hooves—several sets—vibrated the ground beneath Daisy's cheek. Finally able to draw a shallow breath, she pushed up on her elbows and lifted her chin.

Three riders—no, four—were galloping toward her, hooves thrasing up clouds of dust in the lane. One of the men swung off his horse before it had even stopped and rushed to her in a few ground-eating strides.

Daisy blinked in surprise as he dropped to his knees and gathered her up in the same motion. Her head fell back on his arm, and she found herself staring hazily up into Matthew Swift's dark face.

"*Daisy.*" It was a tone she had never heard from him before, rough and urgent. Cradling her in one arm, he ran his free hand over her body in a rapid search for injuries. "Are you hurt?"

Daisy tried to explain that she'd just gotten the wind knocked out of her, and he seemed to understand her incoherent sounds. "All right," he said. "Don't try to talk. Breathe slowly." Feeling her stir against him, he resettled her in his arms. "Rest against me." His hand passed over her hair, smoothing it back from her face. Tiny shivers of reaction ran through her limbs, and he gathered her closer. "Slowly, sweetheart. Easy. You're safe now."

Daisy closed her eyes to hide her astonishment. Matthew Swift was murmuring endearments and holding her in hard, strong arms, and her bones seemed to have melted like boiling sugar.

Years of uncivilized rough-and-tumble with her siblings had taught Daisy to recover quickly from a fall. In any other circumstances she would have sprung up and dusted herself off by now. But every pleasure-saturated cell in her body sought to preserve the moment for as long as possible.

Matthew's gentle fingers stroked the side of her face. "Look at me, sweetheart. Tell me where it hurts."

Her lashes swept upward. His face was right over hers. As she was held in the compass of his extraordinary blue eyes, she felt as if she were floating in layers of color. "You have nice teeth," she told him groggily, "but you know, your eyes are even nicer . . ."

Swift frowned, the pad of his thumb passing over the crest of her cheek. His touch brought a wash of pink to the surface of her skin. "Can you tell me your name?"

She blinked at him. "You've forgotten it?"

"No, I want to know if *you've* forgotten it."

"I would never be so silly as to forget my own name," she said. "I'm Daisy Bowman."

"What is your birthday?"

She couldn't repress a crooked smile. "You wouldn't know if I told you the wrong one."

"Your birthday," he insisted.

"March the fifth."

His mouth curved wryly. "Don't play games, imp."

"All right. It's September the twelfth. How did you know my birthday?"

Instead of replying, Swift looked up and spoke to his companions, who had gathered around them. "Her pupils are the same size," he said. "And she's alert. No broken bones, either."

"Thank God." Westcliff's voice.

Looking over Matthew Swift's broad shoulder, Daisy saw her brother-in-law standing over them. Mr. Mardling and Lord Llandrindon were also there, wearing sympathetic expressions.

Westcliff held a rifle in his hand. He lowered to his haunches beside her. "We were just returning from an afternoon shoot," the earl said. "It was pure chance that we came upon you just as you were charged."

"I could have sworn it was a wild boar," Daisy said in wonder.

"But that can't be," Lord Landrindon remarked with a patronizing chuckle. "Your imagination has gotten the better of you, Miss Bowman. There have been no wild boars in England for hundreds of years."

"But I saw—" Daisy began defensively.

"It's all right," Swift murmured, tightening his hold. "I saw it too."

Westcliff's expression was rueful. "Miss Bowman is not entirely mistaken," he told Llandrindon. "We've had a local problem with some escaped livestock that have farrowed a generation or two of feral litters. Only last month a horsewoman was charged by one of them."

"You mean I was just attacked by an angry pig?" Daisy asked, struggling to a sitting position. Swift kept a supportive arm at her back and tucked her against his warm side.

A last ray of sunlight flashed over the horizon, temporarily blinding her. Turning her face away from it, Daisy felt Swift's chin brush against her hair.

"Not angry," Westcliff said in reference to the pig. "Feral, and therefore dangerous. Domestic pigs set free in the wild can easily become aggressive and quite large. I would estimate the one we just saw to be at least twenty stone." Seeing Swift's perplexity, the earl clarified, "Approximately three hundred pounds."

Swift helped Daisy to her feet, bracing her against his sturdy form. "Slowly," he murmured. "Are you dizzy? Nauseous?"

Daisy felt absolutely fine. But it was so delicious to stand there with him that she said breathlessly, "Perhaps a little."

His hand came up to her head, gently cradling it against his shoulder. Her temperature escalated as she felt the protectiveness of his embrace, the wonderful solidity of his body. All this from Matthew Swift, the most *un*romantic man she had ever known.

So far this visit was producing one surprise after another.

"I'll take you back," Swift said near her ear. Her skin prickled in delighted response. "Do you think you could ride in front of me?"

How topsy-turvy everything had become, Daisy thought, that she should feel a shameless thrill of anticipation at the prospect. She could lean back in his arms as he carried her away on his horse, and she could secretly indulge in a fantasy or two. She would pretend she was an adventuress being abducted by a dashing villain—

"I fear that would not be wise," Lord Llandrindon interrupted with a laugh. "Considering the state of affairs between the two of you . . ."

Daisy blanched, thinking at first that he was referring to those torrid moments in the library. But there was no way Llandrindon could know about that. She hadn't told a soul, and Swift was as close-mouthed as a clam about his private life. No, Llandrindon had to be talking about their rivalry at lawn-bowling.

"I think *I* had better be the one to escort Miss Bowman home," Llandrindon said, "to prevent any chance of violence."

Daisy slitted a glance at the viscount's smiling face and wished he had kept his mouth shut. She parted her lips to protest, but Swift had already replied.

"Perhaps you're right, my lord."

Oh, *drat*. Daisy felt cold and disgruntled as Swift eased her away from the warm shelter of his body.

Westcliff viewed the ground with a grim expression. "I'll have to find the animal and cull it."

"Not on my account, I hope," Daisy said anxiously.

"There is blood on the ground," the earl replied. "The animal is wounded. It's kinder to put it down rather than let it suffer."

Mr. Mardling went to fetch his own gun, saying eagerly, "I'll go with you, my lord!"

In the meanwhile Lord Llandrindon had mounted his horse. "Hand her up to me," he said to Swift, "and I'll return her safely to the manor."

Swift tilted Daisy's face upward and extracted a white handkerchief from his pocket. "If you still feel dizzy by the time we arrive home," he said, carefully wiping the dirt smudges from her face, "I'm going to send for the doctor. Understand?"

Despite his overbearing manner there was an elusive tenderness in his gaze that made Daisy want to crawl inside his coat and huddle against his heartbeat. "Are you coming back too," she asked, "or will you stay with Lord Westcliff?"

"I'm going to follow right behind you." Replacing the handkerchief in his pocket, Swift bent and picked her up easily. "Hold onto me."

Daisy put her arms around his neck, her wrist tingling where it pressed against the hot skin of his nape and the cool silky locks of his hair. He carried her as if she weighed nothing, his chest rock-solid, his breath soft and even against her cheek. His skin carried the scent of sun and outdoors. She could barely restrain herself from nuzzling into his neck.

Bemused by the force of her attraction to him, Daisy remained silent as Swift handed her up to Lord Llandrindon, who was seated on a large bay. The viscount settled her in front of him, where the edge of the saddle dug into her thigh.

Llandrindon was a handsome man, elegant and dark-haired and fine-featured. But the feel of Llandrindon's arms around her, his lean chest, his scent . . . somehow it wasn't *right*. The clasp of his hand at the side of her waist was foreign and intrusive.

Daisy could have wept with frustration as she wondered why she couldn't want him instead of the man who was wrong for her.

"What happened?" Lillian asked as Daisy walked into the Marsden parlor. She was reclining on the settee with a periodical. "You look as if you've been run over by a carriage."

"I had an encounter with an ill-mannered pig, actually."

Lillian smiled and set aside the periodical. "Who would that be?"

"I wasn't speaking in metaphor. It really *was* a pig." Sitting in a nearby chair, Daisy told her about the misadventure, casting it in a humorous light.

"Are you really all right?" Lillian asked in concern.

"Perfectly," Daisy assured her. "And Hubert was fine as well. He arrived at the stables at the same time that Lord Llandrindon and I did."

"That was lucky."

"Yes, it was clever of Hubert to find his way home—"

"No, not the deuced pony. I'm talking about

riding home with Lord Llandrindon. Not that I'm encouraging you to set your cap for him, but on the other hand—"

"He wasn't the one I wanted to ride back with." Daisy stared down at the dirt-stained fabric of her skirts and concentrated on plucking a horse hair from the fine muslin weave.

"One can't blame you for that," Lillian said. "Llandrindon is nice but rather innocuous. I'm sure you would have preferred to ride back with Mr. Mardling."

"No," Daisy said. "I was *very* glad not to have come back with him. The one I really wanted to ride home with was—"

"*No.*" Lillian covered her ears. "Don't say it. I don't want to hear it!"

Daisy stared at her gravely. "Do you really mean that?"

Lillian grimaced. "Bloody hell," she muttered. "Damn and blast. Son of a—"

"When the baby is born," Daisy said with a faint smile, "you'll really have to stop using such foul language."

"Then I will indulge myself to the fullest until he gets here."

"Are you certain it's a he?"

"It had better be, since Westcliff needs an heir and I'm never going through this again." Lillian scrubbed the heels of her hands over her weary eyes. "Since the only choice left was Matthew Swift," she said grumpily, "I assume he was the one you wanted to ride back with."

"Yes. Because . . . I'm attracted to him." It was a relief to say it out loud. Daisy's throat, which had felt pinched and tight, finally dilated to allow her a long, slow breath.

"In a physical sense, you mean?"

"In other ways as well."

Lillian rested her cheek on her hand, which was balled into a sharp-knuckled fist. "Is it because Father wants the match?" she asked. "Are you hoping somehow to win his approval?"

"Oh, no. If anything, Father's approval is a mark *against* Mr. Swift. I don't give a fig about pleasing him—I know very well that's impossible."

"Then I don't understand why you would want a man who is so obviously wrong for you. You're not some madcap, Daisy. Impulsive, yes. Romantic, of a certainty. But you're also practical and intelligent enough to understand the consequences of being involved with him. I think the problem is that you're desperate. You're the last one of us to be unmarried, and then Father delivered this idiotic ultimatum, and—"

"I'm not desperate!"

"If you're considering marrying Matthew Swift, I'd say that's a mark of extreme desperation."

Daisy had never been accused of having a temper—that distinction had always gone to Lillian. But indignation filled her chest like the blast from a steam kettle, and she had to fight to keep from exploding.

Glancing at the curve of her sister's stomach helped her to calm down. Lillian was dealing with many new discomforts and uncertainties. Now Daisy was adding to the problem.

"I said nothing about wanting to marry him," Daisy replied. "I merely want to find out more about him. About what kind of man he is. I don't see the harm in that."

"But you won't," Lillian argued with forceful conviction. "That's the point. He won't show you who he really is, he'll deceive you. His skill in life is to find out what people want and manufacture it for them, all for his own benefit. Look at how he made himself into the son Father always wanted. Now he's going to pretend to be the kind of man you've always wanted."

"He couldn't know that—" Daisy tried to say, but Lillian interrupted in a heedless rush, inflamed beyond the ability to have a rational exchange.

"He has no interest in you, your heart and mind, the person you are . . . he wants controlling shares in the company, and he sees you as the way to get them. Of course he's trying to make you like him . . . he'll charm you out of your knickers until the day after your wedding when you find out that it was all an illusion. He's just like Father, Daisy! He'll crush you, or turn you into someone like Mother. Is that the life you want?"

"Of course not."

For the first time ever Daisy realized she could not talk to her older sister about something important.

There were so many things she wanted to say . . . that not everything Matthew Swift had said and done could have been calculated. That he could have insisted that she ride back with him to the manor and instead he had handed her over to Llandrindon without a protest. She also wanted to confide that Swift had kissed her, and that it had been glorious, and how much that had worried her.

But there was no point arguing when Lillian was in this mood. They would just chase in circles.

The silence unfolded in a smothering blanket.

"Well?" Lillian demanded. "What are you going to do?"

Standing, Daisy rubbed at a spot of dirt on her arms and said ruefully, "To start with, I think I had better take a bath."

"You know what I meant!"

"What would you like me to do?" Daisy asked with a politeness that caused Lillian to scowl.

"Tell Matthew Swift he's a loathsome toad and there's no chance in hell you would ever consider marrying him!"

Chapter 8

 ". . . *and then she* left," *Lillian said* vehemently, "without telling me what *she* was going to do or what she really thought, and damn it all, I *know* there were things she left out—"

"Dear," Annabelle interrupted gently, "are you certain you gave her the opportunity to tell you everything?"

"What do you mean? I was sitting right in front of her. I was conscious and I had two ears. What more opportunity did she need?"

Restless and unable to sleep, Lillian had discovered Annabelle was also awake after having been up with the baby. They had seen each other from the respective balconies of their rooms, and had motioned to meet downstairs. It was midnight. At Annabelle's suggestion they went for a walk in the Marsden gallery, a long rectangular room lined with dour family portraits and priceless works of art. Clad in their dressing gowns, they meandered through the gallery with their arms linked, their pace limited by Lillian's slow shuffle.

Lillian had found herself turning to Annabelle with increasing frequency during the course of the pregnancy. Annabelle understood what she was going through, having experienced it herself quite recently. And Annabelle's calm presence was invariably soothing.

"What I mean," Annabelle said, "is that you may have been so intent on telling Daisy how *you* felt that you forgot to ask how *she* felt."

Lillian spluttered indignantly, "But she—but I—" She stopped and considered the point. "You're right," she admitted gruffly. "I didn't. I was so appalled by the idea of Daisy being attracted to Matthew Swift that I suppose I didn't really want to discuss it. I wanted to tell her what to do and then be finished with it."

They turned at the end of the gallery and proceeded past a row of landscapes. "Do you think there has been any intimacy between them?" Annabelle asked. Seeing Lillian's alarm, she clarified, "Such as a kiss . . . an embrace . . ."

"Oh *God*." Lillian shook her head. "I don't know. Daisy's so innocent. It would be so easy for that snake to seduce her."

"He is genuinely enchanted by her, in my opinion.

What young man wouldn't be? She's a darling, and lovely and clever—"

"And wealthy," Lillian said darkly.

Annabelle smiled. "Wealth never hurts," she allowed. "But in this case, I think there is more to it than that."

"How can you be so sure?"

"Dear, it's obvious. You've seen the way they look at each other. It's just . . . in the air."

Lillian frowned. "May we stop for a moment? My back hurts."

Annabelle complied immediately, helping her ease to one of the cushioned benches that ran down the center of the gallery. "I don't think it will be long until the baby comes," Annabelle murmured. "I would even venture to guess he will arrive a bit sooner than the doctor predicted."

"Thank God. I've never wanted anything so much as to be *un*pregnant." Lillian made a project of trying to see the tips of her slippers over the curve of her stomach. Her mind circled back to the subject of Daisy. "I'm going to be honest with her about my opinions," she said abruptly. "I see Matthew Swift for what he is, even if she doesn't."

"I think she knows your opinions already," Annabelle said dryly. "But ultimately it's her decision to make. I'll hazard a guess that when you were trying to decide your feelings for Lord Westcliff, Daisy didn't try to influence you one way or the other."

"This situation is entirely different," Lillian protested. "Matthew Swift is a reptile! And furthermore, if Daisy married him, he would eventually take her away to America and I would hardly ever see her again."

"And you'd like her to stay under your wing forever," Annabelle murmured.

Lillian turned to give her a baleful stare. "Are you suggesting I'm selfish enough to keep her from leading her own life just so I can keep her near me?"

Unruffled by her ire, Annabelle smiled sympathetically. "It's always been the two of you, hasn't it? You've always been each other's sole source of love and companionship. But it's all changing, dear. You have your own family now, a husband and a child—and you should want nothing less for Daisy."

Lillian's nose began to sting. She looked away from Annabelle, and to her mortification, her eyes turned hot and blurry. "I promise I will like the *next* man she's interested in. No matter who he is. Just as long as he's not Mr. Swift."

"You wouldn't like any man she was interested in." Annabelle's arm slipped around her shoulders as she added affectionately, "You are somewhat possessive, dear."

"And you are incredibly annoying," Lillian said, laying her head on Annabelle's soft shoulder. She continued to sniffle while Annabelle held her in the kind of firm, comforting embrace that Lillian's own mother had never been capable of. It was a relief to cry, but a bit embarrassing as well. "I hate being a watering pot," she mumbled.

"It's because of your condition," Annabelle soothed. "It's perfectly natural. You'll be back to rights after the baby is born."

"It's going to be a he," Lillian told her, wiping her eyes with her fingers. "And then we'll arrange a marriage between our children so Isabelle can be a viscountess."

"I thought you didn't believe in arranged marriages."

"I didn't until now. Our children can't possibly be trusted with a decision as important as whom to marry."

"You're right. We'll have to do it for them."

They chuckled together, and Lillian felt her mood lightening just a little.

"I have an idea," Annabelle said. "Let's go to the kitchen and peek in the larder. I'll bet there's still some gooseberry cake left from dessert. Not to mention the strawberry jam trifle."

Lillian lifted her head and blotted her wet nose on her sleeve. "Do you really think a plate of sweets will make me feel better?"

Annabelle smiled. "It can't hurt, can it?"

Lillian considered the point. "Let's go," she said, and allowed her friend to pull her up from the bench.

The morning sun snapped through the windows as housemaids tugged back the main entrance hall drapes and secured them with tasseled silk ropes. Daisy walked toward the breakfast room, knowing there was little chance any of the guests were awake. She had tried to sleep as long as possible while restless energy coursed through her, demanding an outlet until finally she had jumped up and dressed herself.

Servants were busy polishing brass and woodwork, sweeping carpets, carrying pails and baskets of linens. Farther away were the clangs of metal pots and the clinks of dishes as food was prepared in the kitchen for the morning repast.

The door to Lord Westcliff's private study was open, and Daisy glanced inside the wood-paneled room as she passed. It was a beautiful room, simple and spare with a row of stained-glass windows that shed a rainbow of light across the carpeted floor. Daisy paused with a smile as she saw someone sitting at the massive desk. The outline of his dark head and broad shoulders identified him as Mr. Hunt, who often made use of Westcliff's study when he was at Stony Cross.

"Good morning . . ." she began, pausing as he turned to look at her.

She felt a pang of excitement as she realized it was not Mr. Hunt but Matthew Swift.

He rose from his chair, and Daisy said bashfully, "No, please, I'm sorry to have interrupted . . ."

Her voice trailed away as she noticed there was something different about him. He was wearing a pair of thin, steel-framed spectacles.

Spectacles, on that strong-featured face . . . and his hair mussed as if he had been tugging absently

on the front locks. All that combined with a plenitude of muscles and masculine virility was aston-
ishingly . . . erotic.

"When did you start wearing those?" Daisy
managed to ask.

"About a year ago." He smiled ruefully and removed the spectacles with one hand. "I need them
to read. Too many late nights poring over contracts
and reports."

"They . . . they are very becoming."

"Are they?" Continuing to smile, Swift shook
his head, as if it had not occurred to him to wonder about his appearance. He tucked the spectacles
into the pocket of his waistcoat. "How do you
feel?" he asked softly. It took a moment for Daisy
to realize he was referring to her tumble from the
pony cart.

"Oh, I'm quite well, thank you." He was staring
at her in that way he always had, concentrated,
unwavering. It had always made her uneasy. But
just now, his gaze didn't seem critical. In fact, he
was staring at her if she were the only thing in the
world worth looking at. She fidgeted with the skirts
of her muslin gown, pink with printed flowers.

"You're up early," Swift said.

"I usually am. I can't imagine why some people
stay abed so late in the morning. There's only so
much sleeping one can do." As Daisy finished speaking it occurred to her there was something else
people did in bed besides sleeping, and she turned
scarlet.

Mercifully Swift didn't mock her, though she saw a subtle smile lurking in the corners of his mouth. Discarding the risky subject of sleeping habits, he gestured to the sheaf of papers behind him. "I'm preparing to go to Bristol soon. Some issues have to be settled before we decide to locate the manufactory there."

"Lord Westcliff has agreed that you will manage the project?"

"Yes. Though it seems I'll have to maneuver around an advisory committee."

"My brother-in-law can be a bit controlling," Daisy admitted. "But once he sees how dependable you are, I predict he will loosen the reins considerably."

He gave her a curious glance. "That almost sounds like a compliment, Miss Bowman."

She shrugged with elaborate casualness. "Whatever faults you may have, your dependability is legendary. My father has always said that one may set a clock by your comings and goings."

Sardonic amusement edged his voice. "Dependable. That is the description of an exciting fellow."

Once Daisy would have agreed with the sarcastic statement. When one said a man was "dependable" or "nice," one was damning him with faint praise. But she had spent three seasons observing the caprices of gentlemen who were rakish, absent-minded or irresponsible. Dependability was a wonderful quality in a man. She wondered why she had never appreciated that before.

"Mr. Swift . . ." Daisy tried to sound light, with only marginal success. "I have been wondering about something . . ."

"Yes?" He took a half-step backward as she moved closer, as if it were imperative to maintain a certain distance between them.

Daisy watched him intently. "Since there is no possibility that you and I . . . that marriage is out of the . . . I was wondering, when *do* you plan to marry?"

He looked bemused, then blank. "I don't think marriage would suit me."

"Ever?"

"Ever."

"Why not?" she demanded. "Is it that you value your freedom too much? Or are you planning on becoming a skirt-chaser?"

Swift laughed, the sound so warm that Daisy felt it like a stroke of velvet down her spine. "No. I've always thought it would be a waste of time to pursue hordes of women when one good one would suffice."

"How do you define a good one?"

"Are you asking what kind of woman I would want to marry?" His smile lingered much longer than usual, causing the fine hairs to prickle on the nape of Daisy's neck. "I suppose I would know when I met her."

Striving to seem unconcerned, Daisy wandered to the stained-glass windows. She held a hand up, watching the mosaic of colored light on the paleness

of her skin. "I can predict what she would be like."
She kept her back to Swift. "Taller than me, for one
thing."

"Most women are," he pointed out.

"And accomplished and useful," Daisy continued. "Not a dreamer. She would keep her mind on
practical matters, and manage the servants perfectly, and she would never be tricked by the fish-
monger into buying scrod after it's turned."

"If I did have any thoughts about marriage,"
Swift said, "you've just driven them completely out
of my mind."

"You'll have no difficulty finding her," Daisy
continued, sounding more glum than she would
have wished. "There are hundreds of them in Manhattanville. Maybe thousands."

"What makes you certain I would want a conventional wife?"

Her nerves tingled as she felt him approaching
her from behind.

"Because you're like my father," she said.

"Not entirely."

"And if you married someone different from the
woman I just described, you would eventually come
to think of her as a . . . parasite."

The light pressure of Swift's hands closed over
her shoulders. He turned Daisy to face him. His
blue eyes were warm as he searched hers, and she
had the discomforting suspicion that he was reading her thoughts far too accurately. "I prefer to
think," he said slowly, "that I would never be that

cruel. Or idiotic." His gaze felt to the exposed skin of her chest. With utter gentleness, he traced his thumbs across the winged shape of her collarbones, until gooseflesh rose on her arms beneath her puffed sleeves. "All I would ever ask of a wife," he murmured, "is that she would bear me some affection. That she might be happy to see me at the end of the day."

Her breath quickened beneath the touch of his fingers. "That's not very much to ask."

"Isn't it?"

His fingertips had reached the base of her throat, which rippled from her hard swallow. He blinked and removed his hands promptly, seeming not to know what to do with them until he buried them in his coat pockets.

And yet he didn't move away. Daisy wondered if he felt the same irresistible pull that she did, a perplexing need that could only be appeased by more closeness.

Clearing her throat in a businesslike manner, Daisy straightened her spine and drew up to her full height of five feet and one debatable inch.

"Mr. Swift?"

"Yes, Miss Bowman?"

"I have a favor to ask."

His gaze sharpened. "What is it?"

"As soon as you tell my father definitively that you're not going to marry me, he will be . . . disappointed. You know how he is."

"Yes, I know," Swift said dryly. Anyone acquainted with Thomas Bowman was well aware that for him, disappointment was but a quick stop on the way to high dudgeon.

"I'm afraid it will result in some unpleasant repercussions for me. Father is already unhappy that I haven't brought someone up to scratch. If he assumes I've deliberately done something to foil his plans about you and I . . . well, it will make my situation . . . difficult."

"I understand." Swift knew her father perhaps better than Daisy herself did. "I won't say anything to him," he said quietly. "And I'll do what I can to make things easier for you. I'm leaving for Bristol in two days, three at the most. Llandrindon and the other men . . . none of them are idiots, they have a fair idea of why they were invited here, and they wouldn't have come if they weren't interested. So it shouldn't take long for you to get a proposal out of one of them."

Daisy supposed she should appreciate his eagerness to shove her into the arms of another man. Instead, his enthusiasm made her feel sour and waspish.

And when one felt like a wasp, one's main inclination was to sting.

"I appreciate that," she said. "Thank you. You've been very helpful, Mr. Swift. Especially by providing me with some much-needed experience. The next time I kiss a man—Lord Llandrindon, for example—I'll know much more about what to do."

It filled Daisy with vengeful satisfaction to see the way his mouth tightened.

"You're welcome," he said in a growl.

Perceiving that his hands were half-raised as if he were on the brink of throttling or shaking her, Daisy gave him her sunniest smile and scooted out of his reach.

As the day progressed the early morning sunshine was smothered in clouds that unrolled in a great gray carpet across the sky. Rain began to fall steadily, turning unpaved roads to mud, replenishing the wet meadows and bogs, sending people and animals scurrying to their respective shelters.

This was Hampshire in spring, sly and mercurial, playing pranks on the unsuspecting. If one ventured out with an umbrella on a wet morning, Hampshire would produce sunlight with a magician's flourish. If one went walking without the umbrella, the sky was sure to dump buckets of rain on one's head.

Guests clustered in various ever-changing groups . . . some in the music room, some in the billiards room, some in the parlor for games or tea or amateur theatrics. Many ladies attended to their embroidery or lace work while gentlemen read, talked, and drank in the library. No conversation escaped without at least a nominal discussion of when the storm might end.

Daisy usually loved rainy days. Curling up next

to a hearth fire with a book was the greatest pleasure imaginable. But she was still trapped in a fretful state in which the printed word had lost its magic. She meandered from room to room, discreetly observing the activities of the guests.

Pausing at the threshold of the billiards room, she peered around the doorframe as gentlemen milled lazily around the table with drinks and cue sticks in hand. The clicks of ivory balls provided an arrhythmic undertone to the hum of masculine conversation. Her attention was caught by the sight of Matthew Swift in his shirtsleeves, leaning over the table to execute a perfect bank shot.

His hands were deft on the cue stick, his blue eyes narrowed as he focused on the layout of balls on the table. Those ever-rebellious locks of hair had fallen over his forehead once more, and Daisy longed to push them back. As Swift sank a ball neatly into a side pocket, there was a scattering of applause, some low laughs, and a few coins changing hands. Standing, Swift produced one of his elusive grins and made a remark to his opponent, who turned out to be Lord Westcliff.

Westcliff laughed at the comment and circled the table, an unlit cigar clamped between his teeth as he considered his options. The air of relaxed masculine enjoyment in the room was unmistakable.

As Westcliff rounded the table, he caught sight of Daisy peeking around the doorframe. He winked at her. She pulled back like a turtle jerking into its shell. It was ridiculous of her to creep around the manor trying to catch stolen glimpses of Matthew Swift.

Scolding herself silently, Daisy strode away from the billiards room and toward the main hall and the grand staircase. She bounded up the stairs, not stopping until she reached the Marsden parlor.

Annabelle and Evie were with Lillian, who was half-curled on the settee. Her features were pale and tense, her forehead lightly scored with frown lines. Her slim arms were wrapped around her stomach.

"That's twenty minutes," Evie said, her gaze fastened on the mantel clock.

"They're still not coming regularly," Annabelle remarked. She brushed Lillian's hair and braided it neatly, her slim fingers dexterous in the heavy black locks.

"What aren't coming regularly?" Daisy asked with forced cheer, coming into the room. "And why are you watching the—" She blanched as she suddenly understood. "My God. Are you having birthing pains, Lillian?"

Her sister shook her head, looking perplexed. "Not full-on pains. Just a sort of tightening of my stomach. It started after lunchtime, and then I had one an hour later, and then a half-hour later, and this one came after twenty minutes."

"Does Westcliff know?" Daisy asked breathlessly. "Should I go tell him?"

"*No*," all three of the other women said at once.

"There's no need to worry him yet," Lillian added

in a sheepish tone. "Let Westcliff enjoy the afternoon with his friends. As soon as he finds out, he'll be up here pacing and giving commands, and no one will have any peace. Especially me."

"What about Mother? Shall I fetch her?" Daisy had to ask, even though she was certain of the answer. Mercedes was not a comforting sort of person, and despite the fact that she had given birth to five children, she was squeamish at the mention of any kind of bodily function.

"I'm in enough pain already," Lillian said dryly. "No, don't tell Mother anything yet. She would feel obligated to sit here with me to maintain appearances, and that would make me as nervous as a cat. Right now all I need are the three of you."

Despite her sardonic tone, she reached for Daisy's hand and clung tightly. Childbirth was a frightening business, especially the first time, and Lillian was no exception. "Annabelle says this could happen on and off for days," she told Daisy, crossing her eyes comically. "Which means I may not be as sweet-tempered as usual."

"That's fine, dear. Give us your worst." Retaining Lillian's hand, Daisy sat on the carpeted floor at her feet.

The room was quiet except for the ticking of the mantel clock, and the stroke of the bristled brush against Lillian's scalp. Between the sisters' joined hands, the pressure of their pulses mingled in steady throbs. Daisy was not certain if she was giving comfort to her sister or receiving it. Lillian's time was here, and Daisy was afraid for her, of the pain and possible complications, and the fact that life would never be the same afterward.

She glanced at Evie, who flashed her a smile, and Annabelle, whose face was reassuringly calm. They would help each other through all the challenges and joys and fears of their lives, Daisy thought, and she was suddenly overwhelmed with love for all of them. "I will never live away from you," she said. "I want the four of us to be together always. I could never bear to lose any of you."

She felt Annabelle's slippered toe nudge her leg affectionately. "Daisy . . . you can never lose a true friend."

Chapter 9

As the afternoon spun out into early evening, the storm escalated beyond the usual springtime prank into a full-on assault. Rain-laden wind struck the windows and thrashed the meticulously trimmed hedgerows and trees, while lightning splintered the sky. The four friends stayed in the Marsden parlor, timing Lillian's contractions until they were separated by regular ten-minute intervals. Lillian was subdued and anxious, though she tried to hide it. Daisy suspected her sister found it difficult to surrender to the inevitable process that was taking control of her body.

"You can't possibly be comfortable on the settee," Annabelle finally said, pulling Lillian upright. "Come, dear. Time to go to bed."

"Should I—" Daisy began, thinking Westcliff should finally be summoned.

"Yes, I think so," Annabelle said.

Relieved at the prospect of actually doing something instead of helplessly sitting by, Daisy asked, "And then what? Do we need sheets? Towels?"

"Yes, yes," Annabelle said over her shoulder, hooking a firm arm around Lillian's back. "And scissors and a hot water bottle. And tell the housekeeper to send up some valerian oil, and some tea with dried motherwort and shepherd's purse."

As the others helped Lillian to the master bedroom, Daisy hurried downstairs. She went to the billiards room only to find it empty, then scampered to the library and one of the main parlors. It seemed Westcliff was nowhere to be found. Tamping down her impatience, Daisy forced herself to walk calmly past some guests in the hallway, and headed to Westcliff's study. To her relief, he was there with her father, Mr. Hunt, and Matthew Swift. They were involved in an animated conversation that included phrases such as "distribution network deficiencies" and "profits per unit of output."

Becoming aware of her presence in the doorway, the men looked up. Westcliff rose from his half-seated position on the desk. "My lord," Daisy said, "if I might have a word with you?"

Although she spoke calmly, something in her expression must have alerted him. He didn't waste a second in coming to her. "Yes, Daisy?"

"It's about my sister," she whispered. "It seems her labor has started."

She had never seen the earl look so utterly taken aback.

"It's too early," he said.

"Apparently the baby doesn't think so."

"But . . . this is off-schedule." The earl seemed genuinely baffled that his child would have failed to consult the calendar before arriving.

"Not necessarily," Daisy replied reasonably. "It's possible the doctor misjudged the date of the baby's birth. Ultimately it's only a matter of guesswork."

Westcliff scowled. "I expected far more accuracy than this! It's nearly a month before the projected . . ." A new thought occurred to him, and he turned skull-white. "Is the baby premature?"

Although Daisy had entertained a few private concerns about that, she shook her head immediately. "Some women show more than others, some less. And my sister is very slender. I'm sure the baby is fine." She gave him a reassuring smile. "Lillian has had pains for the past four or five hours, and now they're coming every ten minutes or so, which Annabelle says—"

"She's been in labor for *hours* and no one told me?" Westcliff demanded in outrage.

"Well, it's not technically labor unless the intervals between the pains are regular, and she said she didn't want to bother you until—"

Westcliff let out a curse that startled Daisy. He turned to point a commanding but unsteady finger at Simon Hunt. "Doctor," he barked, and took off at a dead run.

Simon Hunt appeared unsurprised by Westcliff's primitive behavior. "Poor fellow," he said with a slight smile, reaching over the desk to slide a pen back into its holder.

"Why did he call you 'Doctor'?" Thomas Bowman asked, feeling the effects of an afternoon snifter of brandy.

"I believe he wants me to *send* for the doctor," Hunt replied. "Which I intend to do immediately."

Unfortunately there were difficulties in producing the doctor, a venerable old man who lived in the village. The footman sent to summon him returned with the unhappy report that in the process of escorting the doctor to Westcliff's waiting carriage, the old man had injured himself.

"How?" Westcliff demanded, having come outside the bedroom to receive the footman's report. A small crowd of people including Daisy, Evie, St. Vincent, Mr. Hunt, and Mr. Swift were all waiting in the hallway. Annabelle was inside the room with Lillian.

"Milord," the footman said to Westcliff regretfully, "the doctor slipped on a wet paving-stone and fell to the ground before I could catch him. His leg is injured. He says he does not believe the limb is broken, but all the same he cannot come to assist Lady Westcliff."

A wild gleam appeared in the earl's dark eyes. "Why weren't you holding the doctor's arm? For God's sake, he's a fossil! It's obvious he couldn't be trusted to walk by himself on wet pavement."

"If he's all that frail," Simon Hunt asked reasonably, "how was the old relic supposed to be of any use to Lady Westcliff?"

The earl scowled. "That doctor knows more about childbirth than anyone between here and Portsmouth. He has delivered generations of Marsden issue."

"At this rate," Lord St. Vincent said, "the latest Marsden issue is going to arrive all by itself." He turned to the footman. "Unless the doctor had any suggestion of how to replace himself?"

"Yes, milord," the footman said uncomfortably. "He told me there is a midwife in the village."

"Then go fetch her at once," Westcliff barked.

"I've already tried, milord. But . . . she's a bit tap-hackled."

Westcliff scowled. "Bring her anyway. At the moment I'm hardly inclined to quibble over a glass of wine or two."

"Er, milord . . . she's actually *more* than a bit tap-hackled."

The earl stared at him incredulously. "Damn it, how drunk is she?"

"She thinks she's the queen. She shouted at me for stepping on her train."

A short silence followed as the group digested the information.

"I'm going to kill someone," the earl said to no one in particular, and then Lillian's cry from inside the bedroom caused him to turn pale.

"Marcus!"

"I'm coming," Westcliff shouted, and turned to view the footman with a menacing glare. "Find someone," he bit out. "A doctor. A midwife. A bloody sideshow fortune-teller. Just *get . . . someone . . . now.*"

As Westcliff disappeared into the bedroom the air seemed to quiver and smoke in his wake, as if in the aftermath of a lightning strike. A peal of thunder boomed from the sky outside, rattling chandeliers and vibrating the floor.

The footman was near tears. "Ten years in his lordship's service and now I'll be dismissed—"

"Go back to the doctor," Simon Hunt said, "and find out if his leg is better. If not, ask if there is some apprentice or student—who might suffice as a replacement. In the meantime I'll ride for the next village to search for someone."

Matthew Swift, who had been silent so far, asked quietly, "Which road will you take?"

"The one leading east," Hunt replied.

"I'll take the west."

Daisy stared at Swift with surprise and gratitude. The storm would make the errand dangerous, not to mention uncomfortable. The fact that he was willing to undertake it for Lillian, who had made no secret of her dislike, raised him several degrees in Daisy's estimation.

Lord St. Vincent said dryly, "I suppose that leaves me the south. She *would* have to have the baby during a deluge of biblical proportions."

"Would you rather stay here with Westcliff?" Simon Hunt asked in a sardonic tone.

St. Vincent threw him a glance rife with suppressed amusement. "I'll get my hat."

Two hours passed after the men left, while Lillian's labor progressed. The pains became so sharp that they robbed her of breath. She gripped her husband's hand with a bone-crunching force that he didn't seem to feel in the slightest. Westcliff was patient and soothing, wiping her face with a cool damp cloth, giving her sips of motherwort brew, kneading her lower back and legs to help her relax.

Annabelle proved so competent that Daisy doubted a midwife could have done any better. She applied the hot water bottle to Lillian's back and stomach and talked her through the pains, reminding her that if she, Annabelle, had managed to survive this, Lillian certainly could.

Lillian trembled in the aftermath of each hard contraction.

Annabelle held her hand tightly. "You don't have to be quiet, dear. Scream or curse if it helps."

Lillian shook her head weakly. "I don't have the energy to scream. I have more strength if I keep it in."

"I was that way too. Though I warn you, people won't give you nearly as much sympathy if you bear it stoically."

"Don't want sympathy," Lillian gasped, closing her eyes as another pain approached. "Just want . . . it to be *over*."

Watching Westcliff's taut face, Daisy reflected that whether or not Lillian wanted sympathy, her husband was overflowing with it.

"You're not supposed to be in here," Lillian told Westcliff when the contraction was over. She clung to his hand as if it were a lifeline. "You're supposed to be downstairs pacing and drinking."

"Good God, woman," Westcliff muttered, blotting her sweaty face with a dry cloth, "I did this to you. I'm hardly going to let you face the consequences alone."

That produced a faint smile on Lillian's dry lips.

There was a quick, hard rap at the door, and Daisy ran to answer it. Opening it a few inches, she saw Matthew Swift, dripping and muddy and out of breath. Relief swept over her. "Thank God," she exclaimed. "No one else has come back yet. Did you find someone?"

"Yes and no."

Experience had taught Daisy that when one answered "yes and no," the results were seldom what one would have wished for. "What do you mean?" she asked warily.

"He'll be upstairs momentarily—he's washing up. The roads have turned to mud—sinkholes everywhere—thundering like hell—it was a miracle the horse didn't bolt or break its leg." Swift removed his hat and swiped at his forehead with his sleeve, leaving a dirty streak across his face.

"But you did find a doctor?" Daisy pressed, snatching up a clean towel from a basket beside the door and handing it to him.

"No. The neighbors said the doctor went to Brighton for a fortnight."

"What about a midwife—"

"Busy," Swift said tersely. "She's helping two other women in the village who are in labor as we speak. She said it happens sometimes during a particularly bad storm—something in the air brings it on."

Daisy stared at him in confusion. "Then whom did you bring?"

A balding man with soft brown eyes appeared at Swift's side. He was damp but clean—cleaner than Swift, at any rate—and respectable looking. "Evening, miss," he said bashfully.

"His name is Merritt," Swift told Daisy. "He's a veterinarian."

"A what?"

Even though the door was mostly closed, the conversation could be heard by the people in the room. Lillian's sharp voice came from the bed. "You brought me an *animal doctor*?"

"He was highly recommended," Swift said.

Since Lillian was covered with the bedclothes, Daisy opened the door wider to allow her a glimpse of the man.

"How much experience do you have?" Lillian demanded of Merritt.

"Yesterday I delivered puppies from a bulldog bitch. And before that—"

"Close enough," Westcliff said hastily as Lillian clutched his hand at the onset of another cramp. "Come in."

Daisy allowed the man to enter the room, and she stepped outside with another clean towel.

"I would have gone to another village," Swift said, his voice roughened with a note of apology. "I don't know if Merritt will be of any help. But the bogs and creeks have overflowed and the roads are impassable. And I wasn't going to come back without someone." He closed his eyes for a moment, his face drawn, and she realized how exhausting the ride through the storm had been.

Dependable, Daisy thought. Wrapping a corner of the clean towel around her fingers, she wiped at the mud on his face and blotted the rain caught in his day-old beard. The dark bristle of his jaw fascinated her. She wanted to stroke her bare fingers over it.

Swift held still, his head bent to make it easier

for her to reach him. "I hope the others have more success at finding a doctor than I did."

"They may not make it back in time," Daisy replied. "Things have progressed rapidly in the last hour."

He pulled his head back as if her gentle dabbing at his face bothered him. "Aren't you going back in there?"

Daisy shook her head. "My presence is *de trop,* as they say. Lillian hates being crowded, and Annabelle is far more able than I am to help her. But I am going to wait nearby in case . . . in case she calls for me."

Taking the towel from her, Swift scrubbed the back of his head, where the rain had soaked into the thick hair and made it as black and glossy as a seal's pelt. "I'll return soon," he said. "I'm going to wash and change into dry clothes."

"My parents and Lady St. Vincent are waiting in the Marsden parlor," Daisy said. "You can stay with them—it's far more comfortable than waiting here."

But when Swift returned, he didn't go to the parlor. He came to Daisy.

She sat cross-legged in the hallway, leaning back against the wall. Lost in her thoughts, she didn't notice his approach until he was right beside her. Dressed in fresh clothes with his hair still damp, he stood looking down at her.

"May I?"

Daisy wasn't certain what he was asking, but she found herself nodding anyway. Swift lowered himself to the floor in a cross-legged posture identical to hers. She had never sat this way with a gentleman, and had certainly never expected to with Matthew Swift. Companionably he handed her a small glass filled with rich, plum-red liquid.

Receiving it with some surprise, Daisy held it up to her nose for a cautious sniff.

"Madeira," she said with a smile. "Thank you. Although celebration is a bit premature since the baby still isn't here."

"This isn't for celebration. It's to help you relax."

"How did you know what my favorite wine was?" she asked.

He shrugged. "A lucky guess."

But somehow she knew it hadn't been luck.

There was little conversation between them, just an oddly companionable silence. "What time is it?" Daisy would ask every now and then, and he would produce a pocket watch.

Mildly intrigued by the jangle of objects in his coat pocket, Daisy demanded to see what was inside it.

"You'll be disappointed," Swift said as he unearthed the collection of items. He dumped the lot into her lap while Daisy sorted through it all.

"You're worse than a ferret," she said with a grin. There was the folding knife and the fishing line, a few loose coins, a pen nib, the pair of spectacles, a little tin of soap—Bowman's, of course—and a slip of folded waxed paper containing willowbark powder. Holding the paper between thumb and forefinger, Daisy asked, "Do you have headaches, Mr. Swift?"

"No. But your father does whenever he gets bad news. And I'm usually the one who delivers it."

Daisy laughed and picked up a tiny silver match case from the pile in her lap. "Why matches? I thought you didn't smoke."

"One never knows when a fire will be needed."

Daisy held up a paper of straight pins and raised her brows questioningly.

"I use them to attach documents," he explained. "But they've been useful on other occasions."

She let a teasing note enter her voice. "Is there *any* emergency for which you are not prepared, Mr. Swift?"

"Miss Bowman, if I had enough pockets I could save the world."

It was the way he said it, with a sort of wistful arrogance intended to amuse her, that demolished Daisy's defenses. She laughed and felt a warm glow even as she recognized that liking him was not going to improve her circumstances one bit. Bending over her lap, she examined a handful of tiny cards bound with thread.

"I was told to bring both business *and* visiting cards to England," Swift said. "Though I'm not entirely certain what the difference is."

"You must never leave a business card when you're calling on an Englishman," Daisy advised him. "It's bad form here—it implies you're trying to collect money for something."

"I usually am."

Daisy smiled. She found another intriguing object, and she held it up to inspect it.

A button.

Her brow creased as she stared at the front of the button, which was engraved with a pattern of a windmill. The back of it contained a tiny lock of black hair behind a thin plate of glass, held in place with a copper rim.

Swift blanched and reached for it, but Daisy snatched it back, her fingers closing around the button.

Daisy's pulse began to race. "I've seen this before," she said. "It was part of a set. My mother had a waistcoat made for Father with five buttons. One was engraved with a windmill, another with a tree, another with a bridge . . . she took a lock of hair from each of her children and put it inside a button. I remember the way she took a little snip from my hair at the back where it wouldn't show."

Still not looking at her, Swift reached for the discarded contents of his pocket and methodically replaced them.

As the silence drew out, Daisy waited in vain for an explanation. Finally she reached out and took hold of his sleeve. His arm stilled, and he stared at her fingers on his coat fabric.

"How did you get it?" she whispered.

Swift waited so long that she thought he might not answer.

Finally he spoke with a quiet surliness that wrenched her heart. "Your father wore the waistcoat to the company offices. It was much admired. But later that day he was in a temper and in the process of throwing an ink bottle he spilled some on himself. The waistcoat was ruined. Rather than face your mother with the news he gave the garment to me, buttons and all, and told me to dispose of it."

"But you kept one button." Her lungs expanded until her chest felt tight on the inside and her heartbeat was frantic. "The windmill. Which was mine. Have you . . . have you carried a lock of my hair all these years?"

Another long silence. Daisy would never know how or if he would have answered, because the moment was broken by the sound of Annabelle's voice in the hallway. *"Daaaisyyyy!"*

Still clutching the button, Daisy struggled to her feet. Swift rose in one smooth movement, first steadying her, then clamping his hand on her wrist. He held his free hand beneath hers and gave her an inscrutable look.

He wanted the button back, she realized, and let out an incredulous laugh.

"It's mine," she protested. Not because she wanted the dratted button, but because it was strange to realize that he had possessed this tiny part of her, kept it with him for years. She was a little afraid of what it meant.

Swift didn't move or speak, just waited with unyielding patience until Daisy opened her fingers and let the button drop into his palm. He pocketed the object like a possessive magpie and released her.

Bewildered, Daisy hurried toward her sister's room. As she heard the sound of a baby crying, her breath stopped with anxious joy. It was only a few yards to her sister's door, and yet it seemed to be miles.

Annabelle met her at the door, looking strained and weary but wearing a brilliant smile. And there was a tiny bundle of linen and clean toweling in her arms. Daisy put her fingers over her mouth and shook her head slightly, laughing even as her eyes prickled with tears. "Oh my," she said, staring at the red-faced baby, the bright dark eyes, the wealth of black hair.

"Say hello to your niece," Annabelle said, gently handing the infant to her.

Daisy took the baby carefully, astonished by how light she was. "My sister—"

"Lillian's fine," Annabelle replied at once. "She did splendidly."

Cooing to the baby, Daisy entered the room. Lillian was resting against a stack of pillows, her eyes closed. She looked very small in the large bed, her hair braided in two plaits like a young girl's. Westcliff was at her side, looking like he had just fought Waterloo singlehandedly.

The veterinarian was at the washstand, soaping his hands. He threw Daisy a friendly smile, and she grinned back at him. "Congratulations, Mr. Merritt," she said. "It seems you've added a new species to your repertoire."

Lillian stirred at the sound of her voice. "Daisy?"

Daisy approached with the baby in her arms. "Oh, Lillian, she's the most beautiful thing I've ever seen."

Her sister grinned sleepily. "I think so too. Would you—" she broke off to yawn. "Show her to Mother and Father?"

"Yes, of course. What is her name?"

"Merritt."

"You're naming her after the veterinarian?"

"He proved to be quite helpful," Lillian replied. "And Westcliff said I could."

The earl tucked the bedclothes more snugly around his wife's body and kissed her forehead.

"Still no heir," Lillian whispered to him, her grin lingering. "I suppose we'll have to have another one."

"No, we won't," Westcliff replied hoarsely. "I'm never going through this again."

Amused, Daisy glanced down at little Merritt, who was falling asleep in her arms. "I'll show her to the others," she said softly.

Stepping into the hallway, she was surprised to find it was empty.

Matthew Swift was gone.

* * *

When Daisy woke up the next morning, she learned to her relief that Mr. Hunt and Lord St. Vincent had returned safely to Stony Cross Park. St. Vincent had found the south road to be impassable, but Mr. Hunt had had more luck. He had found a doctor in a neighboring village, but the man had balked at riding out in a perilous storm. Apparently it had taken a fair amount of bullying from Hunt to convince him to go. Once they had arrived at Stony Cross Manor, the doctor examined Lillian and Merritt and pronounced them both in excellent condition. In his assessment the baby was small but perfectly formed, with a well-developed pair of lungs.

The guests at the manor received the news of the birth with only a few regretful murmurs about the baby's gender. But seeing Westcliff's face as he held his newborn daughter, and hearing his whispered promises that he was going to buy ponies and castles and entire kingdoms for her, Daisy knew he could not have been any happier had Merritt been a boy.

As she shared breakfast in the morning room with Evie, Daisy was aware of a most peculiar jumble of emotions. Aside from the joy that her niece had been born and her sister was fine, she felt . . . nervous. Lightheaded. Eager.

All because of Matthew Swift.

Daisy was grateful that she had not yet seen him today. After the discoveries she had made last night, she was not certain how she would react to him.

"Evie," she entreated privately, "there is something I need to talk to you about. Will you walk in the gardens with me?" Now that the storm was over, weak gray sunlight seeped through the sky.

"Of course. Although it's rather muddy outside . . ."

"We'll stay on the graveled paths. But it must be out there. This is too private to be discussed indoors."

Evie's eyes widened, and she drank her tea so fast it must have scalded her tongue.

The garden had been disheveled by the storm, leaves and green buds scattered everywhere, twigs and branches lying across the usually immaculate path. But the air was fragrant with the scents of wet earth and rain-drenched petals. Breathing deeply of the invigorating smell, the two friends strolled along the graveled walkway. They knotted their shawls around their arms and shoulders while the breeze pushed at them with the impatience of a child urging them to quicken their pace.

Daisy had seldom known a relief as great as unburdening herself to Evie. She told her about everything that had transpired between herself and Matthew Swift, including the kiss, finishing with the revelation of the button he carried in his pocket. Evie was a better listener than anyone Daisy knew, perhaps because of her struggles with her stammer.

"I don't know what to think," Daisy said miserably. "I don't know how to feel about any of it. I don't know why Mr. Swift seems different now than he did before, or why I am so drawn to him. It was so much easier to hate him. But last night when I saw that blasted button . . ."

"It had never occurred to you until then that he might actually have feelings for you," Evie murmured.

"Yes."

"Daisy . . . is it possible his actions have been calculated? That he is deceiving you, and the button in his pocket was some kind of pl-ploy?"

"No. If you had only seen his face. He was obviously desperate to keep me from realizing what it was. Oh, Evie . . ." Daisy kicked morosely at a pebble. "I have the most horrible suspicion that Matthew Swift might actually be everything I ever wanted in a man."

"But if you married him, he would take you back to New York," Evie said.

"Yes, eventually, and I *can't*. I don't want to live away from my sister and all of you. And I love England—I'm more myself here than I ever was in New York."

Evie considered the problem thoughtfully. "What if Mr. Swift were willing to consider s-staying here permanently?"

"He wouldn't. The opportunities are far greater in New York—and if he stayed here he would always have the disadvantage of not being an aristocrat."

"But if he were willing to try . . ." Evie pressed.

"I still could never become the kind of wife he would need."

"The two of you must have a forthright conversation," Evie said decisively. "Mr. Swift is a mature and intelligent man—surely he wouldn't expect you to become something you're not."

"It's all moot, anyway," Daisy said gloomily. "He made it clear that he won't marry me under any circumstances. That was his exact wording."

"Is it you he objects to, or the concept of marriage itself?"

"I don't know. All I know is he must feel *something* for me if he carries a lock of my hair in his pocket." Remembering the way his fingers had closed over the button, she felt a quick, not unpleasant shiver chase down her spine. "Evie," she asked, "how do you know if you love someone?"

Evie considered the question as they passed a low circular boundary hedge containing an explosion of multi-colored primulas. "I'm sure this is when I'm s-supposed to say something wise and helpful," she said with a self-deprecating shrug. "But my situation was different from yours. St. Vincent and I didn't expect to fall in love. It caught us both unaware."

"Yes, but how did you *know*?"

"It was the moment I realized he was willing to die for me. I don't think anyone, including St. Vincent, believed he was capable of self-sacrifice. It taught me that you can assume you know a person quite well—but that person can s-surprise you. Everything seemed to change from one moment to the next—suddenly he became the most important thing in the world to me. No, not important . . . *necessary*. Oh, I wish I were clever with words—"

"I understand," Daisy murmured, although she felt more melancholy than enlightened. She wondered if she would ever be able to love a man that way. Perhaps her emotions had been too deeply invested in her sister and friends . . . perhaps there wasn't enough left over for anyone else.

They came to a tall juniper hedge beyond which extended a flagstoned walkway that bordered the side of the manor. As they made their way to an opening of the hedge, they heard a pair of masculine voices engaged in conversation. The voices were not loud. In fact, the strictly moderated volume of the conversation betrayed that something secret— and therefore intriguing—was being discussed. Pausing behind the hedge, Daisy motioned for Evie to be still and quiet.

". . . doesn't promise to be much of a breeder . . ." one of them was saying.

The comment was met with a low but indignant objection. "*Timid?* Holy hell, the woman has enough spirit to climb Mont-Blanc with a pen-knife and a ball of twine. Her children will be perfect hellions."

Daisy and Evie stared at each other with mutual astonishment. Both voices were easily recognizable as those belonging to Lord Llandrindon and Matthew Swift.

"Really," Llandrindon said skeptically. "My impression is that she is a literary-minded girl. Rather a bluestocking."

"Yes, she loves books. She also happens to love adventure. She has a remarkable imagination accompanied by a passionate enthusiasm for life and an iron constitution. You're not going to find a girl her equal on your side of the Atlantic or mine."

"I had no intention of looking on your side," Llandrindon said dryly. "English girls possess all the traits I would desire in a wife."

They were talking about *her*, Daisy realized, her mouth dropping open. She was torn between delight at Matthew Swift's description of her, and indignation that he was trying to sell her to Llandrindon as if she were a bottle of patent medicine from a street vendor's cart.

"I require a wife who is poised," Llandrindon continued, "sheltered, restful . . ."

"*Restful?* What about natural and intelligent? What about a girl with the confidence to be herself rather than trying to imitate some pallid ideal of subservient womanhood?"

"I have a question," Llandrindon said.

"Yes?"

"If she's so bloody remarkable, why don't *you* marry her?"

Daisy held her breath, straining to hear Swift's

reply. To her supreme frustration his voice was muffled by the filter of the hedges. "Drat," she muttered and made to follow them.

Evie yanked her back behind the hedge. "No," she whispered sharply. "Don't test our luck, Daisy. It was a miracle they didn't realize we were here."

"But I wanted to hear the rest of it!"

"So did I." They stared at each other with round eyes. "Daisy . . ." Evie said in wonder, ". . . I think Matthew Swift is in love with you."

Chapter 10

$\mathcal{D}$aisy wasn't certain why the notion that Matthew Swift could be in love with her should set her entire world upside-down. But it did.

"If he is," she asked Evie unsteadily, "then why is he so determined to pawn me off on Lord Llandrindon? It would be so easy for him to fall in with my father's plans. And he would be richly rewarded. If on top of that he actually cares for me in the bargain, what could be holding him back?"

"Maybe he wants to find out if you love him in return?"

"No, Mr. Swift's mind doesn't work that way, any more than my father's does. They're men of business. *Predators.* If Mr. Swift wanted me, he wouldn't stop to ask for my permission any more

than a lion would stop and politely ask an antelope
if he would mind being eaten for lunch."

"I think the two of you should have a forthright
conversation," Evie declared.

"Oh, Mr. Swift would only evade and prevari-
cate, exactly as he has done so far. Unless . . ."

"Unless?"

". . . I could find some way to make him let his
guard down. And force him to be honest about
whether he feels anything for me or not."

"How will you do that?"

"I don't know. Hang it, Evie, you know a hundred times more about men than I do. You're married to one. You're surrounded by them at the club.
In your informed opinion, what is the quickest
way to drive a man to the limits of his sanity and
make him admit something he doesn't want to?"

Seeming pleased by the image of herself as a
worldly woman, Evie contemplated the question.
"Make him jealous, I suppose. I've seen civilized
men fight like dogs in the alley behind the club
over the f-favors of a particular lady."

"Hmm. I wonder if Mr. Swift could be provoked
to jealousy."

"I should think so," Evie said. "He's a man, after
all."

In the afternoon Daisy cornered Lord Llandrindon
as he went into the library to replace a book on
one of the lower gallery shelves.

"Good afternoon, my lord," Daisy said brightly,

pretending not to notice the glaze of apprehension in his eyes. She smothered a grin, thinking that after Matthew Swift's campaign on her behalf, poor Llandrindon probably felt like a fox run to ground.

Recovering quickly, Llandrindon summoned a pleasant smile. "Good afternoon, Miss Bowman. May I ask after your sister and the baby?"

"Both are quite well, thank you." Daisy drew closer and inspected the book in his hands. "*History Of Military Cartography*. Well. That sounds quite, er . . . intriguing."

"Oh, it is," Llandrindon assured her. "And wonderfully instructive. Though I fear something was lost in the translation. One must read it in the original German to appreciate the full significance of the work."

"Do you ever read novels, my lord?"

He looked sincerely appalled by the question. "Oh, I never read novels. I was taught from childhood that one should only read books that instruct the mind or improve the character."

Daisy was annoyed by his superior tone. "What a pity," she said beneath her breath.

"Hmm?"

"That's pretty," she amended quickly, pretending to examine the volume's engraved leather binding. She gave him what she hoped was a poised smile. "Are you an avid reader, my lord?"

"I try never to be avid about anything. 'Moderation in all things' is one of my most valued mottoes."

"I don't have any mottoes. If I did I would forever be contradicting them."

Llandrindon chuckled. "Are you admitting to a mercurial nature?"

"I prefer to think of it as being open-minded," Daisy said. "I can see wisdom in a great variety of beliefs."

"Ah."

Daisy could practically read his thoughts, that her so-called openmindedness cast her in a lessthan-favorable light. "I should like to hear more of your mottoes, my lord. Perhaps during a stroll through the gardens?"

"I . . . er . . ." It was unpardonably bold for a girl to invite a gentleman on a walk instead of the other way around. However, Llandrindon's gentlemanly nature would not allow him to refuse. "Of course, Miss Bowman. Perhaps tomorrow—"

"Now would be fine," she said brightly.

"Now," came his weak reply. "Yes. Lovely."

Taking his arm before he had a chance to offer it, Daisy tugged him toward the doorway. "Let's go."

Having no choice but to allow the militantly cheerful young woman to drag him this way and that, Llandrindon soon found himself proceeding down one of the great stone staircases that led from the back terrace to the grounds below. "My lord," Daisy said, "I have something to confess. I am hatching a little plot and I was hoping to enlist your help."

"A little plot," he repeated skittishly. "My help. Quite. That is, er—"

"It's harmless, of course," Daisy continued. "My objective is to encourage a certain gentleman's attentions, as he seems to be somewhat reticent when it comes to courtship."

"Reticent?" Llandrindon's voice was a bare scratch of sound.

Daisy's estimation of his mental capacity sank several degrees as it became apparent that all he could do was repeat her words in a parrotlike fashion. "Yes, reticent. But I have the impression that underneath the reluctant surface a different feeling may exist."

Llandrindon, usually so graceful, tripped on an uneven patch of gravel. "What—what gives you that impression, Miss Bowman?"

"It's just a woman's intuition."

"Miss Bowman," he burst out, "if I have said or done anything to give you the misapprehension that I . . . that I . . ."

"I'm not talking about you," Daisy said bluntly.

"You're not? Then who—"

"I'm referring to Mr. Swift."

His sudden joy was nearly palpable. "*Mr. Swift.* Yes. *Yes.* Miss Bowman, he has sung your praises for endless hours—not that it has been disagreeable to hear about your charms, of course."

Daisy smiled. "I fear Mr. Swift will continue being reticent until something happens to flush him out like a pheasant from a wheat field. But if you wouldn't mind giving the impression that you have indeed taken an interest in me—an outing in the carriage, a stroll, a dance or two—it may give him just the impetus he needs to declare himself."

"It would be my pleasure," Llandrindon said, apparently finding the role of co-conspirator far more appealing than that of matrimonial target. "I assure you, Miss Bowman, I can give a most convincing appearance of courtship."

"I want you to delay your trip for a week."

Matthew, who had been fastening five sheets of paper together with a straight pin, accidently shoved the point of one into his finger. Withdrawing the pin, he ignored the tiny dot of blood on his skin and stared at Westcliff without comprehension. The man had been closeted away with his wife and new-born daughter for at least thirty-six hours, and all of a sudden he had decided to appear the night before Matthew was to leave for Bristol and issue a command that made no sense at all.

Matthew kept his voice under tight control. "May I ask why, my lord?"

"Because I have decided to accompany you. And my schedule will not accommodate a departure on the morrow."

As far as Matthew knew, the earl's current schedule revolved solely around Lillian and the baby. "There is no need for you to go," he said, offended by the implication that he couldn't manage things on his own. "I know more than anyone about the various aspects of this business, and what it will require—"

"You are a foreigner, nonetheless," Westcliff said, his face inscrutable. "And the mention of my name will open doors you won't otherwise have access to."

"If you doubt my negotiating skills—"

"Those aren't at issue. I have complete faith in your skills, which in America would be more than sufficient. But here, in an undertaking of this magnitude, you will need the patronage of someone highly placed in society. Someone like me."

"This isn't the medieval era, my lord. I'll be damned if I need to put on a dog-and-pony show with a peer as part of a business deal."

"Speaking as the other half of the dog-and-pony show," Westcliff said sardonically, "I'm not fond of the idea either. Especially when I have a newborn infant and a wife who hasn't yet recovered from labor."

"I can't wait a week," Matthew exploded. "I've already made appointments. I've arranged to meet with everyone from the dockmaster to the owners of the local waterworks company—"

"Those meetings will be rescheduled, then."

"If you think there won't be complaints—"

"The news that I will be accompanying you next week will be enough to quell most complaints."

From any other man such a pronouncement would have been arrogance. From Westcliff it was a simple statement of fact.

"Does Mr. Bowman know about this?" Matthew demanded.

"Yes. And after hearing my opinion on the matter, he has agreed."

"What am I supposed to do here for a week?"

The earl arched a dark brow in the manner of a man whose hospitality had never been questioned. People of all ages, nationalities and social classes begged for invitations to Stony Cross Park. Matthew was probably the only man in England who *didn't* want to be there.

He didn't care. He had gone too long without any real work—he was tired of idle amusements, tired of small talk, tired of beautiful scenery and fresh country air and peace and quiet. He wanted some activity, damn it all. Not to mention some coal-scented city air and the clamor of traffic-filled streets.

Most of all he wanted to be away from Daisy Bowman. It was constant torture to have her so near and yet never be able to touch her. It was impossible to treat her with calm courtesy when his head was filled with lurid images of holding her, seducing her, his mouth finding the sweetest, most vulnerable places of her body. And that was only the beginning. Matthew wanted hours, days, weeks alone with her . . . he wanted all her thoughts and smiles and secrets. The freedom to lay his soul bare before her.

Things he could never have.

"There are many entertainments available at the estate and its environs," Westcliff said in answer to his question. "If you desire a particular kind of female companionship, I suggest you go to the village tavern."

Matthew had already heard some of the male guests at the estate boasting of a spring evening's revelry with a pair of buxom tavern maids. If only he could be satisfied with something that simple. A solid village wench, instead of a tantalizing will-o'-the-wisp who had wrought some kind of spell over his mind and heart.

Love was supposed to be a happy, giddy emotion. Like the silly verses written on Valentine cards and decorated with feathers and paint and lace. This wasn't at all like that. This was a gnawing, feverish, bleak feeling . . . an addiction that could not be quenched.

This was pure reckless need. And he was not a reckless man.

But Matthew knew if he stayed at Stony Cross much longer, he was going to do something disastrous.

"I'm going to Bristol," Matthew said desperately. "I'll reschedule the meetings. I won't do anything without your leave. But at least I can gather information—interview the local transport firm, have a look at their horses—"

"Swift," the earl interrupted. Something in his quiet tone, a note of . . . kindness? . . . sympathy? . . .

caused Matthew to stiffen defensively. "I understand the reason for your urgency—"

"No, you don't."

"I understand more than you might think. And in my experience, these problems can't be solved by avoidance. You can never run far or fast enough."

Matthew froze, staring at Westcliff. The earl could have been referring either to Daisy, or to Matthew's tarnished past. In either case he was probably right.

Not that it changed anything.

"Sometimes running is the only choice," Matthew replied gruffly, and left the room without looking back.

As it turned out, Matthew did not go to Bristol. He knew he would regret his decision . . . but he had no idea how much.

The days that followed were what Matthew would remember for the rest of his life as a week of unholy torture.

He had been to hell and back at a much earlier time in his life, having known physical pain, deprivation, near-starvation, and bone-chilling fear. But none of those discomforts came close to the agony of standing by and watching Daisy Bowman being courted by Lord Llandrindon.

It seemed the seeds he had sown in Llandrindon's mind about Daisy's charms had successfully taken root. Llandrindon was at Daisy's side constantly, chatting, flirting, letting his gaze travel over her with offensive familiarity. And Daisy was similarly absorbed, hanging on his every word, dropping whatever she happened to be doing as soon as Llandrindon appeared.

On Monday they went out for a private picnic.

On Tuesday they went for a carriage drive.

On Wednesday they went to pick bluebells.

On Thursday they fished at the lake, returning with damp clothes and sun-glazed complexions, laughing together at a joke they didn't share with anyone else.

On Friday they danced together at an impromptu musical evening, looking so well matched that one of the guests remarked it was a pleasure to watch them.

On Saturday Matthew woke up wanting to murder someone.

His mood was not improved by Thomas Bowman's dyspeptic pronouncement after breakfast.

"He's winning," Bowman grumbled, pulling Matthew into the study for a private conversation. "That Scottish bastard Llandrindon has spent hours on end with Daisy, oozing charm and spouting all the nonsense women like to hear. If you had any intention of marrying my daughter, the opportunity has dwindled to almost nothing. You've gone out of your way to avoid her, you've been taciturn and distant, and all week you've worn an expression that would frighten small children and animals. Your notion of wooing a woman confirms everything I've ever heard about Bostonians."

"Perhaps Llandrindon is the best match for her," Matthew said woodenly. "They seem to be developing a mutual affection."

"This isn't about affection, it's about marriage!" The top of Bowman's head began to turn red. "Do you understand the stakes involved?"

"Other than the financial ones?"

"What other kind of stakes could there be?"

Matthew sent him a sardonic glance. "Your daughter's heart. Her future happiness. Her—"

"Bah! People don't marry to be happy. Or if they do, they soon discover it's hog-swill."

Despite his black mood, Matthew smiled slightly. "If you're hoping to inspire me in the direction of wedlock," he said, "it's not working."

"Is this inspiration enough?" Reaching into the pocket of his waistcoat, Bowman extracted a gleaming silver dollar and flipped it upward with his thumb. The coin spun toward Matthew in a bright silver arc. He caught it reflexively, closing it in his palm. "Marry Daisy," Bowman said, "and you'll get more of that. More than one man could spend in a lifetime."

A new voice came from the doorway, and they both glanced toward the speaker.

"Lovely."

It was Lillian, dressed in a pink day-gown and a shawl. She stared at her father with something approaching hatred, her eyes as dark as volcanic glass. "Is anyone in your life more than a mere pawn to you, Father?" she asked acidly.

"This is a discussion between men," Bowman retorted, flushing from guilt, anger, or some combination of the two. "It's none of your concern."

"Daisy is my concern," Lillian said, her voice soft but chilling. "And I'd kill you both before letting you make her unhappy." Before her father could reply, she turned and proceeded down the hall.

Swearing, Bowman left the room and headed in the opposite direction.

Left alone in the study, Matthew slammed the coin onto the desk.

"All this effort for a man who doesn't even care," Daisy muttered to herself, thinking dire thoughts about Matthew Swift.

Llandrindon sat a few yards away on the rim of a garden fountain, obediently holding still as she sketched his portrait. She had never been particularly talented at sketching, but she was running out of things to do with him.

"What was that?" the Scottish lord called out.

"I said you have a fine head of hair!"

Llandrindon was a perfectly nice fellow, pleasant and unexceptional and utterly conventional. Glumly Daisy admitted to herself that in the effort to drive Matthew Swift half-mad with jealousy, she had succeeded only in driving herself half-mad with boredom.

Daisy paused to raise the back of her hand to her lips, stifling a yawn as she tried to appear as if she were immersed in her sketching.

This had been one of the most miserable weeks of her entire life. Day after day of deadly tedium, pretending to enjoy herself in the company of a man who couldn't have interested her less. It wasn't Llandrindon's fault—he had made every effort to be entertaining—but it was clear to Daisy they had nothing in common and never would.

This didn't seem to bother Llandrindon nearly as much as it did her. He could talk about practically nothing for hours. He could have filled entire newspapers with society gossip about people Daisy had never met. And he launched on long discourses about things like his search for the perfect color scheme for the hunting room at his Thurso estate, or the detailed course of studies he had followed at school. There never seemed to be a point to any of these stories.

Llandrindon seemed similarly disinterested in what Daisy had to say. He didn't laugh at the tales of her childhood pranks with Lillian, and if she said something like "Look at that cloud—it's shaped just like a rooster," he stared at her as if she were mad.

He also hadn't liked it when they discussed the poor laws and Daisy questioned his distinctions between the "deserving poor" and the "unworthy poor." "It seems, my lord," she had said, "that the law is designed to punish the people who need help the most."

"Some people are poor because of choices they make through their own moral weaknesses, and therefore one can't help them."

"Such as fallen women, you mean? But what if these women had no other—"

"We will *not* discuss fallen women," he had said, looking horrified.

Conversation with him was limited at best. Especially as Llandrindon found it difficult to follow Daisy's quicksilver transitions between subjects. Long after she had finished talking about one thing, he would keep asking about it. "I thought we were still on the subject of your aunt's poodle?" he had asked in confusion that very morning, and Daisy had replied impatiently, "No, I finished with that five minutes ago—just now I was telling you about the opera visit."

"But how did we go from the poodle to the opera?"

Daisy was sorry that she had enlisted Llandrindon in her scheme, especially as it had proven so ineffective. Matthew Swift had not displayed one second's worth of jealousy—he had been his usual granite-faced self, barely sparing a glance in her direction for days.

"Why are you frowning, sweeting?" Llandrindon asked, watching her face.

Sweeting? He had never used an endearment with her before. Daisy glanced at him over the edge of the sketchbook. He was staring at her in a way that made her uneasy. "Be quiet, please," she said primly. "I'm sketching your chin."

Concentrating on her drawing, Daisy thought it was not half-bad, but . . . was his head really that egg-shaped? Were his eyes that close-set? How strange that a person could be quite attractive, but when one examined them feature by feature, much of their charm faded. She decided sketching people was not her forte. From now on she would stick to plants and fruit.

"This week has had a strange effect on me," Llandrindon ruminated aloud. "I feel . . . different."

"Are you ill?" Daisy asked in concern, closing the sketchbook. "I'm sorry, I've made you sit out in the sun too long."

"No, not that kind of different. What I meant to say is that I feel . . . wonderful." Llandrindon was staring at her in that odd way again. "Better than I ever have before."

"It's the country air, I expect." Daisy stood and brushed her skirts off, and went to him. "It's quite invigorating."

"It's not the country air I find invigorating," Llandrindon said in a low voice. "It's you, Miss Bowman."

Daisy's mouth fell open. "Me?"

"You." He stood and took her shoulders in his hands.

Daisy could only stutter in surprise. "I—I—my lord—"

"These past few days in your company have given me cause for deep reflection."

Daisy twisted to glance at their surroundings, taking in the neatly trimmed hedges covered with bursts of pink climbing roses. "Is Mr. Swift nearby?" she whispered. "Is that why you're talking this way?"

"No, I'm speaking for myself." Ardently Llandrindon pulled her closer, until the sketchbook was nearly crushed between them. "You've opened my eyes, Miss Bowman. You've made me see everything a different way. I want to find shapes in clouds, and do something worth writing a poem about. I want to read novels. I want to make life an adventure—"

"How nice," Daisy said, wriggling in his tightening grasp.

"—with you."

Oh no.

"You're joking," she said weakly.

"I'm besotted," he declared.

"I'm unavailable."

"I'm determined."

"I'm . . . surprised."

"You dear little thing," he exclaimed. "You're everything he said you were. Magic. Thunderstorms wrapped up with rainbows. Clever and lovely and desirable—"

"Wait." Daisy stared at him in astonishment. "Matth—that is, Mr. Swift said that?"

"Yes, yes, yes . . ." And before she could move, speak or breathe, Llandrindon lowered his head and kissed her.

The sketchbook dropped from Daisy's hands. She remained passive in his embrace, wondering if she was going to feel something.

Objectively speaking, there was nothing wrong with his kiss. It wasn't too dry or slobbery, not too hard or soft. It was . . .

Boring.

Drat. Daisy pulled back with a frown. She felt guilty that she had enjoyed the kiss so little. And it made her feel even worse when it appeared Llandrindon had enjoyed it quite a lot.

"My dear Miss Bowman," Llandrindon murmured flirtatiously. "You didn't tell me you tasted so sweet."

He reached for her again, and Daisy danced backward with a little yelp. "My lord, control yourself!"

"I cannot." He pursued her slowly around the fountain until they resembled a pair of circling cats. Suddenly he made a dash for her, catching at the sleeve of her gown. Daisy pushed hard at him and twisted away, feeling the soft white muslin rip an inch or two at the shoulder seam.

There was a loud splash and a splatter of water drops.

Daisy stood blinking at the empty spot where Llandrindon had been, and then covered her eyes with her hands as if that would somehow make the entire situation go away.

"My lord?" she asked gingerly. "Did you . . . did you just fall into the fountain?"

"No," came his sour reply. "You *pushed* me into the fountain."

"It was entirely unintentional, I assure you." Daisy forced herself to look at him.

Llandrindon rose to his feet, water streaming from his hair and clothes, his coat pockets filled to the brim. It appeared the dip in the fountain had cooled his passions considerably.

He glowered at her in affronted silence. Suddenly his eyes widened, and he reached into one of his water-laden coat pockets. A tiny frog leaped from the pocket and returned to the fountain with a quiet *plunk*.

Daisy tried to choke back her amusement, but the harder she tried the worse it became, until she finally burst out laughing. "I'm sorry," she gasped, clapping her hands over her mouth, while irrepressible giggles slipped out. "I'm so—oh *dear*—" And she bent over laughing until tears came to her eyes.

The tension between them disappeared as Llandrindon began to smile reluctantly. He stepped from the fountain, dripping from every surface. "I believe when you kiss the toad," he said dryly, "he is supposed to turn into a prince. Unfortunately in my case it doesn't seem to have worked."

Daisy felt a rush of sympathy and kindness, even as she snorted with a few last giggles. Approaching him carefully, she placed her small hands on either side of his wet face and pressed a friendly, fleeting kiss on his lips.

His eyes widened at the gesture.

"You are someone's handsome prince," Daisy

said, smiling at him apologetically. "Just not mine. But when the right woman finds you . . . how lucky she'll be."

And she bent to pick up her sketchbook and went back to the manor.

It was a small and peculiar twist of fate that the path Daisy chose should take her beside the bachelor's house. The small residence was set apart from the main house, close enough to the riverside bluff that it provided magnificent views of the water. A few of the male guests had elected to take advantage of the privacy of the bachelor's house. Now it was empty since the hunting party had ended yesterday and most of the guests had taken their leave.

Except for Matthew Swift, of course.

Preoccupied with her thoughts, Daisy trudged along the path beside an ironstone wall that edged the bluff. Her amusement melted into moroseness as she thought of her father, who was determined to marry her to Matthew Swift . . . and Lillian, who wanted her to marry anyone *but* Swift . . . and her mother, who would be satisfied with nothing less than a peer. Mercedes was not going to be happy once she learned that Daisy had rebuffed Llandrindon.

Thinking over the past week, Daisy realized that her attempt to capture Matthew's attention had not been a game to her. It mattered desperately. She had never wanted anything in her life as much as the chance to speak to him sincerely, honestly, holding nothing back. But instead of forcing his feelings to the surface, she had only managed to uncover her own.

When she was with him, she felt the promise of something more wonderful, more exciting than anything she had read or dreamed about.

Something *real*.

It was incredible that a man she had always thought of as cold and passionless had turned out to be someone with so much gentleness and sensuality and tenderness. Someone who had secretly carried a lock of her hair in his pocket.

Becoming aware of someone's approach, Daisy glanced upward and felt her entire body quake.

Matthew was coming from the manor, looking dark and surly as he walked in ground-eating strides.

A man in a hurry with no place to go.

His momentum stopped abruptly as he saw her, his face turning blank.

They stared at each other in the charged silence.

Daisy's brows rushed downward in a scowl. It was either that or fling herself at him and start weeping. The depth of her yearning shocked her.

"Mr. Swift," she said unsteadily.

"Miss Bowman." He looked as though he would rather be anywhere but there with her.

Her nerves crackled with expectant heat as he reached for the sketchbook in her hand.

Without thinking, she let him take it.

His eyes narrowed as he looked down at the book, which was open to her sketch of Llandrindon. "Why did you draw him with a beard?" he asked.

"That's not a beard," Daisy said shortly. "It's shadowing."

"It looks as if he hasn't shaved in three months."

"I didn't ask for your opinion on my artwork," she snapped. She grabbed the sketchbook, but he refused to release it. "Let go," she demanded, tugging with all her might, "or I'll . . ."

"You'll what? Draw a portrait of me?" He released the book with a suddenness that caused her to stumble back a few steps. He held up his hands defensively. "No. Anything but that."

Daisy rushed at him and whacked his chest with the book. She hated it that she felt so alive with him. She hated the way her senses drank in his presence like dry earth absorbing rain. She hated his handsome face and virile body, and the mouth that was more tempting than any man's mouth had a right to be.

Matthew's smile vanished as his gaze slid over her and lingered on the torn seam at her shoulder. "What happened to your dress?"

"It was nothing. I had a sort of . . . well, a *scuffle,* you might call it, with Lord Llandrindon."

It was the most innocent way Daisy could think of to describe the encounter, which of course had been harmless. She was certain no lurid connotations could be attached to "scuffle."

However, it appeared that Swift's definition of the word was far more expansive than hers. Suddenly his expression turned dark and frightening, and his blue eyes blazed.

"I'm going to kill him," he said in a guttural voice. "He dared to—*where is he?*"

"No, no," Daisy said hastily, "you misunderstood—it wasn't like that—" Dropping the sketchbook, she threw her arms around him, using all her weight to restrain him as he headed toward the garden. She might as well have tried to hold back a charging bull. With the first few steps she was carried bodily with him. "*Wait!* What gives you the right to do anything where I'm concerned?"

Breathing heavily, Matthew stopped and glared down into her flushed face. "Did he touch you? Did he force you to—"

"You're nothing but a dog in the manger," Daisy cried hotly. "You don't want me—why should you care if someone else does? Leave me alone and go back to your plans for building your big sodding factory and making mountains of money! I hope you become the richest man in the world. I hope you get everything you want, and then someday you'll look around and wonder why no one loves you and why you're so unh—"

Her words were crushed into silence as he kissed her, his mouth hard and punishing. A wild thrill shot through her, and she turned her face away with a gasp. "—happy," she managed to finish, just before he clasped her head in his hands and kissed her again.

This time his mouth was gentler, shifting with sensuous urgency to find the most perfect fit. Daisy's hammering heart sent a rush of pleasure-heated blood through her dilating veins. She fumbled to grip his muscled wrists, her fingertips pressed against the throb of a pulse that was no less frenzied than her own.

Every time she thought Matthew would end the kiss he searched her more deeply. She responded feverishly, her knees weakening until she feared she might collapse to the ground like a rag doll.

Breaking the contact between their lips, she managed an anguished whisper. "Matthew . . . take me somewhere."

"No."

"Yes. I need . . . I need to be alone with you."

Panting raggedly, Matthew folded his arms around her, bringing her against his hard chest. She felt the desperate crush of his lips against her scalp.

"I can't trust myself that far," he finally said.

"Just to talk. Please. We can't stay out in the open like this. And if you leave me now I'll die."

Even aroused and in turmoil, Matthew couldn't prevent a smothered laugh at the dramatic statement. "You won't die."

"Just to talk," Daisy repeated, clinging to him. "I won't . . . I won't tempt you."

"Sweetheart." He let out a serrated breath.

"You tempt me just by being in the same room with me."

Her throat turned hot, as if she had just swallowed sunlight. Sensing that any more coaxing would push him in the opposite direction, Daisy stayed silent. She pressed against him, letting the silent communication of their bodies melt his resolve.

With a quiet groan, Matthew took her hand and tugged her toward the bachelor's house. "God help us both if anyone sees."

Daisy was tempted to quip that in that case he would be forced to marry her, but she held her tongue and hurried up the steps with him.

Chapter 11

It was dark and cool inside the house, which was paneled in gleaming rosewood and filled with heavy furniture. The windows were shrouded in jewel-colored velvets with silk fringe trim. Retaining Daisy's hand in his, Matthew led her through the house to a room in the back.

As Daisy stepped across the threshold, she realized it was his bedroom. Her skin prickled with excitement beneath the binding of her corset. The room was tidy, smelling of beeswax and wood polish, the window covered with cream-colored lace that let in the daylight.

A few articles were neatly arranged on the dresser; a comb, a toothbrush, tins of toothpowder and soap, and on the washstand, a razor and strop. No pomades, waxes, colognes or creams, no cravat pins or rings. One could hardly call him a dandy.

Matthew closed the door and turned toward her. He seemed very large in the small room, his broad frame dwarfing their civilized surroundings. Daisy's mouth went dry as she stared at him. She wanted to be close to him . . . she wanted to feel all his skin against hers.

"What is there between you and Llandrindon?" he demanded.

"Nothing. Only friendship. On my side, that is."

"And on his side?"

"I suspect—well, he seemed to indicate that he would not be averse to—you know."

"Yes, I know," he said thickly. "And even though I can't stand the bastard, I also can't blame him for wanting you. Not after the way you've teased and tempted him all week."

"If you're trying to imply that I've been acting like some femme fatale—"

"Don't try to deny it. I saw the way you flirted with him. The way you leaned close when you talked . . . the smiles, the provocative dresses . . ."

"Provocative dresses?" Daisy asked in bemusement.

"Like that one."

Daisy looked down at her demure white gown, which covered her entire chest and most of her arms. A nun couldn't have found fault with it. She glanced at him sardonically. "I've been trying for days to make you jealous. You would have saved me a lot of effort if you'd just admitted it straight off."

"You were deliberately trying to make me jealous?" he exploded. "What in God's name did you think *that* would accomplish? Or is turning me inside out your latest idea of an entertaining hobby?"

A sudden blush covered her face. "I thought you might feel something for me . . . and I hoped to make you admit it."

Matthew's mouth opened and closed, but he couldn't seem to speak. Daisy wondered uneasily what emotion was working on him. After a few moments he shook his head and leaned against the dresser as if he needed physical support.

"Are you angry?" she asked apprehensively.

His voice sounded odd and ragged. "Ten percent of me is angry."

"What about the other ninety percent?"

"That part is just a hairsbreadth away from throwing you on that bed and—" Matthew broke off and swallowed hard. "Daisy, you're too damned innocent to understand the danger you're in. It's taking all the self-control I've got to keep my hands off you. Don't play games with me, sweetheart. It's too easy for you to torture me, and I'm at my limit. To put to rest any doubts you might have . . . I'm jealous of every man who comes within ten feet of you. I'm jealous of the clothes on your skin and the air you breathe. I'm jealous of every moment you spend out of my sight."

Stunned, Daisy whispered, "You . . . you certainly haven't shown any sign of it."

"Over the years I've collected a thousand memories of you, every glimpse, every word you've ever said to me. All those visits to your family's home, those dinners and holidays—I could hardly wait to walk through the front door and see you." The corners of his mouth quirked with reminiscent amusement. "You, in the middle of that brash, bull-headed lot . . . I love watching you deal with your family. You've always been everything I thought a woman should be. And I have wanted you every second of my life since we first met."

Daisy was filled with an agony of regret. "I was never even nice to you," she said sorrowfully.

"I was damn glad you weren't. If you had been, I probably would have gone up in flames on the spot." Matthew stayed her with a gesture as she moved toward him. "No. Don't. As I told you before, I can't marry you under any circumstances. That's not going to change. But it has nothing to do with how much I want you." His eyes glowed like molten sapphire as he glanced over her slight form. "My God, how I want you," he whispered.

Daisy ached with the desire to throw herself into his arms. "I want you too. So much that I don't think I can let you go without knowing why."

"If it was possible to explain my reasons, believe me, I would have by now."

Daisy forced herself to ask the question she feared most. "Are you already married?"

Matthew's gaze shot to hers. "God, no."

Relief swept over her. "Then anything else can be resolved as long as you'll tell me—"

"If you were just a bit more worldly," Matthew said moodily, "you wouldn't use phrases like 'anything else can be resolved.'" He made his way to the other side of the dresser, leaving a clear path to the door.

He was silent for a long moment, as if considering some weighty matter.

Daisy was still and silent, holding his gaze. All she could offer him was patience. She waited without a word, without even blinking.

Matthew looked away from her, his expression distant. His eyes turned hard and flat as chips of polished cobalt. "A long time ago," he eventually said, "I made an enemy, a powerful one, through no fault of my own. Because of his influence I was forced to leave Boston. And I have good reason to believe this man's grievance will come back to haunt me someday. I've lived with that sword hanging over my head for years. I don't want you anywhere near me when it drops."

"But there must be something that can be done," Daisy said eagerly, determined to confront this unknown enemy with every means at her disposal. "If you'll just explain more, tell me his name and—"

"No." The word was quiet, but it contained a finality that caused her to fall abruptly silent. "I've been as honest with you as I can, Daisy. I hope you won't betray my confidence." He gestured to the door. "Now it's time for you to go."

"Just like that?" she asked in bewilderment. "After what you just told me, you want me to leave?"

"Yes. Try not to let anyone see you."

"It's not fair that you get to speak your piece without letting me—"

"Life is seldom fair," he said. "Even for a Bowman."

Daisy's thoughts raced as she stared at his hard profile. This wasn't mere obstinacy on his part. This was conviction. He had left no room for argument, no opening for negotiation.

"Shall I go to Llandrindon, then?" she asked, hoping to provoke him.

"Yes."

Daisy scowled. "I wish you'd be consistent. A few minutes ago you were ready to make mincemeat of him."

"If you want him, I have no right to object."

"If you want me, you have every right to say something!" Daisy strode to the door. "Why does everyone always claim women are illogical when men are a hundred times more so? First they want something, then they don't, then they make irrational decisions based on secrets they won't explain and no one is supposed to question them because a man's word is final."

As she reached for the doorknob, she saw the

key in the lock, and her hand paused in mid-air.

She glanced at Matthew, who was firmly planted on the other side of the dresser to keep a safe distance between them.

Although Daisy was the mildest-tempered of all the Bowmans, she was by no means a coward. And she would not accept defeat without a fight.

"You're forcing me to take desperate measures," she said.

His reply was very soft. "There's nothing you can do."

He had left her no choice.

Daisy turned the key in the lock and carefully withdrew it.

The decisive *click* was abnormally loud in the silence of the room.

Calmly Daisy tugged the top edge of her bodice away from her chest. She held the key above the narrow gap.

Matthew's eyes widened as he understood what she intended. *"You wouldn't."*

As he started around the dresser, Daisy dropped the key into her bodice, making certain it slipped beneath her corset. She sucked in her stomach and midriff until she felt the cold metal slide to her navel.

"Damn it!" Matthew reached her with startling speed. He reached out to touch her, then jerked his hands back as if he had just encountered open flame. "Take it out," he commanded, his face dark with outrage.

"I can't."

"I mean it, Daisy!"

"It's fallen too far down. I'll have to take my dress off."

It was obvious he wanted to kill her. But she could also feel the force of his longing. His lungs were working like bellows, and scorching heat radiated from his body.

His whisper contained the ferocity of a roar. "Don't do this to me."

Daisy waited patiently.

The next move was his.

He turned his back to her, the seams of his coat straining over bunched muscles. His fists clenched as he struggled to master himself. He took a shuddering breath, and another, and when he spoke his voice sounded thick, as if he had just awakened from a heavy sleep.

"Take off your gown."

Trying not to antagonize him any more than was necessary, Daisy replied in an apologetic tone. "I can't do it by myself. It buttons up the back."

Matthew said something in a muffled voice that sounded very foul. After an eternity of silence he turned to face her. His jaw could have been cast in iron. "I'm not going to fall apart that easily. I can resist you, Daisy. I've had years of practice. Turn around."

Daisy obeyed. As she bent her head forward, she could actually feel his gaze travel over the endless row of pearl buttons.

"How do you ever get undressed?" he muttered. "I've never seen so many blasted buttons on one garment."

"It's fashionable."

"It's ridiculous."

"You can send a letter of protest to Godey's *Lady's Book*," she suggested.

Giving a scornful snort, Matthew began on the top button. He tried to unfasten it while avoiding contact with her body.

"It helps if you slide your fingers beneath the placket," Daisy said. "And then you can pop the button through the—"

"Quiet," he snapped.

She closed her mouth.

Matthew battled with the buttons for another minute. With an exasperated grunt he followed her advice, slipping two fingers between her dress and her skin. As she felt his knuckles brush high on her spine, a shiver of delight ran down her back.

His progress was excruciatingly slow. Daisy could feel him fumbling with the same buttons over and over again.

"May I sit down, please?" she asked mildly. "I'm tired of standing."

"There's no place to sit."

"Yes there is." Breaking away from him, Daisy went to the four-poster bed and tried to climb onto it. Unfortunately the bed was an antique Sheraton, built high to avoid winter drafts and allow for a trundle below. The top of the mattress was level with her breasts. Hoisting herself upward, she tried to lever her hips onto the mattress.

Gravity defeated her.

"Usually," Daisy said, struggling and squirming with her feet dangling, "there's a stair-step provided—" She grabbed handfuls of the counterpane. "—for beds this tall." Straining to hook a knee over the edge of the mattress, she continued, "Good God . . . if someone fell out of this bed at night . . . it would be *fatal*."

She felt Matthew's hands clamp around her waist. "The bed's not that tall," he said. Picking her up as if she were a child, he deposited her on the mattress. "It's just that you're short."

"I'm not short. I'm . . . vertically disadvantaged."

"Fine. Sit up." His weight depressed the mattress behind her and his hands returned to the back of her dress.

Feeling the slight tremor of his fingers against her skin, Daisy was emboldened to remark, "I've never been attracted to tall men before. But you make me feel—"

"If you don't keep quiet," he interrupted curtly, "I'm going to strangle you."

Daisy felt silent, listening to the rhythm of his breath as it turned deeper, less controlled. By contrast his fingers became more certain in their task, working along the row of pearls until her dress gaped open and the sleeves slipped from her shoulders.

"Where is it?" he asked.

"The key?"

His tone was deadly. "Yes, Daisy. The key."

"It fell inside my corset. Which means . . . I'll have to take that off too."

There was no reaction to the statement, no sound or movement. Daisy twisted to glance at Matthew.

He seemed dazed. His eyes looked unnaturally blue against the flush on his face. She realized he was occupied with a savage inner battle to keep from touching her.

Feeling hot and prickly with embarrassment, Daisy pulled her arms completely out of her sleeves. She worked the dress over her hips, wriggling out of the filmy white layers, letting them slide to the floor in a heap.

Matthew stared at the discarded dress as if it were some kind of exotic fauna he had never seen before. Slowly his eyes returned to Daisy, and an incoherent protest came from his throat as she began to unhook her corset.

She felt shy and wicked, undressing in front of him. But she was encouraged by the way he seemed unable to tear his gaze from each newly revealed inch of pale skin. When the last metal hook came apart, she tossed the web of lace and stays to the floor. All that remained over her breasts was a crumpled chemise.

The key had dropped into her lap. Closing her fingers around the metal object, she risked a cautious glance at Matthew.

His eyes were closed, his forehead scored with

furrows of pained concentration. "This isn't going to happen," he said, more to himself than to her.

Daisy leaned forward to tuck the key into his coat pocket. Gripping the hem of her chemise, she stripped it over her head. A tingling shock chased over her naked upper body. She was so nervous that her teeth had begun to chatter. "I just took my chemise off," she said. "Don't you want to look?"

"No."

But his eyes had opened, and his gaze found her small, pink-tipped breasts, and the breath hissed through his clenched teeth. He sat without moving, staring at her as she untied his cravat and unbuttoned the layers of his waistcoat and shirt. She blushed everywhere but continued doggedly, rising to her knees to tug the coat from his shoulders.

He moved like a dreamer, slowly pulling his arms from the coat sleeves and waistcoat.

Daisy pushed his shirt open with awkward determination, her gaze drinking in the sight of his chest and torso. His skin gleamed like heavy satin, stretched taut over broad expanses of muscle. She touched the powerful vault of his ribs, trailing her fingertips to the rippled tautness of his midriff.

Suddenly Matthew caught her hand, seemingly undecided whether to push it away or press it closer.

Her fingers curled over his. She stared into his dilated blue eyes. "Matthew," she whispered. "I'm here. I'm yours. I want to do everything you've ever imagined doing with me."

He stopped breathing. His will foundered and collapsed, and suddenly nothing mattered except the demands of a desire that had been denied too long. With a rough groan of surrender, he lifted her onto his lap. Heat sank through the layers of their clothes, and Daisy gasped as the soft notch of her body cradled an unfamiliar hardness.

Matthew took her mouth with his, while his hands slid in restless paths over her body. As his fingers cupped the firm undercurve of her breast, her blood coursed frantically and the ache in her flesh became sharp and volatile. She fumbled with his shirt, trying to push her hands beneath it, trying to tear it away from his body.

Easing her down to the bed, Matthew paused to rip the shirt off, baring the magnificent contours of his chest and shoulders. He lowered his body to hers, and she moaned in pleasure at the feel of his naked skin. The familiar scent of him was all around her, the luxurious spice of clean male skin. He possessed her mouth with lavishly sensual kisses, his hands coursing tenderly over her half-dressed body. His thumb rubbed a lazy circle over her nipple, making it harder, darker, until she arched in helpless supplication.

Understanding the wordless plea, he bent and took the tip of her breast into his mouth. He tugged lightly, his tongue bringing fresh sparks of warmth to the surface of her skin. Daisy whimpered and shivered in his arms. Her nerves sent wild messages through her body as he moved to her other breast, kissing the peak into bright rosy distention.

"Do you know what I want from you?" she heard him ask hoarsely. "Do you understand what's going to happen if we don't stop?"

"Yes."

Matthew lifted his head and gave her a doubtful glance.

"I'm not as innocent as you might think," Daisy said earnestly. "I'm very well read."

He turned his face away, and she had the impression he was fighting a smile. Then he looked back at her with piercing tenderness. "Daisy Bowman," he said unevenly, "I'd spend eternity in hell for one hour with you."

"Is that how long it takes? An hour?"

His reply was rueful. "Sweetheart, at this point it would be a miracle if I lasted one minute."

She curled her arms around his neck. "You have to make love to me," she told him. "Because if you don't, I'll never stop complaining about it."

Matthew cradled her body against his, and kissed her forehead, and he was silent for so long that she was afraid he was going to refuse her. But then his warm hand moved slowly down her body, and her heart gave an excited leap. He wrapped the tapes of her drawers around his fingers and pulled to loosen them.

Her tummy rose and fell with her labored breathing, and embarrassment flooded her as his hand slipped beneath the fragile fabric. He was touching the fleece of private hair, the curls flattened against the vulnerable mound. He played with the soft locks, fluffing, stroking. The tip of his ring finger brushed over a place so sensitive that she jerked in surprise. Staring into her flushed face, Matthew gently parted the closed flesh.

"Daisy, love," he whispered, "You're so soft . . . so dainty . . . where shall I touch you? Here? Or here . . ."

"There," she sobbed, as his fingers slid to just the right spot. "Yes . . . oh, there . . ."

His mouth moved in hot open kisses over her throat and down to her breast, while at the same time his fingers slipped farther between her legs. As he kneaded her intimately, she became aware of a disconcerting moisture in that secret place. She hadn't expected that. Which made her wonder if she was quite as well-informed as she had previously thought.

Consternated, she began to say something but was abruptly silenced as she felt his finger nudge inside her. *That* was not something she had expected, either.

Matthew's head lifted from her breast, his eyes filled with drowsy heat. He watched her face as he searched inside her body with a lightly massaging rhythm that drove her to an unbearable height of pleasure. She strained upward and moaned anxiously, returning his kisses with uncontrolled fervor.

"Do you like that?" he whispered.

"Yes, I . . ." She fought to speak between helpless gasps. "I thought . . . it was going to hurt."

"Not from this." A smile touched his mouth. "Later, however, you might have cause for complaint." A shimmer of sweat gathered on his face as he felt the pulsing of her body around his exploring finger. "I don't know if I can be gentle," he said raggedly. "I've wanted you for too long."

"I trust you," she whispered.

Matthew shook his head, easing his hand away from her. "You have terrible judgment. You're in bed with the last man in the world you should trust, and you're about to make the biggest mistake of your life."

"Is this your idea of seductive banter?"

"I thought I should give you one last warning. Now you're doomed."

"Oh, good." Daisy moved to help him as he stripped off her drawers and stockings.

Her eyes widened as he began to unbutton his trousers. Curious but shy, she reached down to help him. A shaky endearment left his lips as he felt her small, cool hand slip beneath the unbuttoned placket of his falls. She stroked carefully, learning the length and hardness of him, loving the way his body trembled. "How should I touch you?" she whispered.

Matthew shook his head with an unsteady laugh. "Daisy . . . I'd rather you didn't just now."

"Did I do it wrong?" she asked in worry.

"No, no—" He gathered her against him, kissing

her cheek, her ear, her hair. "You do it too well."

His hands swept over her in sensitive strokes as he urged her back against the pillows. He undressed and levered his body over hers, and she shivered at the delicious textures of him, hairiness and smoothness and heat. Too many things were happening at once—she couldn't compass all of it—the moist, hot drift of his mouth, the long coaxing fingers, the brush of his hair against her breasts, her stomach . . .

The silky swirl of his tongue in the hollow of her navel sent fire licking through her veins. Hazily aware of the area his mouth was traversing, she stirred beneath him.

Not seeming to realize just where he was kissing her, Matthew persisted, sliding lower until Daisy let out a muffled yelp and pushed hard at his encroaching head.

"What is it?" he asked, rising to his elbows.

Crimson with mortification, Daisy could hardly bring herself to explain. "You were too close to my . . . well, you accidentally . . ."

As her voice faded, understanding dawned in Matthew's eyes. Quickly he bent his head to hide his expression, and a tremor ran through his shoulders. He replied with great care, still looking away from her. "It wasn't accidental. I meant to do that."

Daisy was astonished. "But you were going to kiss me right on my—" She broke off as his gaze met hers, laughter dancing in his blue eyes.

He wasn't embarrassed at all—he was *amused*.

"You're not shocked, are you?" he asked. "I thought you were well read."

"Well, no one would ever write about something like *that*."

He shrugged, his eyes glowing. "You're the literary authority."

"You're making fun of me," she said.

"Just a little," he whispered, and kissed her stomach again. Her legs jerked against his restraining hands.

She began to chatter nervously as she felt his mouth wander to her hip. "In s-some of the novels I've read, there were certain parts, of course . . ." She inhaled sharply at the sensation of his teeth gently scoring over her inner thigh. ". . . but . . . I suppose they were written so euphemistically that I didn't qu-quite understand . . . oh, *please,* I don't think you should do that—"

"What about this?"

"*Definitely* not that." She twisted to escape him.

But his hands had hooked beneath her knees and he held them apart as he did wicked things with his tongue. She began to shiver as he found the sensitive flesh he had touched before, and his mouth was soft and hot and demanding, suckling until rapture flooded her from that place where his mouth possessed her, and when she begged him to stop he tormented her even more, licking, nuzzling deeper and deeper, and suddenly the pleasure uncoiled and she was crying out in dazzling relief.

After a long time Matthew moved upward to hold her. Fiercely she wrapped her arms and legs around him. He settled between her wide-open thighs, shaking with the effort to be gentle. She was invaded by a sundering thrust, and Matthew murmured love words against her throat, trying to soothe her even as he pushed farther, taking her, holding her.

When they were completely joined he went still, trying not to cause her further pain. He was so hard inside her, and Daisy absorbed the curious feeling of being possessed, of being utterly helpless and at the same time . . . in this moment he belonged to her utterly. She knew she filled his mind and heart even as he filled her body. Wanting to give him the same pleasure he had given her, she arched her hips.

"Daisy . . . no, wait . . ."

She lifted again, and again, straining to be closer to him. He groaned and began to press downward in a subtle rhythm. Crushing his mouth over hers, he shuddered from the intensity of his climax.

They were both silent for minutes afterward, while Matthew held her close and cradled her head against his shoulder. He withdrew from her carefully and hushed her with his lips as she protested.

"Let me take care of you."

Daisy didn't understand what he meant, but she was so enervated that she lay with her eyes closed as he left the bed. He returned soon with a damp cloth, neatly wiping her perspiring body and the stinging flesh between her thighs.

When he lowered beside her, she burrowed against him, sighing in pleasure as he drew the covers over them. She moved until her ear rested on the sturdy beat of his heart.

Daisy supposed she ought to feel ashamed, locking herself in his bedroom and demanding to be seduced. Instead she felt triumphant. And strangely precarious, as if she were balanced on the edge of a new kind of intimacy that went beyond the physical.

She wanted to know everything about him—she had never known such devouring curiosity about another person. But perhaps a little patience was in order until they both had time to adjust to their new circumstances.

As the warmth of their bodies mingled beneath the bedclothes, Daisy was filled with the overwhelming urge to sleep. She had never suspected how nice it would be to lie quietly in a man's arms, breathing his scent, his strength surrounding her.

"Don't fall asleep," she heard him warn. "We have to get you out of here."

"I'm not sleeping. I'm just . . ." she paused to yawn hugely. ". . . resting my eyes."

"Only for a minute." His hand passed over her hair and down her back in a long stroke. That was all it took to lull her into sweet, dark oblivion.

* * *

Daisy awakened to the patter of rain on the roof, and the waft of a moisture-heavy breeze from the open window. The Hampshire weather had decided to cool the afternoon with a spontaneous shower, the kind that usually lasted no more than a half-hour and left the ground spongy and fragrant.

Blinking, Daisy registered her unfamiliar surroundings, the masculine bedroom . . . the vivid strangeness of a naked muscular body at her back. And the stirring of someone's breath in her hair. She tensed in surprise but lay quietly, wondering if Matthew was awake. His breathing didn't change. But gradually his arm slid across her body, his fingers spreading over her front.

Gently he settled her back against him, and they watched the rain in silence. Daisy tried to remember if there had ever been a time in her life when she had felt so safe and content. No, she decided. Nothing could compare to this.

Feeling her smile against his arm, Matthew murmured, "You like the rain."

"Yes." She explored the hairy surface of his leg with her toes, rather amazed at how long his calves were. "Some things are always better when it's raining. Like reading. Or sleeping. Or this."

"Lying in bed with me?" He sounded amused.

Daisy nodded. "It feels as if we're the only two people in the world."

He traced the line of her collarbone, and the side

of her throat. "Did I hurt you, Daisy?" he whispered.

"Well, it was rather uncomfortable when you—" she stopped and blushed. "But I expected that. My friends told me it improves after the first time."

His fingertips wandered to the outline of her ear, and the blood-heated curve of her cheek. There was a smile in his voice as he said, "I'll do my best to see that it does."

"Are you sorry it happened?" Her fingers clenched as she waited tensely for his answer.

"Good Lord, no." He brought her small fist to his mouth and kissed it open, and flattened her palm against the side of his face. "It's what I've wanted most in my entire life. And the one thing I knew I could never have. I'm surprised. Shocked, even. But never sorry."

Daisy turned and snuggled against him, sandwiching one of his thighs between her own.

The rain beat out a brisk song against the side of the house, some of it coming through the window. Considering the idea of getting out of bed, Daisy shivered a little, and felt Matthew draw the covers higher over her bare shoulder.

"Daisy," he asked without heat, "where is the damn key?"

"I put it in your coat pocket," she said helpfully. "Didn't you see? No? . . . well, I suppose you were distracted at the time." She trailed her hand over his chest, letting her palm graze the point of his nipple. "You're probably angry with me for locking us in the bedroom."

"Enraged," he agreed. "I insist you do it every night after we're married."

"Are we going to get married?" Daisy whispered, raising her head.

His eyes were warm, but there was no hint of pleasure in his voice. "Yes, we're going to marry. Although you'll probably hate me for it someday."

"Why in the world would I . . . *oh*." Daisy remembered what he had told her about the likelihood of his past catching up to him someday. "I could never hate you," she said. "And I'm not afraid of your secrets, Matthew. Whatever comes, I'll face it with you. Although you should know I find it exasperating when you throw out comments like that and refuse to explain."

There was a sudden catch of laughter in his chest. "That's only one of many reasons you find me exasperating."

"True." She crawled on top of him and nuzzled his chest like an inquisitive kitten. "But I like exasperating men much more than the nice ones."

Two notches appeared between his dark brows. "Such as Llandrindon?"

"Yes, he's much nicer than you." Experimentally Daisy put her mouth over his nipple and touched it with her tongue. "Does that feel the same to you as it does to me?"

"No. Although the effort is appreciated." He

tilted her face upward. "Did Llandrindon kiss you?"

She nodded slowly in the framework of his hands. "Just once."

Jealousy entered his voice. "Did you like it?"

"I wanted to. I tried to." She closed her eyes and turned her cheek into his palm. "But it wasn't at all like your kisses."

"Daisy," he whispered, turning until she was tucked beneath him once more. "I didn't mean for this to happen." His fingers investigated the fragile angles of her face, the smiling curve of her lips. "But now it seems impossible that I held out as long as I did."

Her nerves, sated as they were, stirred beneath the caress of his fingertips. "Matthew . . . what will happen next? Will you speak to my father?"

"Not yet. In the interest of preserving at least a semblance of decorum, I'm going to wait until I return from Bristol. By that time most of the guests will have left, and the family will be able to deal with the situation in relative privacy."

"My father will be overjoyed. But Mother will have conniptions. And Lillian . . ."

"Will explode."

Daisy sighed. "My brothers aren't too fond of you, either."

"Really," he said in mock surprise.

Daisy stared worriedly into his shadowed face. "What if you change your mind about me? What if you come back and tell me that you were wrong, you don't want to marry me, and—"

"No," Matthew said, stroking the rampant black waves of her hair. "There's no turning back. I've taken your innocence. I'm not going to avoid my responsibility."

Disgruntled by the choice of words, Daisy frowned.

"What's the matter?" he asked.

"The way you put it . . . your *responsibility* . . . as if you have to atone for some terrible mistake. It's not the most romantic thing to say, especially in present circumstances."

"Oh." Matthew grinned suddenly. "I'm not a romantic man, sweetheart. You knew that already." He bent his head and kissed the side of her neck, and nipped at her ear. "But I *am* responsible for you now." He worked his way down to her shoulder. "For your safety . . . your welfare . . . your pleasure . . . and I take my responsibilities very seriously . . ."

He kissed her breasts, drawing the taut peaks into the melting heat of his mouth. His hand parted her thighs and played gently between them.

A moan of pleasure slipped from her throat, and he smiled. "You make the sweetest sounds," he murmured. "When I touch you like this . . . and this . . . and the way you cry out when you come for me . . ."

Her face burned. She tried to be quiet, but in

another moment he had coaxed another helpless moan from her.

"Matthew . . . ?" Her toes curled as she felt him slip lower, his tongue tickling the hollow of her navel.

His voice was muffled by the covers that tented over his head. "Yes, chatterbox?"

"Are you going to do—" she paused with a gasp as she felt him push her knees apart, "—what you did before?"

"It would seem so."

"But we've already . . ." The puzzle of why he would want to make love to her twice in a row was suddenly abandoned. She felt him investigating the tender juncture of her thigh and groin, the insides of her legs, and she went weak. Soft, artful nibbling . . . lazy strokes of his tongue . . . toying with the sore opening of her body . . . easing upward until he found a place that made her sob and groan, yes, there, *yes* . . .

He teased her with maddening delicacy, slowly moving away, then returning with warm, rapid flicks . . . she groped for his head between her thighs and held him there, arching and shivering and pulsing with pleasure.

He brought her steadily upward to a height of impossible rapture, above the storm, above the sky itself . . . and when she regained awareness, she was in his arms, her pounding heartbeat soothed by the gentle sound of spring rain.

Chapter 12

Since most of the estate guests were
leaving on the morrow, dinner that night was a
long and elaborate affair. Two long tables set with
crystal and Sèvres china glittered in the light shed
by chandeliers and candelabrum. An army of foot-
men dressed in full livery of blue, mustard and
black with gold braiding moved deftly around the
guests, refilling water and wine glasses, serving
each remove with quiet precision.

It was a magnificent affair. Unfortunately Daisy
had never been less interested in eating. It was a
pity she couldn't do justice to the meal, which featured Scottish salmon, steaming roast joints, venison
haunch accompanied by sausages and sweetbreads,
and elaborate vegetable casseroles dressed with
cream and butter and truffles. For dessert there were

platters of luxury fruits; raspberries, nectarines, cherries, peaches and pineapples, as well as a surfeit of cakes, tarts, and syllabubs.

Daisy forced herself to eat, laugh, and converse in as natural a manner as possible. But it was not easy. Matthew was seated a few places away on the other side of the table, and whenever their gazes caught, she nearly choked on whatever she happened to be chewing.

Conversation flowed around her, and she responded to it vaguely while her mind remained fixed on the memory of what had happened a few hours earlier. Those who knew her well, her sister and friends, seemed to notice that she was not quite herself. Even Westcliff had given her a few speculative glances.

Daisy felt overheated in the bright, stuffy room, the blood rushing easily to her cheeks. Her body was oversensitive, her undergarments chafing, her corset unbearable, her garters pinching around her thighs. Every time she moved there were reminders of the afternoon with Matthew; the soreness between her legs, the stings and twitches in unexpected places. And yet her body ached for more . . . more of Matthew's hands, his restless mouth, his hardness inside her . . .

Feeling her face flame once again, Daisy devoted herself to buttering a piece of bread. She glanced at Matthew, who was conversing with a lady to his left.

Sensing Daisy's furtive regard, Matthew looked

in her direction. The depths of blue kindled with heat and his chest moved as he inhaled deeply. He dragged his attention back to his companion, focusing on her with a flattering interest that sent the lady into giggling effusiveness.

Daisy lifted a glass of watered wine to her lips and made herself pay attention to a conversation on her right . . . something about touring the lake districts and the Scottish Highlands. Soon, however, her mind drifted back to her own situation.

She did not regret her decision . . . but she was not so naive as to believe everything would be easy from now on. Quite the opposite. There was the issue of where they were to live, and when Matthew would take her back to New York, and if she could learn to be happy far away from her sister and friends. There was also the unanswered question about whether she would be an adequate wife for a man who so fully inhabited a world she had never quite found a way to fit in. And last, the not-insignificant question of what kind of secrets Matthew was harboring.

But Daisy remembered the soft, vibrant note in his voice when he had said, *"You've always been everything I thought a woman should be."*

Matthew was the only man who had ever wanted her just as she was. (One had to discount Llandrindon since his infatuation had flared up just a bit too quickly and would likely subside with equal speed.)

In this regard, Daisy reflected, her marriage to Matthew would not be unlike Lillian's with Westcliff. As two strong-willed people with very different sensibilities, Lillian and Westcliff often argued and negotiated . . . and yet this didn't seem to weaken their marriage. Quite the opposite, in fact—their union seemed all the better for it.

She considered her friends' marriages . . . Annabelle and Mr. Hunt as a harmony of similar dispositions . . . Evie and Lord St. Vincent with their opposite natures, as necessary to each other's existence as day and night. It was impossible to say that any of these pairings was superior to the others.

Perhaps, in spite of all she had heard about the ideal of a perfect marriage, there was no such thing. Perhaps every marriage was a unique creation.

It was a comforting thought.

And it filled her with hope.

After the interminable dinner Daisy pleaded a headache rather than endure the ritual of tea and gossip. It was half true, actually—the combination of light, noise, and emotional strain had caused her temples to throb painfully. With a pained smile, she made her excuses and headed toward the grand staircase.

But as she reached the main hall, she heard her sister's voice.

"Daisy? I want to talk with you."

Daisy knew Lillian well enough to recognize the edge in her tone. Her older sister was suspicious, and worried, and she wanted to thrash out issues and problems until everything had been discussed exhaustively.

Daisy was far too weary. "Not now, please," she said, giving her sister a placating smile. "Can it wait until later?"

"No."

"I have a headache."

"So do I. But we're still going to talk."

Daisy struggled with a rush of exasperation. After all her patience with Lillian, the years of unquestioning support and loyalty, it didn't seem too much to ask that Lillian refrain from badgering her.

"I'm going to bed," Daisy said, her steady gaze daring her sister to argue. "I don't want to explain anything, especially when it's obvious you have no intention of listening. Good night." Seeing the stricken look on Lillian's face, she added more gently, "I love you." She stood on her toes, kissed her sister's cheek, and went to the staircase.

Lillian fought the temptation to follow Daisy up the stairs. She became aware of someone at her elbow, and she turned to see Annabelle and Evie, both of them looking sympathetic.

"She won't talk to me," she told them numbly.

Evie, usually hesitant to touch her, slipped her arm through Lillian's. "L-let's go to the orangery," she suggested.

* * *

The orangery was by far Lillian's favorite room in the manor, the walls constructed of long glass windows, the floor wrought with fancy iron grill-work that let in gently warmed air from stoves down below. Orange and lemon trees filled the room with fresh citrus fragrance, while scaffolding loaded with tropical plants added exotic top notes to the scent. Torchlight from outside sent intricate shadows through the room.

Finding a small grouping of chairs, the three friends sat together. Lillian's shoulders slumped as she said glumly, "I think they've done it."

"Who's done what?" Evie asked.

"Daisy and Mr. Swift," Annabelle murmured with a touch of amusement. "We're speculating that they've had, er . . . carnal knowledge of each other."

Evie looked perplexed. "Why do we think that?"

"Well, you were sitting at the other table, dear, so you couldn't see, but at dinner there were . . ." Annabelle raised her brows significantly. ". . . *undercurrents*."

"Oh." Evie shrugged. "It's just as well I wasn't at your table, then. I'm never any good at reading undercurrents."

"These were *obvious* undercurrents," Lillian said darkly. "It couldn't have been any clearer if Mr. Swift had leapt onto the table and made an announcement."

"Mr. Swift would never be so vulgar," Evie said decisively. "Even if he is an American."

Lillian's face scrunched in a ferocious scowl. "Whatever happened to 'I could never be happy with a soulless industrialist'? What happened to 'I want the four of us to be together always'? Curse it all, I can't believe Daisy's done this! Everything was going so well with Lord Llandrindon. What could have possessed her to sleep with Matthew Swift?"

"I doubt there was much sleeping involved," Annabelle replied, her eyes twinkling.

Lillian gave her a slitted glare. "If you have the bad taste to be amused by this, Annabelle—"

"Daisy was never interested in Lord Llandrindon," Evie volunteered hastily, trying to prevent a quarrel. "She was only using him to provoke Mr. Swift."

"How do you know?" the other two asked at the same time.

"Well, I-I . . ." Evie made a helpless gesture with her hands. "Last week I m-more or less inadvertently suggested that she try to make him jealous. And it worked."

Lillian's throat worked violently before she could manage to speak. "Of all the asinine, sheepheaded, moronic—"

"Why, Evie?" Annabelle asked in a considerably kinder tone.

"Daisy and I overheard Mr. Swift t-talking to

Lord Llandrindon. He was trying to convince Llandrindon to court her, and it became obvious that Mr. Swift wanted her for himself."

"I'll bet he planned it," Lillian snapped. "He must have known somehow that you would over-hear. It was a devious and sinister plot, and you fell for it!"

"I don't think so," Evie replied. Staring at Lillian's crimson face, she asked apprehensively, "Are you going to shout at me?"

Lillian shook her head and dropped her face in her hands. "I'd shriek like a banshee," she said through the screen of her fingers, "if I thought it would do any good. But since I'm fairly certain Daisy has been intimate with that reptile, there is probably nothing anyone can do to save her now."

"She may not want to be saved," Evie pointed out.

"That's because she's gone stark raving mad," came Lillian's muffled growl.

Annabelle nodded. "Obviously. Daisy has slept with a handsome, young, wealthy, intelligent man who is apparently in love with her. What in God's name can she be thinking?" She smiled compassionately as she heard Lillian's profane reply, and settled a gentle hand between her friend's shoulders. "Dearest," she murmured, "as you know, there was a time when it didn't matter to me whether I married a man I loved or not . . . it seemed enough just to get my family out of the desperate situation we were in. But when I thought about what it would be like to share a bed with my husband . . . to spend the rest of my life with him . . . I knew Simon was the only choice." She paused, and sudden tears glittered her eyes. Beautiful, self-possessed Annabelle, who hardly ever cried. "When I'm ill," she continued in a husky voice, "when I'm afraid, when I need something, I know he will move heaven and earth to make everything all right. I trust him with every fiber of my being. And when I see the child we created, the two of us mingled forever in her . . . my God, how grateful I am that I married Simon. We've all been able to choose our own husbands, Lillian. You have to allow Daisy the same freedom."

Lillian shook off her hand irritably. "He's not the same caliber as any of our husbands. He's not even the same quality as St. Vincent, who may have been a devious skirt-chasing scoundrel, but at least he has a heart." She paused and muttered, "No offense intended, Evie."

"That's all right," Evie said, her lips quivering as if she were trying to suppress a laugh.

"The point is," Lillian fretted, "I'm all for Daisy having the freedom of choice, as long as she doesn't make the wrong one."

"Dear—" Annabelle began in a careful attempt to correct the flaw in her logic, but Evie interrupted softly.

"I th-think it's Daisy's right to make a mistake. All we can do is give her our help if she asks for it."

"We can't help her if she ends up in bloody New York!" Lillian retorted.

Evie and Annabelle didn't argue with her after that, tacitly agreeing there were some problems that mere words couldn't solve, and some fears that couldn't be soothed. They did what friends do when all else has failed . . . they sat with her in companionable silence . . . and let her know they cared.

A hot bath helped to soothe Daisy's body and relax her frazzled nerves. She stayed in the steaming water until she was boneless and sweltering, and her headache had faded. Feeling renewed, she dressed in a ruffled white nightgown and began to brush her hair, while a pair of maids came to take away the bath.

The bristles ran through her hair until the waist-length locks formed a gleaming ebony river. She stared through the open doorway that lead to the balcony, into the damp spring night. The starless sky was the color of black plums.

Smiling absently, Daisy heard the click of the bedroom door behind her. Assuming one of the maids had returned to collect a towel or a soap dish, she continued to stare outside.

Suddenly she felt a touch on her shoulder, followed by the warmth of a large hand sliding across her chest. Startled, she rose to her feet and was slowly pulled back against a hard masculine body.

Matthew's deep voice tickled her ear. "What were you thinking about?"

"You, of course." Daisy rested against him, her fingers coming up to stroke the hairy surface of his forearm to the edge of his rolled-up shirtsleeves. Her gaze returned to the outside view. "This room used to belong to one of the earl's sisters," she said. "I was told that her lover—a stable boy, actually— used to climb up to the balcony to visit her. Just like Romeo."

"I hope the reward was worth the risk," he said.

"Would you have taken such a risk for my sake?"

"If it was the only way I could be with you. But it makes no sense to climb two stories to the balcony when a perfectly good door is available."

"Using the door isn't nearly as romantic."

"Neither is breaking your neck."

"How pragmatic," Daisy said with a laugh, turning in his arms. Matthew's clothes were scented with outside air and the acrid trace of tobacco. He must have gone out to the back terrace with some of the gentlemen after dinner. Huddling deeper into his embrace, she smelled the starch of his shirt and the clean, familiar fragrance of his skin. "I love the way you smell," she said. "I could walk blindfolded into a room filled with a hundred men and I would find you right away."

"Another parlor game," he said, and they snickered together.

Catching at his hand, Daisy tugged him toward the bed. "Come lie with me."

Matthew shook his head, resisting. "I'll only stay a few minutes. Westcliff and I are leaving at first light." His gaze slid hungrily over the prim ruffled nightgown. "And if we go anywhere near that bed, I won't be able to keep from making love to you."

"I wouldn't mind," Daisy said shyly.

He pulled her into his arms and hugged her carefully. "Not so soon after your first time. You need to rest."

"Then why are you here?"

Daisy felt his cheek rubbing against the top of her head. Even after all that had happened between them, it seemed impossible that Matthew Swift was holding her so tenderly. "I just wanted to say good night," he murmured. "And to tell you . . ."

Daisy looked up with a questioning glance, and he stole a kiss as if he couldn't help himself. ". . . you don't ever have to worry that I would change my mind about marrying you," he said. "In fact, you would have a damn difficult time getting rid of me now."

"Yes," Daisy said, smiling at him. "I know you're dependable."

Forcing himself to let go of her, Matthew went

reluctantly to the door. He opened it a cautious crack and glanced outside to ascertain the hallway was empty.

"Matthew," she whispered.

He glanced over his shoulder at her. "Yes?"

"Come back to me soon."

Whatever he saw in her face caused his eyes to blaze in the shadow-tricked atmosphere. He gave her a short nod and left while he was still able.

Chapter 13

Matthew quickly discovered that traveling in Bristol with Lord Westcliff was a far different matter than navigating the port city by himself. He had originally planned to stay at an inn located in the central part of Bristol. With Westcliff as his companion, however, they took up temporary residence with a wealthy shipbuilding family. Matthew gathered there had been many such invitations extended by prosperous families in the area, all eager to host the earl in the finest style possible.

Everyone was either a friend of Westcliff's, or wanted to be. Such was the power of an ancient aristocratic name. To be fair, it was more than a name and title that inspired such enthusiasm for Westcliff . . . he was known as a political progressive, not to mention a skillful businessman, both of which made a man very sought-after in Bristol.

The city, second only to London in its volume of trade, was undergoing a period of explosive development. As the commercial areas expanded and the old city walls crumbled, narrow roads were being widened and new thoroughfares appeared on what seemed a daily basis. Most significantly, a harborside railway system connecting the Temple Mead station to the docks had just been completed. As a result, there was no better place in Europe to establish a manufacturing business.

Matthew had grudgingly admitted to Westcliff that his presence had made their negotiations and meetings much easier. Not only did Westcliff's name open doors, it practically inspired people to give him the entire building. And Matthew privately acknowledged there was a great deal to be learned from the earl, who possessed reams of knowledge about business and manufacturing.

When they discussed locomotive production, for example, the earl was not only conversant with principles of design and engineering, he could also name the dozen varieties of bolts used on their latest broad-gauge locomotives.

Without modesty, Matthew had never met another man who could rival his own ability to understand and retain vast quantities of technical knowledge. Until Westcliff. It made for interesting conversation, at least to the two of them. Anyone else taking part in the discussion would have started snoring after five minutes.

For his part, Marcus had embarked on the week in Bristol with a dual purpose, officially to accomplish certain business-related goals . . . but unofficially to decide what to make of Matthew Swift.

It hadn't been easy for Marcus to leave Lillian's side. He had discovered that while the events of childbirth and infancy were perfectly ordinary when they happened to other people, they were monumentally important when his own wife and child were involved. Everything about his daughter fascinated him: her pattern of sleeping and waking, her first bath, the way she wiggled her toes, the sight of her at Lillian's breast.

Although it was not unheard of for an upperclass lady to nurse her own child, it was far more common to hire a lactating maid for that purpose. However, Lillian had abruptly changed her mind after Merritt was born. "She wants me instead," Lillian had told Marcus. He hadn't dared to point out that the baby was hardly capable of a discussion on the matter and would likely be just as content with a wet nurse.

Marcus's fear that his wife might succumb to childbed fever receded day by day as Lillian returned to her old self, healthy and slender and vigorous. His relief was vast. He had never known such overwhelming love for one person, nor had he anticipated that Lillian would so quickly become his essential requirement for happiness. Anything that was in his power to do for Lillian would be done. And in light of his wife's worry over her sister,

Marcus had decided to form some definitive conclusions about Matthew Swift.

As they met with representatives of the Great Western railway, the dockmaster, and various councilmen and administrators, Marcus was impressed by the way Swift acquitted himself. Until now he had only seen Swift interact with the well-to-do guests at Stony Cross, but it immediately became apparent that he could relate easily to a variety of people, from elderly aristocrats to burly young dock laborers. When it came to bargaining, Swift was aggressive without being ungentlemanly. He was calm, steady, and sensible, but he also possessed a dry sense of humor that he used to good effect.

Marcus could see the influence of Thomas Bowman in Swift's tenacity and his willingness to stand by his opinions. But unlike Bowman, Swift had a natural presence and confidence that people intuitively responded to. Swift would do well in Bristol, Marcus thought. It was a good place for an ambitious young man, offering as many, if not more, opportunities than London.

As for how Matthew Swift would suit Daisy . . . well, that was more ambiguous. Marcus was loath to make judgments in such matters, having learned from experience that he was not infallible. His initial opposition to Annabelle and Simon Hunt's marriage was a case in point. But a judgment would have to be made. Daisy deserved a husband who would be kind to her.

After a meeting with the railway representatives,

Marcus and Swift walked along Corn Street through a covered market filled with fruit and vegetable stalls. Recently the pavement had been raised to protect pedestrians from mud splashes and street refuse. The street was lined with shops featuring goods such as books, toiletries, and glass objects made from local sandstone.

Stopping at a tavern, the two went inside for a simple meal. The tavern was filled with all manner of men from wealthy merchants to common shipyard laborers.

Relaxing in the raucous atmosphere, Marcus lifted a tankard of dark Bristol ale to his lips. It was cold and bitter, sliding down his throat in a pungent rush and leaving a mellow aftertaste.

As Marcus considered various ways to open the subject of Daisy, Swift surprised him with a blunt statement. "My lord, there is something I would like to discuss with you."

Marcus adopted a pleasantly encouraging expression. "Very well."

"It turns out that Miss Bowman and I have reached an . . . understanding. After considering the logical advantages on both sides, I have made a sensible and pragmatic decision that we should—"

"How long have you been in love with her?" Marcus interrupted, inwardly amused.

Swift let out a tense sigh. "Years," he admitted. He dragged his hand through his short, thick hair, leaving it in ruffled disarray. "But I didn't know what it was until recently."

"Does my sister-in-law reciprocate?"

"I think—" Breaking off, Swift took a deep draw of his ale. He looked young and troubled as he admitted, "I don't know. I hope in time . . . oh, hell."

"In my opinion, it would not be difficult for you to win Daisy's affections," Marcus said in a kinder tone than he had planned. "From what I have observed, it is a good match on both sides."

Swift looked up with a self-derisive smile. "You don't think she would be better off with a poetry-spouting country gentleman?"

"I think that would be disastrous. Daisy doesn't need a husband as unworldly as she." Reaching for the wooden platter of food between them, Marcus cut a portion of pale Wensleydale cheese and sandwiched it between two thick slices of bread. He regarded Swift speculatively, wondering why the young man seemed to take so little pleasure in the situation. Most men displayed considerably more enthusiasm at the prospect of marrying the women they loved.

"Bowman will be pleased," Marcus remarked, watching closely for Swift's reaction.

"Pleasing him has never been any part of this. Any implication to the contrary is a serious underestimation of all Miss Bowman has to offer."

"There's no need to leap to her defense," Marcus replied. "Daisy is a charming little scamp, not to mention lovely. Had she a bit more confidence, and far less sensitivity, she would have learned by now to attract the opposite sex with ease. But to her credit, she doesn't have the temperament to treat love as a game. And few men have the wits to appreciate sincerity in a woman."

"I do," Swift said curtly.

"So it would seem." Marcus felt a stab of sympathy as he considered the younger man's dilemma. As a sensible man with a laudable aversion to melodrama, it was more than a little embarrassing for Swift to find himself wounded by one of Cupid's arrows. "Although you haven't asked for my support of the match," Marcus continued, "you may rely on it." ·

"Even if Lady Westcliff takes exception?"

The mention of Lillian caused a little ache of longing in Marcus's chest. He missed her even more than he had expected. "Lady Westcliff," he replied dryly, "will reconcile herself to the fact that every once in a great while something may not happen as she wishes. And if you prove to be a good husband to Daisy over time, my wife will change her opinion. She is a fair-minded woman."

But Swift still looked troubled. "My lord—" His hand clenched around the handle of his tankard, and he stared at it fixedly.

Seeing the shadow that passed across the young man's face, Marcus stopped chewing. His instincts told him something was very wrong. *Damn it all,* he thought, *can nothing involving the Bowmans ever be simple?*

"What would you say about a man who builds

his life on a lie . . . and yet that life has become more worthwhile than his original one ever could have been?"

Marcus resumed chewing, swallowed hard, and took his time about drinking a large quantity of ale. "But it all hinges upon a falsehood?" he finally asked.

"Yes."

"Did this man rob someone of his rightful due? Cause physical or emotional harm to someone?"

"No," Swift said, looking at him directly. "But it did involve some legal trouble."

That made Marcus feel marginally better. In his experience even the best of men could not avoid occasional legal problems of one kind or another. Perhaps Swift had once been misled into some questionable business deal or indulged in some youthful indiscretions that would prove embarrassing if brought to light all these years later.

Of course, Marcus did not weigh questions of honor lightly, and news of past legal trouble was hardly what one would want to hear from a prospective brother-in-law. On the other hand, Swift appeared to be a man of good bearing and character. And Marcus had found much about him to like.

"I'm afraid I will have to withhold my support of the match," Marcus said with care, "until I have an understanding of the particulars. Is there anything more you can tell me?"

Swift shook his head. "I'm sorry. God, I wish I could."

"If I give you my word that I will not betray your confidence?"

"No," Swift whispered. "Again, I'm sorry."

Marcus sighed heavily and leaned back in his chair. "Unfortunately I can't solve or even mitigate a problem when I have no idea what the bloody problem is. On the other hand, I believe people deserve second chances. And I would be willing to judge a man for who he has become instead of what he was. That being said . . . I will have your word on something."

Swift looked up, his blue eyes wary. "Yes, my lord?"

"You will tell Daisy everything before you marry her. You will lay out the issues in full, and let her decide whether she wants to proceed. You will *not* take her as your wife without giving her the complete and unvarnished truth."

Swift didn't blink. "You have my word."

"Good." Marcus signaled the tavern maid to come to the table.

After this, he needed something much stronger than ale.

Chapter 14

With Westcliff and Matthew Swift
away in Bristol, the estate seemed abnormally quiet.
To Lillian and Daisy's relief, Westcliff had arranged
for their parents to accompany a neighboring family on a jaunt to Stratford-on-Avon. They would
attend a week of banquets, plays, lectures, and musical events, all part of Shakespeare's two hundred
and eightieth birthday festival. Just how Westcliff
had managed to prod the Bowmans into going was
a mystery to Daisy.

"Mother and Father couldn't be less interested
in the Bard," Daisy marveled to Lillian, soon after
the carriage conveying her parents had departed.
"And I can't believe Father would have opted to go
to a festival instead of Bristol."

"Westcliff had no intention of letting Father go with them," Lillian said with a rueful grin.

"Why not? It's Father's business, after all."

"Yes, but when it comes to negotiations, Father is too crass for British tastes—he makes it quite difficult for everyone to come to an agreement. So Westcliff arranged the trip to Stratford with such expediency that Father didn't have a chance to object. And after Westcliff oh-so-casually informed Mother about all the noble families she would be rubbing elbows with at the festival, Father didn't have a prayer."

"I imagine Westcliff and Mr. Swift will do well in Bristol," Daisy said.

Lillian's expression immediately became guarded. "No doubt they will."

Daisy noticed that without their friends as a buffer, she and Lillian had fallen into an excessively careful manner of speaking. She didn't like it. They had always been so free and open with each other. But suddenly it seemed they were obliged to avoid certain subjects as if they were trying to ignore an elephant in the room. An entire herd of elephants, actually.

Lillian had not asked if Daisy had slept with Matthew. In fact, Lillian seemed disinclined to talk about Matthew at all. Nor did she ask why Daisy's budding relationship with Lord Llandrindon had evaporated, or why Daisy had no apparent interest in going to London to finish the season.

Daisy had no desire to broach any of these subjects either. Despite Matthew's reassurances before he had left, she felt uneasy and restless, and the last thing she wanted was to have an argument with her sister.

Instead they focused on Merritt, taking turns holding, dressing, and bathing her as if she were a little doll. Although there were two nursery maids available to care for the infant, Lillian had been reluctant to give her over to them. The simple fact was, she enjoyed being with the infant.

Before Mercedes had left, she had warned that the baby would become too accustomed to being held. "You'll spoil her," she had told Lillian, "and then no one will ever be able to put her down."

Lillian had retorted that there was no shortage of arms at Stony Cross Manor, and Merritt would be held as often as she liked.

"I intend for her childhood to be different from ours," Lillian told Daisy later, while they pushed the baby in a perambulator through the garden. "The few memories I have of our parents are of watching Mother dress for evenings out or going to Father's study to confess our latest mischief. And getting punished."

"Do you remember," Daisy asked with a smile, "how Mother used to scream when we roller-skated on the pavement and knocked people over?"

Lillian chuckled. "Except when it was the Astors, and then it was all right."

"Or when the twins planted a little garden and

we pulled up all the potatoes before they were ripe?"

"Crabbing and fishing on Long Island . . ."

"Playing rounders . . ."

The afternoon of "remember when" filled the sisters with a mutual glow. "Who would have ever thought," Daisy said with a grin, "that you would end up married to a British peer, and that I would be . . ." She hesitated. ". . . a spinster."

"Don't be silly," Lillian said quietly. "It's obvious you're not going to be a spinster."

That was the closest they came to discussing Daisy's relationship with Matthew Swift. However, in pondering Lillian's unusual restraint, Daisy realized that her sister wanted to avoid a rift with her. And if that meant having to include Matthew Swift in the family, Lillian would do her best to tolerate him. Knowing how difficult it was for her sister to hold back her opinions, Daisy longed to throw her arms around her. Instead, she moved to take the handles of the perambulator.

"My turn to push," Daisy said.

They continued to walk.

Daisy resumed their reminiscing. "Remember overturning the canoe on the pond?"

"With the governess in it," Lillian added, and they grinned at each other.

The Bowmans were the first to return on Saturday. As one might have expected, the Shakespeare festival had been unmitigated torture for Thomas.

"Where is Swift?" he demanded the minute he entered the manor. "Where is Westcliff? I want a report on the negotiations."

"They're not back yet," Lillian replied, meeting him in the entrance hall. She sent her father a gently caustic glance. "Aren't you going to ask how I am, Father? Don't you want to know how the baby is faring?"

"I can see with my own eyes that you're well enough," Bowman retorted. "And I assume the baby is well or you would already have informed me otherwise. When are Swift and Westcliff expected to return?"

Lillian rolled her eyes heavenward. "Momentarily."

But it became apparent the travelers had encountered a delay, probably as a result of the difficulties of going anywhere in spring. The weather was unpredictable, the country roads were often in need of repair, carriages were easily damaged, and horses were subject to injuries such as bog spavins or capped hocks.

As evening approached and there was still no sign of Westcliff and Matthew, Lillian declared they might as well go in to dinner or the cook would be cross.

It was a relatively small affair attended by the Bowmans and two local families, including the vicar and his wife. Midway through the meal, the butler entered the dining hall and murmured something to Lillian. She smiled and turned pink, her eyes brightening with excitement as she informed the table that Westcliff had arrived and would be joining them soon.

Daisy kept a calm expression in place as if it were a mask that had been plastered onto her face. Beneath the surface, however, a riot of expectation pumped through her veins. Realizing her dining utensils trembled visibly in her hands, she put them down and rested her hands in her lap. She listened to the conversation with only half a mind, the other half fixed on the doorway.

When the two men finally appeared in the dining hall after having washed and changed from the journey, Daisy's heart pounded too fast to allow for a full breath.

Matthew's glance swept the company at large, and he bowed as Westcliff did. Both of them appeared collected and remarkably fresh. One would think they had been absent for seven minutes instead of seven days.

Before going to his place at the head of the table, Westcliff went to Lillian. Since the earl was never given to public demonstrations, it astonished everyone, including Lillian, when he cupped her face in his hands and kissed her full on the mouth. She flushed and said something about the vicar being there, making Westcliff laugh.

Meanwhile, Matthew took the empty place beside Daisy's. "Miss Bowman," he said softly.

Daisy couldn't manage a word. Her gaze lifted to his smiling eyes, and it seemed that emotions sprang from her in a fountain of warmth. She had to look away from him before she did something foolish. But she remained intensely aware of his body next to hers.

Westcliff and Matthew entertained the group with an account of how their carriage had gotten stuck in mire. Luckily they had been helped by a passing farmer with an ox-drawn wagon, but in the process of freeing the vehicle, all participants had been covered with mud from head to toe. And apparently the episode had left the ox in quite an objectionable temper. By the time the story was finished, everyone at the table was chuckling.

The conversation turned to the subject of the Shakespeare festival, and Thomas Bowman launched into an account of the visit to Stratford-on-Avon. Matthew asked a question or two, seeming fully engaged in the conversation.

Suddenly Daisy was startled to feel his hand slide into her lap beneath the table. His fingers closed over hers in a gentle clasp. And all the while he took part in the conversation, talking and smiling easily. Daisy reached for her wine with her free hand and brought it to her lips. She took one sip, and then another, and nearly choked as Matthew played lightly with her fingers beneath the table. Sensations that had lain quiescent for a week kindled into vibrant life.

Still not looking at her, Matthew gently slid something over her ring finger, past the knuckle, until it fit neatly at the base. Her hand was returned to her lap as a footman came to replenish the wine in their glasses.

Daisy looked down at her hand, blinking at the sight of the glittering yellow sapphire surrounded by small round diamonds. It looked like a white-petaled flower. Her fingers closed tightly, and she averted her face to hide a betraying flush of pleasure.

"Does it please you?" Matthew whispered.

"Oh, yes."

That was the extent of their communication at dinner. It was just as well. There was too much to be said, all of it highly private. Daisy steeled herself for the usual long rituals of port and tea after dinner, but she was gratified when it seemed that everyone, even her father, was inclined to retire early. As it appeared the elderly vicar and his wife were ready to return home, the group dispersed without much fanfare.

Walking with Daisy from the dining hall, Matthew murmured, "Will I have to scale the outside wall tonight, or are you going to leave your door unlocked?"

"The door," Daisy replied succinctly.

"Thank God."

Approximately an hour later Matthew carefully tried the handle of Daisy's bedroom door and eased his way in. The small room was lit with the glow of a bedside lamp, its flame dancing in the breeze from the balcony.

Daisy sat in bed reading, her hair plaited in a

neat braid that trailed over her shoulder. Dressed in a demure white gown with intricate ruching across the front, she looked so clean and innocent that Matthew felt vaguely guilty coming to her with desire coursing in hot thrills through his body. But as she looked up from her book, her dark eyes lured him irresistibly closer.

She set the book aside, the lamplight slipping over her profile. Her skin looked as cool and perfect as polished ivory. He wanted to warm it with his hands.

The corners of Daisy's mouth curled upward as if she could read his thoughts. As she turned the covers back, the yellow sapphire glittered on her finger. Matthew was momentarily surprised by his own response to the sight, the flash of primal possessiveness. Slowly he obeyed her gesture to come to the bed.

He sat on the edge of the mattress, his nerves sizzling as Daisy gathered up the loose folds of her nightgown. She crawled into his lap with the delicacy of a cat. The scent of sweet female skin filled his nostrils, and her weight settled on his thighs. Linking her slender arms around his neck, she said gravely, "I missed you."

His palms charted the shape of her body; the tender curves, the slender waist, the firm heart-shaped bottom. But as enchanting as he found Daisy's physical charms, they didn't affect him a fraction as intensely as the warm, lively intelligence of her nature.

"I missed you too."

Daisy's fingers played in his hair, the delicate touch sending jolts of pleasure from the base of his skull to his groin. Her voice turned provocative. "Did you meet many women in Bristol? Westcliff mentioned something about a dinner, and a soirée given by your host—"

"I didn't notice any women." Matthew found it hard to think over the exquisite writhing desire. "You're the only one I've ever wanted."

She touched the tip of her nose to his in a playful nudge. "You weren't celibate in the past, however."

"No," Matthew admitted, closing his eyes as he felt the caress of her breath against his skin. "It's a lonely feeling, wishing the woman in your arms was someone else. Not long before I left New York, I realized that every woman I'd been with in the past seven years had resembled you in some way. One would have your eyes, another your hands, or your hair . . . I thought I would spend the rest of my life searching for little reminders of you. I thought—"

Her mouth pressed against his, absorbing the raw confession. Her lips parted, and he needed no further invitation to kiss her, the gentle ingress of his tongue deepening until he had taken her mouth fully. The soft shapes of her breasts brushed against his chest with every inhalation.

He lowered Daisy to her back, catching the hem of her nightgown and drawing it upward. She helped him to remove the garment, wriggling a little to slide it over her head. The grace of the movement sent his pulse firing through his over-heated veins. She lay naked before him, her far-spreading blush overlaid with a spill of candleglow, her limbs drawn modestly tight against her body. He drank in the sight of her while he stripped off his own clothes.

Laying beside her, Matthew devoted himself to teasing away her shyness. He caressed her shoulders, her throat, the vulnerable wing of her collarbone. Gradually the heat of his skin transferred to the coolness of hers, her flesh seeming to ignite beneath his patient touch. Gasping, she twined her supple body around his, and he hushed her with his mouth, whispering that the windows were open and she must be quiet.

His lips seared a leisurely path to her breasts, catching at the soft peaks until they tightened against his mouth. Hearing the constricted sounds she made, he smiled and drew his tongue lightly around her nipple. He played with her until she clenched her hand over her own mouth, panting.

Finally Daisy twisted away and buried a tormented groan in the bedclothes. "I can't," she whispered, shivering. "I can't keep quiet."

Matthew laughed softly and kissed the center of her spine. "But I'm not going to stop," he murmured, flipping her back over. "And think of the trouble it will cause if we're caught."

"Matthew, please—"

"Hush." He let his mouth wander over her body

without constraint, kissing, biting tenderly, until she twisted in restless confusion. At times she rolled away, her slender fingers digging into the mattress like cat's claws. He coaxed her onto her back each time, whispering endearments and promises, giving her his mouth to quiet her, his gently playful fingers to fill and soothe her swollen flesh. When she was taut in every limb and her skin gleamed with perspiration, Matthew finally settled between her shaking thighs.

Her body tensed as she felt the hardness of him easing intimately inside her . . . and then she moaned and flushed as he searched for the right rhythm. He knew he had found it when her knees hitched upward, instinctively clamping his hips.

"Yes, hold me . . ." Matthew whispered, stroking her over and over again, while her inner muscles began to throb violently. He had never known such ecstasy, thrusting in her exquisite tightness, rooting himself deeper as she jerked helplessly upward into the weight of his body. He followed her every movement, giving her what she needed, both of them intent on her pleasure.

Daisy covered her mouth with her hand once more, her eyes widening. Gripping her wrist, Matthew pulled her hand away and opened her mouth with his own, and plundered her deeply with his tongue. Her violent shudders pulled him into climax, eliciting a low groan from his chest as he came in hard, soul-wrenching quivers.

When the last ripples had eased, Matthew was overcome with a lethargy more consuming than any he had ever known. Only the thought of crushing Daisy was enough to prod him to roll onto his side. She made a disgruntled sound and reached for him, seeking the warmth of his body. He moved to help her, cradling her head in the crook of his arm, and somehow managed to drag the disheveled bedclothes over them both.

The temptation to sleep was overwhelming, but Matthew didn't dare allow himself. He didn't trust himself to awaken before the maid came to light the grate in the morning. He was far too replete, and the feel of Daisy's small form snuggled against his was too tempting to resist.

"I have to leave," he whispered against her hair.

"No, stay." Her face turned, her lips nuzzling the bare skin of his chest. "Stay all night. Stay forever."

He smiled and kissed her temple. "I would. But somehow I think your family would take exception to my debauching you before we were properly betrothed."

"I don't feel debauched."

"I do," Matthew said.

Daisy smiled. "I'd better marry you, then." Her small hand moved over his body in tentative exploration. "Ironically," she commented, "this will be the first time I've ever done anything to please my father."

With a sympathetic murmur, Matthew gathered

Daisy close against him. He knew her father as well as anyone, having become well acquainted with the man's tempers, his self-absorption, his impossible standards. And yet he understood what it had required for Bowman to build a great fortune from scratch, the sacrifices he'd had to make. Bowman had discarded everything that would have gotten in the way of achieving his goals. Including closeness with his wife and children.

For the first time it occurred to Matthew that Bowman and his family would benefit from someone acting as a mediator, to ease their communications with each other. If such a thing were in his power, he would find a way to do it.

"You," he whispered in Daisy's hair, "are the best thing he's ever done. Someday he'll realize that."

He felt her smile against his skin. "I doubt it. But it's nice of you to say so. You don't have to be concerned on that account, you know. I reconciled myself to the way he was a long time ago."

Once again Matthew was taken unaware by the extent of the feelings she inspired in him, his own limitless desire to fill her with happiness.

"Whatever you need," he whispered, "Whatever you want, I'll get it for you. Just tell me."

Daisy stretched comfortably, a pleasant shiver running through her limbs. She touched his lips with her fingers, tracing the smoothness. "I want to know what your five-dollar wish was for."

"Is that all?" He smiled beneath her exploring fingertips. "I wished you would find someone who wanted you as much as I did. But I knew it wouldn't come true."

The candlelight slid over Daisy's delicate features as she raised her head to look at him. "Why not?"

"Because I knew no one could ever want you as much as I do."

Daisy levered herself farther over him until her hair tumbled in a dark curtain around them both.

"What was your wish?" Matthew asked, combing his fingers through the fall of shimmering hair.

"That I could find the right man to marry." Her tender smile stopped his heart. "And then you appeared."

Chapter 15

After an unusually long sleep Matthew ventured downstairs. Servants were busy cleaning miles of stone-flagged, carpeted, or parqueted floors, while others trimmed lamps, replaced candlesticks, and polished the brasses.

As soon as Matthew approached the morning room, a maid offered to bring him a breakfast tray out to the back terrace if he so desired. Since it promised to be a beautiful day, Matthew accepted the offer readily.

Sitting at one of the outside tables, he watched the progress of a small brown hare hopping along the carefully tended grounds.

His quiet contemplation was interrupted by the sound of the french doors opening. Glancing up expectantly, Matthew saw that instead of the maid with the breakfast tray, it was the considerably less welcome sight of Lillian Bowman. He groaned inwardly, knowing at once that Westcliff had told her about his betrothal to Daisy.

However, it seemed the earl must have exerted some calming influence on his wife. Not that Lillian looked happy, of course . . . but Matthew took it as a good sign that she wasn't approaching him with an ax in hand.

Yet.

Lillian made a motion for him to remain in his chair as she approached. He stood anyway.

Lillian's face was set and her voice was controlled as she said, "There's no need to look at me as if I were a descending plague of Egypt. I am capable of rational discourse on occasion. May I have a word with you?"

She sat before he could help her with the chair.

Regarding her warily, Matthew reoccupied his own chair and waited for her to speak. Despite the tension-fraught atmosphere, he almost smiled as he reflected he had often seen the same expression on Thomas Bowman's face. Lillian was bullishly determined to have her way, yet she was mindful of the fact that a shouting match, no matter how satisfying, would accomplish nothing.

"You and I are both aware," Lillian said with forced composure, "that even though I can't stop this blighted marriage from happening, I can make the proceedings quite unpleasant for everyone. Especially you."

"Yes, I'm aware of that." Matthew's response was completely free of sarcasm. Whatever else he thought of Lillian, he knew her love for Daisy was unimpeachable.

"Then I want to dispense with the cat-footing," Lillian said, "and have a man-to-man conversation."

Matthew sternly bit back a smile. "Good," he replied in an equally businesslike manner. "So do I." He thought he could possibly come to like Lillian. If nothing else, one always knew where one stood with her.

"The only reason I'm willing to tolerate the idea of you as a brother-in-law," Lillian continued, "is because my husband seems to think well of you. And I'm willing to take his opinion into consideration. Although he is not infallible."

"That may be the first time I've heard anyone make such a remark about the earl."

"Yes, well . . ." Lillian surprised him with a faint smile. "It's why Westcliff married me. My willingness to regard him as a mere mortal is something of a relief after all the incessant worship." Her dark eyes, rounder and less exotic than Daisy's, met his in a searching gaze. "Westcliff asked me to try and be impartial. That's not easy when my sister's future hangs in the balance."

"My lady," Matthew said earnestly, "if I can

give you any assurance that might set your mind at ease—"

"No. Wait. Let me set out my opinion of you first."

Matthew remained politely silent.

"You have always embodied the worst of my father," Lillian said. "The coldness, the ambition, the self-centeredness. Except you're worse because you're able to disguise it far more adeptly than he does. You're what my father would have been if he'd been blessed with good looks and a little sophistication. I think that in winning you Daisy must somehow feel she has finally succeeded with Father." Her brows came together as she continued. "My sister has always compelled to love unlovable creatures . . . the strays, the misfits. Once she loves someone, no matter how many times they betray or disappoint her, she will take them back with open arms. But you won't appreciate that any more than Father does. You'll take what you want, and give her very little in return. And when you inevitably hurt her, I will be the first in a line of people waiting to slaughter you. By the time I finish with you, there won't be enough left for the others to pick over."

"So much for impartiality," Matthew said. He respected her brutal honesty even though he was smarting from it. "May I respond with the same frankness you've just shown me?"

"I hope you will."

"My lady, you don't know me well enough to assess how much like your father I may or may not be. It's no crime to be ambitious, particularly when you've started with nothing. And I'm not cold, I'm from Boston. Which means I'm not prone to displaying my emotions for all and sundry to see. As far as being self-centered, you have no way of knowing how much I've done, if anything, for other people. But I'll be damned if I recite a list of my past good deeds in hopes of winning your approval." He leveled a cool stare at her. "Regardless of your opinions, the marriage is going to happen, because both Daisy and I want it. So I have no reason to lie to you. I could say I don't give a damn about Daisy, and I would still get what I want. But the fact is, I'm in love with her. I have been for a long time."

"You've been secretly in love with my sister for years?" Lillian asked with blistering skepticism. "How convenient."

"I didn't define it as 'in love.' All I knew was that I had a persistent, all-consuming . . . preference for her."

"*Preference?*" Lillian looked momentarily outraged, and then she surprised him by laughing. "My God, you really are from Boston."

"Believe it or not," Matthew muttered, "I wouldn't have chosen to feel this way about Daisy. It would have been far more convenient to find someone else. The devil knows I should be given some credit for being willing to take on the Bowmans as in-laws."

"Touché." Lillian continued to smile, leaning her chin on her hand as she stared at him. Suddenly her voice contained a delicately inquiring edge that raised the hairs on the back of his neck. "I find it peculiar that a Boston Swift should use the phrase 'starting with nothing' . . . Have I been mistaken all these years in believing you came from a well-to-do background?"

Damn it all, she was clever. Realizing he'd made a slip, Matthew replied smoothly. "The main branch of the Swifts is affluent. But I am one of the proverbial poor cousins, which is why I was obliged to take a profession."

Her brows lifted slightly. "And would the affluent Swifts have allowed their poorer cousins to dwell in abject poverty, as you implied?"

"A slight exaggeration on my part," Matthew said. "But I'm certain you won't preoccupy yourself with it to the extent of missing the main point."

"I believe I've managed to grasp your point, Mr. Swift." Lillian vacated her chair, obliging him to rise to his feet. "One more thing. Do you believe Daisy would be happy if you took her back to live in New York?"

"No," Matthew said quietly. He saw a flash of surprise in her eyes. "It's obvious that you—and her friends—are essential to her happiness."

"Then you . . . you would be willing to make a

permanent home here? Even if my father objected?"

"Yes, if that's what Daisy wants." Matthew tried to control a sudden surge of annoyance, with limited results. "I'm not afraid of your father's temper, my lady, nor am I a puppet on a string. The fact that I work for him doesn't mean I've surrendered free will and the full use of my brain. I can find gainful employment in Britain whether or not I'm employed by Bowman Enterprises."

"Mr. Swift," Lillian said sincerely, "you don't know how tempting it is for me to believe you."

"And that means . . . ?"

"I suppose it means I'll try to be nicer to you."

"Starting when?" he shot back.

One corner of her mouth tilted upward. "Next week, maybe."

"I'm looking forward to it," Matthew muttered, resuming his seat as she left.

As expected, Mercedes Bowman received the news of Daisy's betrothal to Matthew Swift with poor grace. Having made such a brilliant marriage for her first daughter, she had longed to do the same for her second. It mattered little to Mercedes that Matthew Swift would undoubtedly acquire a fortune developing business interests on two continents. It mattered even less that Daisy had found a man who seemed to understand and even delight in her eccentricities.

"Who cares if he's good at making money?"

Mercedes had grumbled to her daughters as they sat in the Marsden parlor. "Manhattanville was *swarming* with enterprising men who had large fortunes. Why did we come here if not to find a gentleman who stood for something more? I do wish, Daisy, that you might have been able to attract a man of refinement and breeding."

Lillian, who was feeding the baby, replied in a sardonic tone. "Mother, if Daisy married the royal prince of Luxembourg it still wouldn't change the fact that the Bowmans are from common stock, and Grandmother—Lord love her—was a dockside washwoman. This preoccupation with nobility is a bit excessive, isn't it? Let's put it to rest and try to be happy for Daisy."

Indignation caused Mercedes to puff out her cheeks temporarily, causing her narrow face to resemble a set of inflated fireplace bellows. "You don't like Mr. Swift any more than I do," she retorted.

"No," Lillian said frankly. "But much as I hate to admit it, that puts us in a minority. Swift is liked by everyone in the northern hemisphere, including Westcliff and his friends, my friends, the servants, the neighbors—"

"You are exaggerating—"

"—children, animals and the higher order of plants," Lillian finished sardonically. "If root vegetables could talk, I've no doubt they would say they like him, too."

Daisy, who was sitting by the window with a

book, looked up with a sudden grin. "His charm doesn't extend to poultry," she said. "He has a problem with geese." Her smile turned quizzical. "Thank you for being so accommodating, Lillian. I expected you to make a fuss about the betrothal."

Her older sister let out a rueful sigh. "I've reconciled myself to the fact that it would be easier to push a pea with my nose from here to London than to try and stand in the way of this marriage. Besides, you will be far more accessible in Bristol than you would have been with Lord Llandrindon in Thurso."

The mention of Llandrindon nearly caused Mercedes to weep. "He said there were lovely walks in Thurso," she said mournfully. "And Viking history. I would have *so* loved to learn about the Vikings."

Lillian snorted. "Since when have you been interested in warlike pagans with silly-looking headgear?"

Daisy looked up from her book again. "Are we talking about Grandmother again?"

Mercedes leveled a glare at them both. "It seems I have no choice but to accept this match gracefully. I will endeavor to find some small consolation in the fact that at least this time I will be able to plan a proper wedding." She had never quite forgiven Lillian and Marcus for having eloped to Gretna Green, thereby depriving her of the grand festivities she had always dreamed of planning.

Lillian smiled smugly at Daisy. "I don't envy you, dear."

"It won't be pleasant," Daisy warned Matthew later that day, as they sat at the grassy edge of a millpond located far on the western outskirts of the village. "The ceremony will be designed to make the world take notice of the Bowmans."

"Just the Bowmans?" he asked. "Aren't I supposed to be featured in the ceremony?"

"Oh, the groom is the most insignificant part of it," she said cheerfully.

She had meant to amuse Matthew, but his smile didn't reach his eyes. He stared across the millpond with a distant expression.

The stone water mill with its twelve-foot wheel had long been abandoned in favor of a more productive mill closer to the heart of Stony Cross. With its charming stepped gable roof and half-timbered facade, the millhouse possessed a rough-cast charm that was enhanced by the rustic scenery.

While Matthew cast a baited hook into the pond with an expert flick of his wrist, Daisy dangled her bare feet into the water. Every now and then the wriggle of her toes would invite adventurous minnows to dart forward.

She studied Matthew while he appeared to brood on some troublesome matter. His profile was strong and distinctive, with a straight, sturdy nose, sharply defined lips, a severely perfect jaw. She took pleasure in the sight of his dishevelment, the shirt dampened in patches, the trousers scattered with dry leaves, the thick hair rumpled and hanging over his forehead.

There was a fascinating duality about Matthew that Daisy had never encountered in another man. At some moments he was the aggressive, sharp-eyed, buttoned-up businessman who rattled off facts and figures with ease.

At other times he was a gentle, understanding lover who shed his cynicism like an old coat and engaged her in playful debates about which ancient culture had the best mythology, or what Thomas Jefferson's favorite vegetable had been. (Although Daisy was convinced it was green peas, Matthew had made an excellent case for tomatoes.)

They had long conversations about subjects like history and progressive politics. For a man from a conservative Brahmin background, he had a surprising awareness of reform issues. Usually in their relentless climb up the social ladder, enterprising men forgot about those who had been left on the bottom rungs. Daisy thought it spoke well of Matthew's character that he had a genuine concern for those less fortunate than himself.

In their discussions they had begun to lay out tentative plans for the future . . . they would have to find a house in Bristol that was large enough for entertaining. Matthew insisted it would have a view of the sea, and a library room for Daisy's books, and—he added gravely—a high wall around the house so he could ravish her in the garden without being seen.

Mistress of her own house . . . Daisy had never been able to envision it before. But the idea of arranging things exactly as she wanted, establishing a home that suited her own preferences, was starting to sound very inviting.

Their communication often left something to be desired, however. For all the thoughts Matthew was willing to share with Daisy, there were many more that remained inaccessible. Sometimes talking with him was like ambling along a lovely winding path through all kinds of interesting scenery, only to run directly into a stone wall.

When Daisy pressed Matthew to discuss his past, he made only vague references to Massachusetts and growing up near the Charles River. Information about his family was stubbornly withheld. So far he had been unwilling to discuss which members of the Swift clan would be attending the wedding ceremony. And yet surely he wasn't going to be completely unrepresented.

One would think Matthew hadn't existed before he started to work for her father at the age of twenty. Daisy longed to break through the stubborn barrier of secrets. It was maddening to feel herself forever on the verge of an elusive discovery. Their relationship seemed the embodiment of some Hegelian theory . . . something always in the process of becoming something else, never attaining completion.

Bringing her thoughts back to the present, Daisy decided to regain Matthew's attention. "Of course," she said casually, "we don't have to have a wedding ceremony at all. We can simply adhere to the classic marriage-by-purchase. Give my father a cow, and we'll be done with it. Or perhaps we'll do a handfasting ritual. Of course, there's always the ancient Greek practice in which I would cut off all my hair as a sacrifice and dedicate it to Artemis, followed by a ritual bath in a sacred spring—"

Suddenly Daisy found herself flat on her back, the sky partially blocked by Matthew's dark form. She let out a gasp of laughter at the suddenness with which he had thrown aside his fishing rod and pounced on her. His blue eyes gleamed with mischief. "I would consider the cow exchange or the handfasting," he said. "But I draw the line at marrying a hairless bride."

Daisy relished the weight of him pressing her back against the spongy grass, the scents of earth and herbs all around them. "What about the ritual bath?" she asked.

"That you can do. In fact . . ." His long fingers reached for the buttons at the front of her dress. ". . . I think you should practice. I'll help you."

Daisy squirmed and shrieked as he began to tug her gown open. "This is not a sacred spring, this is a slimy old millpond!"

But Matthew persisted, chuckling at her efforts

to evade him as he pulled her gown to her waist. In defiance of propriety, and as a concession to the unseasonable warmth outside, Daisy had gone without a corset. She pushed hard at Matthew's rock-solid chest, and he rolled easily, taking her with him. The world spun crazily, the blue and white sky blurring. She found herself sprawled on his chest while her chemise was pulled inexorably over her head.

"Matthew—" she protested, her voice muffled in the linen garment.

Removing the chemise completely, Matthew tossed it aside. His hands hooked beneath her arms, lifting until she dangled as helplessly as a kitten. His breath quickened as he stared at her pale, rosy-tipped breasts.

"Put me down," Daisy insisted, blushing as she was displayed before his avid gaze. Although she had lain with him twice, she was still too innocent to be cavalier about making love in the open.

Matthew obeyed, hoisting her further over him until his mouth had closed over a taut nipple.

"No," she managed to say, "that's not what I . . . *oh* . . ."

He suckled her breasts in turn, using his teeth and tongue, playing, soothing. After pausing long enough to remove the rest of her clothes, he kissed her deeply. She yanked at his shirt, her fingers clumsy with agitation.

Matthew reached down to help her, pulling his

shirt off and gently bringing her naked chest against his. The warm friction of his skin sent all coherent thoughts tumbling out of reach. Wrapping her arms around his neck, Daisy crushed her mouth over his, hard and eager and passionate.

Her eyes flew open in surprise as she felt his smothered laugh against her lips.

"Have a little patience, sweetheart," he whispered. "I'm trying to go slowly."

"Why?" Daisy asked, her mouth feeling hot and sensitive. She touched her tongue experimentally to the center of her bottom lip, and his lashes lowered as he followed the tiny movement.

His voice had become raspy. "Because it will give you more pleasure."

"I don't need more pleasure," Daisy said. "This is all I can possibly stand."

He laughed quietly. Cradling the side of her face in his strong hand, he coaxed her closer. The tip of his tongue found the subtle indentation of her lower lip and lingered for a burning moment, causing her to inhale unsteadily. His mouth sealed over hers in a lush kiss, his tongue searching and stroking.

Gradually he lowered her to the ground onto his discarded shirt. The thin cloth retained the alluring fragrance of his skin, and Daisy luxuriated in the familiar masculine incense. Her eyes closed against the white glow of the sun as his body covered hers. He had unfastened the top of his trousers, the fabric brushing all along her tingling legs. Aroused by the sensation of being naked against his half-clothed body, Daisy parted her thighs as he settled between them.

"I want to be part of you," he whispered. "I want forever with you."

"Yes, yes . . ." She tried to hold him with her arms and legs, wrapping him in her supple strength.

He entered her slowly, and where there had been soreness before, there was now only pleasure at the exquisite inner pressure of his body filling hers. Easing deeper in patient degrees, he resisted her efforts to hurry him. Daisy writhed and fought to take him in, panting in excitement and exertion, moaning as he caught her hips in her hands and forced her to be still.

"Easy . . ." His voice was wickedly soft. "Just a little patience."

She needed all of him, *now*. Her body was throbbing, her nerves brimming with sensation. "Please . . ." Her mouth ached for the pressure of his, until she could barely form words. "I c-can't just *lie* here while you—"

"Yes you can."

He held torturously still inside her while his hands coasted over her body in artful investigation. Daisy twisted restlessly beneath him, her desire rising with each persuasive caress, her moans absorbed in the sensuous play of his lips. With every shift of his hardness inside her the heat danced higher, brighter, and she arched into him tightly, lifting against his weight.

Matthew relented with a muffled laugh, taking control of the rhythm as he courted her with long strokes. His body scalded hers, invading and pleasuring relentlessly. "There's no hurry, Daisy." His voice became husky and thick. "No reason to . . . yes, just like that . . . sweet love, yes . . ." His head dropped over her shoulder, his breath striking her skin. The muscles in his arms bulged as he sank his fingers into the ground on either side of her, as if he could secure them both to the earth.

Daisy felt like a wild creature, pinned against the grass by the primal rhythm of his hips. Her body caught and retained a tense arch, all her flesh seeking his, her senses focused on the shuddering satisfaction that began where their bodies were joined, spreading outward to the tips of her fingers and toes.

Matthew reached his own pinnacle, his body trembling in the slender circle of her arms. And as he laid his head on her chest, his breath fanning rapidly over her breast, the current of delight hummed through the place where she still clasped him.

Daisy knew he loved her . . . she could feel it in every thump of his heartbeat as it pressed against her. He had admitted it to Westcliff, and to Lillian, but for some reason he had not told Daisy herself.

To Daisy, love was not an emotion that should

be approached in careful degrees. She wanted to throw herself into it wholeheartedly, with trust and pure honesty . . . things Matthew was apparently not ready for.

But someday, she promised herself, there would be no barriers between them. Someday . . .

Chapter 16

The Stony Cross May Day festival had been celebrated for centuries, beginning as a pagan celebration of the end of winter and the return of the soil's fertility. It had evolved into a three-day event that included games, feasting, dancing, and every imaginable revelry.

Local gentry, farmers and townspeople all mingled freely during the festival, despite the protests from clergy and other conservative-minded people who said that the May Day festival was nothing but an excuse to indulge in fornication and public drunkenness. As Lillian remarked slyly to Daisy, it seemed the louder the complaints about the sins that occurred on May Day, the higher the attendance rate.

The oval village green was lit with torches. Farther off a massive bonfire sent gigantic plumes of smoke up to the cloud-weighted sky. It had been overcast all day, the air thick with humidity and charged with the promise of a storm to come. Luckily, however, the storm seemed to be kept in restraint by the pagan deities, and the festivities were taking place as planned.

With Matthew at her side, Daisy browsed the row of wooden stalls that had been erected along High Street, filled with fabrics, toys, millinery, silver jewelry, and glassware. She was determined to see and do as much as possible in a short time, for Westcliff had strongly advised them to return to the manor well before midnight.

"The later the hour, the more unrestrained the merrymaking tends to become," the earl had said meaningfully. "Under the influence of wine—and behind the concealment of masks—people tend to do things they would never think of doing in the light of day."

"Oh, what's a little fertility ritual here or there?" Daisy had scoffed cheerfully. "I'm not so innocent that I—"

"We'll be back early," Matthew had told the earl.

Now as they made their way through the exuberantly crowded village, Daisy understood what Westcliff had meant. It was still early evening, and already it appeared that copiously flowing wine had loosened inhibitions. People were embracing, arguing, laughing and playing. Some were laying floral wreaths at the base of the oldest oak trees, or pouring wine at the roots, or . . .

"Good Lord," Daisy said, her attention caught by a perplexing sight in the distance, "what are they doing to that poor tree?"

Matthew's hands clasped her head and firmly aimed her face in another direction. "Don't look."

"Was it some form of tree-worship or—"

"Let's go watch the rope-dancers," he said with sudden enthusiasm, guiding her to the other side of the green.

They walked slowly past fire-swallowers, conjurors and tumblers, pausing to purchase a skin of new wine. Daisy drank carefully from the wine-skin, but a drop escaped from the corner of her lips. Matthew smiled and began to reach into his pocket for a handkerchief, then appeared to think better of it. Instead he ducked his head and kissed away the wine droplet.

"You're supposed to be protecting me from impropriety," she said with a grin, "and instead you're leading me astray."

The backs of his knuckles stroked gently against the side of her face. "I'd like to lead you astray," he murmured. "In fact, I'd like to lead you straight into those woods and . . ." He seemed to lose his train of thought as he stared into her soft, dark eyes. "Daisy Bowman," he whispered. "I wish—"

But she was never to find out what his wish was, because she was abruptly pushed into him as a crowd jostled past. Everyone was bent on obtaining a view of a pair of jugglers who had clubs and hoops spinning in the air between them. In the rush the wineskin was knocked from Daisy's hands and trampled underfoot. Matthew put his arms around her protectively.

"I dropped the wine," Daisy said regretfully.

"Just as well." His mouth lowered to her ear, his lips brushing the delicate outer rim. "It might have gone to my head. And then you might have taken advantage of me."

Daisy smiled and snuggled against his hard form, her senses delighting in the reassuring warmth of his embrace. "Are my designs on you that obvious?" she asked in a muffled voice.

He nuzzled into the soft space beneath her earlobe. "I'm afraid so."

Tucking her against his side, Matthew guided her through the crush of bodies until they reached the open space beside the booths. He bought her a paper cone of roasted nuts . . . a marzipan rabbit . . . a silver rattle for baby Merritt, and a painted cloth doll for Annabelle's daughter. As they walked the length of High Street toward the waiting carriage, Daisy was stopped by a gaudily dressed woman wearing scarves shot with metallic thread, and jewelry made of beaten gold.

The woman's face reminded Daisy exactly of the apple dolls she and Lillian had made when they were children. They had carved faces in the sides of the peeled fruit and let them dry into brown,

charmingly furrowed heads. Black beads for eyes
and soft tufts of carded wool for the hair . . . yes,
this woman looked exactly the same.

"A fortune for the lady, sir?" the woman asked
Matthew.

Glancing at Daisy, Matthew raised a sardonic
brow.

She grinned, knowing full well he had no patience
with mysticism, superstitions, or anything to do
with the supernatural. He was far too practical to
believe in things that couldn't be proved by empiri-
cal evidence.

"Just because you don't believe in magic," Daisy
told him playfully, "doesn't mean it can't happen.
Don't you want a little peek into the future?"

"I'd prefer to wait until it gets here," came his
dour reply.

"Only a shilling, sir," the fortune-teller pressed.

Matthew heaved a sigh as he shifted his packages and reached inside his pocket. "This shilling,"
he told Daisy, "would be better spent at the booths,
on a hair ribbon or a smoked chub."

"Coming from someone who threw a five-dollar
piece into the wishing well—"

"Making a wish had nothing to do with it,"
he said. "I only did that to get your attention."

Daisy laughed. "And so you did. *But*—" she
glanced at him significantly, "—your wish came
true, didn't it?" Taking the shilling, she transferred
it to the fortune-teller. "What is your method of
divination?" she asked the woman blithely. "Do

you have a crystal ball? Do you use tarot cards or read palms?"

For an answer, the woman took a silver-backed looking glass from the waist of her skirts and handed it to Daisy. "Look at your reflection," she intoned solemnly. "It is the gateway to the world of spirits. Keep staring—don't look away."

Matthew sighed and raised his gaze heavenward.

Obediently Daisy stared at her own expectant reflection, seeing the torchlight flicker across her features. "Are you going to stare into it too?" she asked.

"No," the fortune teller replied. "I only need to see your eyes."

Then . . . silence. Farther along the street, people sung May carols and beat drums. Staring into her own eyes, Daisy saw tiny gold glints of reflected light, like sparks wafting upward from a bonfire. If she looked hard enough, long enough, she could half-convince herself the silvered glass really was the gateway to some mystical world. Perhaps it was her imagination, but she could actually feel the intensity of the fortune-teller's concentration.

With an abruptness that startled Daisy, the woman took the looking glass from her hands. "No good," she said tersely. "I can see nothing. I will give your shilling back."

"No need," Daisy replied in bemusement. "It's not your fault if my spirit is opaque."

Matthew's voice was so dry one could light a

match off it. "We'll be just as happy if you'd make up something," he told the woman.

"She can't make up something," Daisy protested. "That would be abusing her gift."

Studying the fortune-teller's corrugated features, Daisy thought she seemed sincerely disgruntled. She must have seen or thought something that had bothered her. Which was probably a good indication to leave well enough alone. But if she didn't find out what it was, Daisy knew herself well enough to be certain the curiosity would drive her mad.

"We don't want the shilling back," she said. "Please, you *must* tell me something. If it's bad news, I would be better off knowing, wouldn't I?"

"Not always," the woman said darkly.

Daisy drew closer to her, until she could smell a sweet odor of figs, and some herbal essence . . . bay leaves? Basil? "I want to know," she insisted.

The fortune-teller gave her a long, considering glance. Finally she spoke with great reluctance. "Sweet the night a heart was given, bitter turns the day. A promise made in April . . . a broken heart in May."

A broken heart? Daisy didn't like the sound of that.

She felt Matthew come up behind her, one hand settling at Daisy's waist. Although she couldn't see his expression, she knew it was sardonic. "Will two shillings inspire something a little more optimistic?" he asked.

The fortune-teller ignored him. Tucking the

handle of the looking glass at her waist, she said to Daisy, "Make a charm of cloves tied in cloth. He must carry it for protection."

"Against what?" Daisy asked anxiously.

The woman was already striding away from them. Her opulently hued skirts moved like river reeds as she headed to the crowd at the end of the street in search of more business.

Turning to Matthew, Daisy glanced up at his impassive face. "What could you need protection from?"

"The weather." He held his hand palm upward, and Daisy realized that a few fat, cold raindrops had splashed on her head and shoulders.

"You were right," she said, brooding over the ominous fortune. "I should have gone for the smoked chub instead."

"Daisy . . ." His free hand slid behind the nape of her neck. "You didn't believe that load of nonsense, did you? That crone has memorized a few verses, any one of which she'll recite for a shilling. The only reason she gave us an ill omen was because I didn't pretend to believe in her magic looking-glass."

"Yes, but . . . she seemed genuinely sorry."

"There was nothing genuine about her, or anything she said." Matthew drew her closer, regardless of who might see them. As Daisy looked up at him, a raindrop spattered on her cheek, and another near the corner of her mouth. "It wasn't real," Matthew said softly, his eyes like blue midnight. He kissed her strongly, urgently, right there on the public street with the taste of rain absorbed between their lips. "This is real," he whispered.

Daisy pressed against him eagerly, standing on her toes to fit her body against the firm contours of his. The jumble of packages threatened to fall, and Matthew fought to retain them while his mouth consumed Daisy's. She broke the kiss with a sudden chuckle. A vigorous rumble of thunder caused the ground to vibrate beneath their feet.

In the periphery of her vision, people were scattering to the coverage provided by shops and stalls. "I'll race you to the carriage," she told Matthew, and picked up her skirts as she broke into a full-bore run.

Chapter 17

By the time the carriage had reached the end of the graveled drive, rain was coming down in flat, heavy sheets, and wind battered the sides of the vehicle. Thinking of the revelers in the village, Matthew reflected with amusement that many amorous inclinations were surely being drowned in the downpour.

The carriage stopped, the vehicle's roof roaring from the impact of relentless rain. Ordinarily a footman would come to the carriage door with an umbrella, but the strength of this deluge would whip the device right out of his hands.

Matthew removed his coat and wrapped it around Daisy, pulling it up until it covered her head and shoulders. It was hardly adequate protection, but it would shield her between the carriage and the front door of the manor.

"You'll get wet," Daisy protested, glancing at his shirtsleeves and waistcoat.

He began to laugh. "I'm not made of sugar."

"Neither am I."

"Yes you are," he murmured, making her blush. He smiled at the sight of her face peeking out from the folds of the coat, like a little owl in the woods. "You're wearing the coat," he said. "It's just a few yards to the door."

There came a hasty knock, and the carriage opened to reveal a footman struggling manfully with an umbrella. A gust of wind snapped it inside-out. As Matthew jumped out of the carriage, he was immediately soaked by the pounding rain. He clapped the footman on the shoulders. "Go inside," he shouted over the storm. "I'll help Miss Bowman in."

The footman nodded and retreated hastily to the manor.

Turning back to the carriage, Matthew reached inside, plucked Daisy out, and set her carefully on the ground. He guided her along the puddled ground and up the front steps, not stopping until they had crossed the threshold.

The warmth and light of the entrance hall surrounded them. Wet shirt fabric clung to Matthew's shoulders, and a pleasant shiver chased through him at the thought of sitting before a hearth fire.

"Oh, dear," Daisy said, smiling as she reached up to push a swath of dripping hair off his forehead. "You're soaked through."

A housemaid hurried to them with an armload of fresh toweling. Nodding to her in thanks, Matthew scrubbed his hair roughly and blotted the water from his face. He bent his head to let Daisy smooth his hair as best she could with her fingers.

Becoming aware of someone's approach, Matthew glanced over his shoulder. Westcliff had come into the entrance hall. His expression was austere, but there was something in his eyes, a touch of frowning concern, that sent a chill of apprehension through Matthew's veins.

"Swift," the earl said quietly, "we've received unexpected visitors this evening. They have not yet revealed their purpose in coming to the estate unannounced—other than to say it is some business involving you."

The chill intensified until it seemed ice crystals had formed in his muscles and bones. "Who are they?" Matthew asked.

"A Mr. Wendell Waring, of Boston . . . and a pair of Bow Street constables."

Matthew did not move or react as he silently absorbed the news. A sickening wave of despair went through him.

Christ, he thought. How had Waring found him here in England? How . . . oh Christ, it didn't matter, it was all over. All these years he had stolen from fate . . . now fate would have its reckoning. His heart thumped with an insane urge to run. But there was no place to run to, and even if there was—he was weary of living in dread of this day.

He felt Daisy's small hand slip into his, but he didn't return the pressure of her fingers. He stared at Westcliff's face. Whatever was in his eyes caused the earl to sigh heavily.

"Damn," Westcliff murmured. "It's bad, isn't it?"

Matthew could only manage a single nod. He pulled his hand from Daisy's. She did not try to touch him again, her bewilderment almost tangible.

After a long moment of contemplation, Westcliff squared his shoulders. "Well, then," he said decisively, "let's go and sort this out. Whatever comes of it, I will stand by as your friend."

A brief, incredulous laugh escaped Matthew's lips. "You don't even know what it is."

"I don't make idle promises. Come. They're in the large parlor."

Matthew nodded, drymouthed and resolute. He was surprised that he was functioning as if nothing was happening, as if his entire world wasn't about to be blown apart. It seemed almost as if he was watching from outside himself. Fear had never done that to him before. But maybe that was because he'd never had this much to lose.

He saw Daisy walking ahead of him, her face

lifting as Westcliff murmured something to her. She gave the earl a quick nod, seeming to take reassurance from him.

Matthew dropped his gaze to the floor. The sight of her caused a sharp pain in his throat, as if it had been pierced with a stiletto. He willed the blanketing numbness to come back, and mercifully it did.

They entered the parlor. Matthew felt like the damned on judgment day as he saw Thomas, Mercedes, and Lillian. His gaze swept the room, just as he heard a man's voice bark, "That's him!"

All at once there was a bright burst of pain in his head, and his legs collapsed as if they had turned to sand. The brightness shrank like an imploding star, darkness closing in, but his mind pushed at it in bewilderment, struggling feebly for consciousness.

Matthew became dimly aware that he was on the floor—he felt the scratchy wool pile of the carpet beneath his cheek. Wetness trickled from his mouth. He swallowed against a salty taste. A soft groan vibrated in his throat. As he concentrated on the pain, he identified its source at the back of his head. He had been struck, clubbed, by some hard object.

Sizzling light streaked across his vision as he felt himself being hauled upward, his arms jerked forward. Someone was shouting . . . men bellowing, a woman's sharp cry . . . Matthew blinked to clear his eyes, but they wouldn't stop watering against the biting pain. His wrists were compressed in a heavy iron loop. Handcuffs, he realized, and the familiar-awful heft of them filled him with dull panic.

Gradually the voices became recognizable to his buzzing ears. There was Westcliff raging—

". . . dare to come into my home and assault one of my guests . . . do you know who I am? Remove those *now,* or I'll see you all rotting in Newgate!"

And a new voice—

"Not after all these years. I won't chance the possibility of his escape."

The speaker was Mr. Wendell Waring, the patriarch of a wealthy New England family. The man Matthew despised second-most in the world, the first one being Waring's son Harry.

It was strange how a sound or a scent could bring back the past so damn easily, no matter how Matthew would have liked to forget it.

"Just *where,*" Westcliff asked acidly, "do you expect him to flee to?"

"I have permission to secure the fugitive by any means of my choosing. You have no right to object."

It would have been a massive understatement to say Wescliff was unaccustomed to being told by anyone that he had no right to do something, especially in his own home. It would have been an even greater understatement to say that Westcliff was enraged.

The argument thundered more violently than the storm outside, but Matthew lost track as he felt a gentle touch on his face. He jerked backward and heard Daisy's quiet murmur.

"No. Be still."

She was wiping his face with a dry cloth, clearing his eyes and mouth, pushing his damp hair back. He sat with his manacled hands in his lap, fighting to suppress a howl of misery as he looked at her.

Daisy's face was white but remarkably calm. Distress had brought crimson flags to the crests of her cheeks, the color standing out in stark relief against her pale skin. She lowered herself to her knees on the carpet beside his chair to examine the metal cuffs on his hands. A single iron band was closed around his wrist and fastened with a lock-case attached to another, larger loop that a constable would use to lead him.

Lifting his head, Matthew registered the presence of two oversized officers dressed in the standard uniform of white summer trousers, black high-collared tailcoats, and hardened top hats. They stood by in grim silence while Wendell Waring, Westcliff, and Thomas Bowman argued heatedly.

Daisy was fumbling with the lock case of the cuffs. Matthew's heart twisted painfully as he saw that she was prying at it with a hair pin. The Bowman sisters' lock-picking skills were infamous, garnered over years of their parents' foiled attempts at discipline. But Daisy's hands were trembling too badly for her to manage the unfamiliar lock—and it was obviously pointless to try and free him. God, if only he could spirit her away from this ugliness, from the wreck of his past . . . from himself. "No," Matthew said softly. "It's not worth it. Daisy, please—"

"Here, now," one of the officers said as he saw Daisy's meddling. "Step away from the prisoner, miss." Realizing she was ignoring him, the constable stepped forward with his hands half-raised. "Miss, I told you—"

"Don't you touch her," Lillian snapped, her voice containing a ferocity that caused a temporary silence in the room. Even Westcliff and Waring paused in momentary surprise.

Glaring at the dumbfounded constable, Lillian went to Daisy and nudged her aside. She spoke to the constables with stinging scorn. "Before you take a step in my direction, I'd advise you to consider what it will do to your careers when it is made known that you manhandled the Countess of Westcliff in her own home." She extracted a pin from her own hair and took Daisy's place, kneeling before Matthew. In a matter of seconds the lock clicked open and the loop fell from his wrists.

Before Matthew could thank her, Lillian stood and continued her tirade against the constables. "A fine pair you are, taking orders from an ill-bred Yankee to abuse the household that offered you shelter from a storm. Obviously you are too dull-witted to be aware of all the financial and political support my husband has given the New Police. With a lift of his finger, he could have the Home Secretary *and* the chief magistrate of Bow Street replaced within a matter of days. So if I were you—"

"Beg pardon, but we 'as no choice, milady," one of the beefy constables protested. "We're under orders to bring Mr. Phaelan to Bow Street."

"Who the bloody hell is Mr. Phaelan?" Lillian demanded.

Appearing awestruck by the countess's fluent swearing, the constable said, "That one, there." He pointed at Matthew.

Conscious that all eyes were on him, Matthew made his face expressionless.

Daisy was the first one in the room to move. She took the jangling handcuffs from Matthew's lap and went to the door, where a small coterie of curious servants had gathered. After a quick whispered exchange she returned to occupy a chair near Matthew's.

"And to think I predicted it would be a dull evening at home," Lillian said dryly, taking a chair on Matthew's other side as if to help defend him.

Daisy spoke gently to Matthew. "Is that your name? Matthew Phaelan?"

He couldn't answer, every muscle of his body tensing in rejection of the sound.

"It is," Wendell Waring shrilled. Waring was one of those unfortunate men whose high-pitched voices were inadequate to match their lofty physical proportions. Other than that, Waring was distinguished in bearing and appearance, with a thick ruff of silver hair, perfectly groomed side whiskers and an impenetrable white beard. He reeked of Old Boston, with his old-fashioned tailoring and expensive but well-worn tweed coat, and the air of self-assurance that could only have been produced in a family boasting generations of Harvard scholars. His eyes were like unfaceted quartz stones, hard and light and completely without luster.

Striding to Westcliff, Waring thrust a handful of papers at him. "Proof of my authority," he said venomously. "There you have a copy of a diplomatic requisition of provisional arrest from the American Secretary of State. A copy of an order from the British Home Secretary Sir James Graham to the chief magistrate at Bow Street, to issue a warrant for the arrest of Matthew Phaelan, alias Matthew Swift. Copies of sworn information attesting to—"

"Mr. Waring," Westcliff interrupted with a softness that in no way mitigated the danger in his tone, "you may bury me where I stand with copies of everything from arrest warrants to the Gutenberg Bible. That does not mean I will surrender this man to you."

"You have no choice! He is a convicted criminal who will be extradited to the United States, regardless of anyone's objections.

"*No choice?*" Westcliff's dark eyes widened, and a flush worked over his face. "By God, my patience has seldom been tested to its limit as it is now! This property you are standing on has been in my family's possession for five centuries, and on this land, in this house, I am the authority. Now, you will proceed to tell me in the most deferential manner you can manage, what grievance you have with this man."

Marcus, Lord Westcliff in a rage was an impressive sight. Matthew doubted that even Wendell Waring, who was friends with presidents and men of influence, had encountered a man with more natural command. The two constables looked uneasily between the two men.

Waring did not look at Matthew as he replied, as if the sight of him was too repulsive to tolerate. "You all know the man sitting before you as Matthew Swift. He has deceived and betrayed everyone he has ever chanced to meet. The world will be well served when he is exterminated like so much vermin. On that day—"

"Pardon, sir," Daisy interrupted with a politeness that bordered on mockery, "but I for one would prefer to receive the unembellished version. I have no interest in your opinions of Mr. Swift's character."

"His last name is *Phaelan,* not Swift," Waring retorted. "He is the son of an Irish drunkard. He was brought to the Charles River orphanage as an infant after the mother had died in childbirth. I had the misfortune of becoming acquainted with Matthew Phaelan when I purchased him at the age of eleven to act as companion and valet to my son Harry."

"You purchased him?" Daisy repeated acidly.

"I wasn't aware orphans could be bought and sold."

"Hired, then," Waring said, his gaze swerving to her. "Who are you, brazen miss, that you dare to interrupt your elders?"

Suddenly Thomas Bowman entered the discussion, his mustache twitching angrily. "She is my daughter," he roared, "and she may speak as she wishes!"

Surprised by her father's defense of her, Daisy smiled at him briefly, then returned her attention to Waring. "How long was Mr. Phaelan in your employ?" she prompted.

"For a period of seven years. He attended my son Harry at boarding school, did his errands, cared for his personal effects, and came home with him on the holidays." His gaze rushed to Matthew, the eyes suddenly glazed with weary accusation.

Now that his quarry had been secured, some of Waring's fury faded to grim resolution. He seemed like a man who had carried a heavy burden for far too long. "Little did we know we were harboring a serpent in our midst. On one of Harry's holidays at home, a fortune in cash and jewelry was stolen from the family safe. One of the items was a diamond necklace that had belonged to the Warings for a century. My great-grandfather had acquired it from the estate of the Archduchess of Austria. The theft could only have been accomplished by someone in the family, or by a trusted servant who had access to the safe key. All the evidence pointed to one person. Matthew Phaelan."

Matthew sat quietly. Stillness outside, chaos within. He contained it with fierce effort, knowing he would gain nothing by letting go.

"How do you know the lock wasn't picked by a thief?" he heard Lillian ask coolly.

"The safe was fitted with a detector lock," Waring replied, "which stops working if the lever tumblers are manipulated by a lock pick. Only a regulator key or the original key will open it. And Phaelan knew where the key was. From time to time he was sent to fetch money or personal possessions from the safe."

"He's not a thief!" Matthew heard Daisy burst out angrily, defending him before he could defend himself. "He would never be capable of stealing anything from anyone."

"A jury of twelve men did not agree with that assessment," Waring barked, his anger reinvigorated. "Phaelan was convicted of grand larceny and sentenced to the state prison for fifteen years. He escaped before they could deliver him, and he disappeared."

Having assumed Daisy would withdraw from him now, Matthew was astonished to realize she had come to stand beside his chair. The light pressure of her hand settled on his shoulder. He didn't respond outwardly to her touch, but his senses hungrily absorbed the weight of her fingers.

"How did you find me?" Matthew asked hoarsely,

forcing himself to look at Waring. Time had changed the man in subtle ways. The creases on his face were a little deeper, his bones more prominent.

"I've had men looking for years," Waring said with a touch of sneering melodrama that his fellow Bostonians would surely have found excessive. "I knew you couldn't remain hidden forever. There was a large anonymous donation made to Charles River Orphanage—I suspected you were behind it, but it was impossible to break through the armament of lawyers and sham business fronts. Then it struck me that you might have taken it upon yourself to find the father who had abandoned you so long ago. We tracked him down, and for the price of a few drinks he told us everything we wanted to know—your assumed name, your address in New York." Waring's contempt scattered through the air like a swarm of black flies as he added, "You were sold for the equivalent of five gills of whisky."

Matthew's breath caught. Yes, he had found his father, and had decided against all reason or caution to trust him. The need for connection with someone, something, had been too overpowering. His father was a wreck of a human being—there had been painfully little Matthew had been able to do for him aside from finding a place for him to live and paying for his upkeep.

Whenever Matthew had managed to visit in secret, there had been bottles piled everywhere. "If you ever need me," he had told his father, pressing a folded note into his hand, "send for me at this address. Don't share it with anyone, understand?" His father, childlike in his dependency, had said yes, he understood.

If you ever need me . . . Matthew had wanted desperately to be needed by someone.

This was the price for that self-indulgence.

"Swift," Thomas Bowman asked, "are Waring's claims true?" The familiar bluster was tempered with a note of appeal.

"Not entirely." Matthew allowed himself a cautious survey of the room. The things he had expected to see on their faces—accusation, fear, anger—were not there. Even Mercedes Bowman, who was not exactly what anyone would call a compassionate woman, was regarding him with what he could almost swear was kindliness.

Suddenly he realized he was in a different position than he had been all those years ago, when he had been poor and friendless. He had been armed only with the truth, which had proved a poor weapon indeed. Now he had money and influence of his own, not to mention powerful allies. And most of all Daisy, who was still standing at his shoulder, her touch feeding strength and comfort into his veins.

Matthew's eyes narrowed in defiance as he met Wendell Waring's accusing stare. Whether he liked it or not, Waring would have to listen to the truth.

Chapter 18

"*I was Harry Waring's servant,*" Matthew began gruffly. "And a good one, even though I knew he regarded me as something less than a human being. In his view servants were like dogs. I existed only for his convenience. My job was to assume blame for his misdeeds, take his punishments, repair what he broke, fetch what he needed. Even at an early age Harry was an arrogant wastrel who thought he could get away with anything short of murder because of his family's name—"

"I won't have him maligned!" Waring burst out furiously.

"You've had your turn," Thomas Bowman bellowed. "Now I want to hear Swift."

"His name isn't—"

"Let him speak," Westcliff said, his cold voice settling the rising ferment.

Matthew gave the earl a short nod of thanks. His attention was diverted as Daisy resumed her place in the nearby chair. She inched the piece of furniture closer until his right leg was half-concealed in the folds of her skirts.

"I went with Harry to Boston Latin," Matthew continued, "and then to Harvard. I slept in the servants' quarters in the basement. I studied his friends' lecture notes for the classes Harry had missed and I wrote papers for him—"

"That's a lie!" Waring cried. "*You,* who had been educated by ancient nuns at an orphanage— you're mad to think anyone would believe you."

Matthew allowed himself one mocking smile. "I learned more from those ancient nuns than Harry did from a string of private tutors. Harry said he didn't need an education since he had a name and money. But I had neither, and my only chance was to learn as much as possible in the hopes of climbing up some day."

"Climb up to *where?*" Waring asked in patent disdain. "You were a servant—an *Irish* servant— you had no hope of becoming a gentleman."

A curious half-smile crossed Daisy's face. "But that is precisely what he did in New York, Mr. Waring. Matthew earned a place for himself in business and society—and he most certainly became a gentleman."

"Under the guise of a false identity," Waring shot back. "He's a fraud, don't you see?"

"No," Daisy replied, looking straight at Matthew, her eyes bright and dark. "I see a gentleman."

Matthew wanted to kiss her feet. Instead he dragged his gaze away from her and continued. "I did everything I could to keep Harry at Harvard, while he seemed hell-bent on earning expulsion. The drinking and gaming and . . ."

Matthew hesitated as he reminded himself that there were ladies present. ". . . other things," he continued, "became worse. The monthly expenditures far outstripped his allowance, and the gambling debt grew to such unmanageable proportions that even Harry began to worry. He was afraid of the repercussions he would face once his father learned the extent of his trouble. Being Harry, he looked for the easy way out. Which explains the holiday at home when the safe was robbed. I knew at once Harry had done it."

"Poisonous lies," Waring spat.

"Harry pointed the finger at me," Matthew said, "rather than admit he had robbed the safe to take care of his debts. He had decided I would have to be sacrificed so he could save his own skin. Naturally the family took their son's word over mine."

"Your guilt was proven in court," Waring said harshly.

"*Nothing* was proven." Anger bolted through

Matthew, and his breath deepened as he struggled for control. He felt Daisy's hand seeking his, and he took it. His grip was too tight, but he couldn't seem to moderate it.

"The trial was a farce," Matthew said. "It was rushed to keep the papers from reporting too closely on the case. My court-appointed lawyer literally slept through most of it. There was no evidence to connect me to the theft. A servant of one of Harry's classmates had come forward with the claim that he'd overheard Harry and two friends plotting to incriminate me, but he was too afraid to testify."

Seeing that Daisy's fingers were turning white from the pressure of his, Matthew forced his hand to loosen. His thumb brushed gently over the points of her knuckles. "I had a stroke of luck," he continued more quietly, "when a reporter for the *Daily Advertiser* wrote an article exposing Harry's past gambling debts, and revealing that those same debts had coincidentally been cleared right after the robbery. As a result of the article there was a growing public outcry at the obvious travesty of the proceedings."

"And yet you were still convicted?" Lillian asked in outrage.

Matthew smiled wryly. "Justice may be blind," he said, "but it loves the sound of money. The Warings were too powerful, and I was a penniless servant."

"How did you escape?" Daisy asked.

The shadow of a bitter smile lingered. "That was

as much a surprise to me as it was to everyone else. I had been loaded in the prison wagon—it left for the state prison before the sun had come up. The wagon stopped on an empty stretch of road. Suddenly the door was unlocked, and I was pulled outside by a half-dozen men. I assumed I was going to be lynched. But they said they were sympathetic citizens determined to right a wrong. They set me free—the guards of the prison wagon put up no resistance—and I was given a horse. I made it to New York, sold the horse, and started a new life."

"Why did you choose the name Swift?" Daisy asked.

"By that time I had learned the power of a well-respected name. And the Swifts are a large family with many branches, which I thought would make it easier to get by without close scrutiny."

Thomas Bowman spoke then, threatened pride cutting him to the quick. "Why did you come to me for a position? Did you think to make a dupe of me?"

Matthew looked directly at him, remembering his first impression of Thomas Bowman . . . a powerful man willing to give him a chance, too preoccupied with his business to ask probing questions. Canny, bull-headed, flawed, single-minded . . . the most influential masculine figure in Matthew's life.

"Never," Matthew said sincerely. "I admired what you had accomplished. I wanted to learn from you. And I . . ." His throat tightened. ". . . I came to regard you with respect and gratitude, and the greatest affection."

Bowman's face reddened with relief, and he nodded slightly, his eyes glittering.

Waring had the look of a man undone, his composure shattering like cheap glass. He glared at Matthew with quivering hatred. "You're trying to soil my son's memory with your lies," he said. "I won't allow it. You assumed if you came to a foreign country no one would—"

"His memory?" Matthew looked up alertly, stunned. "Harry is dead?"

"Because of you! After the trial there were rumors, lies, doubts that never disappeared. Harry's friends avoided him. The stain on his honor—it ruined his life. If you had admitted your guilt—if you had served the time you owed—Harry would still be with me. But people's filthy suspicions built over time, and living in that shadow caused Harry to drink and live recklessly."

"From all appearances," Lillian said sardonically, "your son was already doing that before the trial."

Lillian had a singular talent for pushing people over the edge. Waring was no exception.

"He's a convicted criminal!" Waring charged toward her. "How dare you believe him over me!"

Westcliff reached them in three strides, but Matthew had already moved in front of Lillian, protecting her from Waring's wrath.

"Mr. Waring," Daisy said in the tumult, "please

collect yourself. Surely you can see that you're doing your own cause no good with this behavior." Her calm lucidity seemed to reach through his fury.

Waring gave Daisy an oddly beseeching stare. "My son is dead. Phaelan is to blame."

"This won't bring him back," she said quietly. "It won't serve his memory."

"It will bring me peace," Waring cried.

Daisy's expression was grave, her gaze pitying. "Are you certain of that?"

They could all see it didn't matter. He was beyond reason.

"I've waited many years and traveled thousands of miles for this moment," Waring said. "I won't be denied. You've seen the papers, Westcliff. Even you are not above the law. The constables are under orders to use force if necessary. You will surrender him to me now, tonight."

"I don't think so." Westcliff's eyes were as hard as rock. "It would be madness to travel on a night like this. Spring storms in Hampshire can be violent and unpredictable. You will stay the night at Stony Cross Park while I consider what is to be done."

The constables looked vaguely relieved at this suggestion, as no sensible man would want to venture into the deluge.

"And give Phaelan the opportunity to escape once again?" Waring asked contemptuously. "No. You will hand him into my custody."

"You have my word he will not flee," Westcliff said readily.

"Your word is useless to me," Waring retorted. "It is obvious you have taken his side."

An English gentleman's word was everything. It was the highest possible insult to distrust it. Matthew was surprised Westcliff didn't detonate on the spot. His taut cheeks vibrated with outrage.

"Now you've done it," Lillian muttered, sounding rather awestruck. Even in her worst arguments with her husband, she had never dared to impugn his honor.

"You will remove this man," Westcliff told Waring in a lethal tone, "over my dead body."

In that moment Matthew realized the situation had gone far enough. He saw Waring's hand dip into his coat pocket, the fabric sagging with some heavy object, and he saw the butt of a pistol. Of course. A gun was sound insurance in the event the constables proved ineffective.

"Wait," Matthew said. He would say or do whatever was necessary to keep the pistol from being brought out. Once that happened, the confrontation would escalate to a degree of danger from which it would be impossible for anyone to back down. "I'll go with you." He stared at Waring, willing him to relax. "The process has been set in motion. God knows I can't avoid it."

"No," Daisy cried, throwing her arms around his neck. "You won't be safe with him."

"We'll leave right now," Matthew told Waring,

while he carefully disengaged Daisy's grasp and pushed her behind the shield of his body.

"I can't allow—" Westcliff began.

Matthew interrupted firmly. "It's better this way." He wanted the half-crazed Waring and the two constables away from Stony Cross Park. "I'll go with them, and everything will be resolved in London. This isn't the time or place for dispute."

The earl swore quietly. An able tactician, Westcliff understood that for the moment he did not have the upper hand. This was not a battle that could be won by brute force. It would require money, legalities, and political wire-pulling.

"I'm coming to London with you," Westcliff said curtly.

"Impossible," Waring replied. "The carriage seats four. It will accommodate only myself, the constables, and the prisoner."

"I will follow in my carriage."

"I will accompany you," Thomas Bowman said decisively.

Westcliff pulled Matthew aside, keeping his hand on his shoulder in a brotherly clasp as he spoke quietly. "I know the Bow Street magistrate quite well. I will see that you are brought before him as soon as we reach London—and at my request you will be discharged at once. We will stay at my private residence while we wait for a formal requisition from the American ambassador. In the meantime I will assemble a regiment of lawyers and every bit of political influence at my disposal."

Matthew could barely trust himself to speak. "Thank you," he managed.

"My lord," Daisy whispered, "will they succeed in extraditing Matthew?"

Westcliff's features hardened in arrogant certainty. "Absolutely not."

Daisy let out a huff of unsteady laughter. "Well," she said, "I am willing to take your word, my lord, even if Mr. Waring is not."

"By the time I'm finished with Waring . . ." Westcliff muttered, and shook his head. "Pardon. I will tell the servants to ready my carriage."

As the earl strode away, Daisy stared up into Matthew's face. "There's so much I understand now," she said. "Why you didn't want to tell me."

"Yes, I—" His voice was hoarse. "I knew it was wrong. I knew I would lose you when you found out."

"You didn't think I would understand?" Daisy asked gravely.

"You don't know how it was before. No one would believe me. The facts didn't matter. And having gone through that, I couldn't believe anyone would ever have faith in my innocence."

"Matthew," she said simply, "I will always believe everything you tell me."

"Why?" he whispered.

"Because I love you."

The words devastated him. "You don't have to say that. You don't—"

"I love you," Daisy insisted, gripping his waist-coat in her hands. "I should have said it before—I wanted to wait until you trusted me enough to stop hiding your past from me. But now that I know the worst—" She paused with a wry smile. "This *is* the worst, isn't it? There's nothing else you want to confess?"

Matthew nodded dazedly. "Yes. No. This is it."

Her expression turned shy. "Aren't you going to say you love me, too?"

"I haven't the right," he said. "Not until this is resolved. Not until my name is—"

"Tell me," Daisy said, jerking his coat a little.

"I love you," Matthew muttered. Holy hell, it felt good to say it to her.

She tugged again, this time as a gesture of possession, an assertion. Matthew resisted, his hands coming to her elbows, feeling the heat of her skin through the damp fabric of her dress. Despite the inappropriateness of the situation, his body pulsed with desire. *Daisy, I don't want to leave you . . .*

"I'm coming to London too," he heard her murmur.

"No. Stay here with your sister. I don't want you to be part of this."

"A bit late for that now, isn't it? As your fiancée I have more than a passing interest in the outcome."

Matthew lowered his head over hers, his mouth lightly touching her hair. "It will be more difficult for me if you're there," he said quietly. "I need to know you're safe here in Hampshire." Taking her hands from his waistcoat, he brought her fingers to his lips and kissed them ardently. "Go to the well for me tomorrow," he whispered. "I'm going to need another five-dollar wish."

Her fingers tightened on his. "I'd better make it ten."

Matthew turned as he became aware of someone approaching from behind. It was the pair of constables, looking disgruntled. "It's procedure for lawbreakers to wear 'andcuffs while they're being transported to Bow Street," one of them said. He gave Daisy an accusing glance. "Pardon, miss, but what did you do with the cuffs that was removed from Mr. Phelan?"

Daisy looked back at him innocently. "I gave them to a maidservant. I'm afraid she's very forgetful. She probably misplaced them."

"Where should we start looking?" the officer asked with a puff of impatience.

Her expression did not change as she replied, "I would suggest a thorough search of all the chamberpots."

Chapter 19

Because of the hasty nature of their departure, Marcus and Bowman brought few personal effects aside from a quickly packed change of clothes and the most basic toiletries. Sitting in opposite seats of the family carriage, they engaged in very little conversation. Wind and rain battered the vehicle, and Marcus thought with concern about the driver and horses.

It was foolhardy to travel in this weather, but Marcus was damned if he would let Matthew Swift . . . Phaelan . . . be whisked away from Stony Cross with no protection whatsoever. And it was obvious that Wendell Waring's quest for vengeance had reached an irrational extreme.

Daisy had been astute in her remarks to Waring, that making someone else pay for the crime that

Harry had committed would neither bring his son back nor serve his memory. But in Waring's mind this was the last thing he could do for his son. And perhaps he had convinced himself that putting Matthew in prison would prove Harry's innocence.

Harry Waring had tried to sacrifice Matthew to cover up his own corruption. Marcus wasn't about to allow Wendell Waring to succeed where his son had failed.

"Do you doubt him?" Thomas Bowman asked suddenly. He looked more troubled than Marcus had ever seen him. No doubt this was acutely painful for Bowman, who loved Matthew Swift like a son. Possibly even more than his own sons. It was no wonder the two had formed a strong bond— Swift, a fatherless young man, and Bowman, in need of someone to guide and mentor.

"Are you asking if I doubt Swift? Not in the slightest. I found his version infinitely more believable than Waring's."

"So did I. And I know Swift's character. I can assure you that in all my dealings with him, he has always been principled and honest to a fault."

Marcus smiled slightly. "Can one be honest to a fault?"

Bowman shrugged, and his mustache twitched with reluctant amusement. "Well . . . extreme honesty can sometimes be a business liability."

A crack of lighting came uncomfortably close, causing Marcus's nape to prickle in warning. "This is madness," he muttered. "They'll have to stop at a tavern soon, if they can even make it past the Hampshire border. A few of the local creeks are stronger than some rivers. Given enough headwater surge, the roads will be impassable."

"God, I hope so," Thomas Bowman said fervently. "Nothing would delight me more than to see Waring and those two bumbling idiots being forced to return to Stony Cross Manor with Swift."

The carriage slowed and came to an abrupt halt, the rain pounding like fists against the lacquered exterior.

"What's this?" Bowman lifted the curtain to peer outside the window, but could see nothing except blackness and water pouring down the glass.

"Damn it," Marcus said.

A panicked thumping at the door, and it was wrenched open. The driver's white face appeared. With his black top hat and cloak blending into the gloom, he looked like a disembodied head. "Milord," he gasped, "there's been an accident ahead—ye must come see—"

Marcus sprang out of the carriage, a shock of cold rain striking him with stunning force. He yanked the carriage lantern from its holder and followed the driver to a creek crossing just ahead.

"Christ," Marcus whispered.

The carriage carrying Waring and Matthew had stopped on a simple wooden beam bridge, one side of which had twisted away from the bank and was now angled diagonally across the creek. The force of the raging current had collapsed part of the bridge, leaving the carriage's back wheels half-submerged in the water while the team of horses struggled in vain to pull it out. Swaying back and forth in the water like a child's toy, the bridge threatened to detach from the other bank.

There was no way to reach the stranded carriage. The bridge had broken away on the side closest to them, and it would be suicidal to try and cross the current.

"My God, no," he heard Thomas Bowman exclaim in horror.

They could only watch helplessly as the driver of Waring's carriage fought to save the team, frantically unbuckling straps from carriage shafts.

At the same time, the uppermost door of the sinking carriage was pushed open, and a figure began to crawl out with obvious difficulty.

"Is it Swift?" Bowman demanded, going as close to the bank as he dared. "Swift!" But his bellow was swallowed in the crash of the storm and the roar of the current, and the angry creaks of the disintegrating bridge.

Then everything seemed to happen at once. The horses stumbled off the bridge to the safety of the bank. Movement on the bridge, a dark figure or two, and with a chilling, almost majestic slowness the heavy carriage eased into the water. It half-sank, retaining marginal buoyancy for a few moments . . . but then the carriage lanterns were extinguished, and the vehicle drifted sideways as the raging current swept it downstream.

* * *

Daisy had slept only fitfully, unable to stop her racing thoughts. She had woken repeatedly in the night, wondering what would happen to Matthew. She was afraid for his well-being. Only the knowledge that Westcliff was with him—or at least close by—kept her reasonably calm.

She kept reliving the moments in the parlor when Matthew had finally revealed the secrets of his past. How vulnerable and alone he had looked. What a burden he had carried all these years . . . and what courage and imagination it had taken for him to reinvent himself.

Daisy knew she wasn't going to be able to wait in Hampshire for very long. She wanted desperately to see Matthew, to reassure him, to defend him against the world if necessary.

Earlier in the evening Mercedes had asked Daisy if the revelations about Matthew had affected her decision to marry him.

"Yes," Daisy had replied. "It's made me even more determined than before."

Lillian had joined the conversation, admitting that she was far more predisposed to like Matthew Swift after what they had learned about him. "Although," she had added, "it would be rather nice to know what your future married name is going to be."

"Oh, what's in a name?" Daisy had quoted, pulling a piece of paper from a lap desk and fidgeting with it.

"What are you doing?" Lillian had asked. "Don't say you're going to write a letter *now*?"

"I don't know what to do," Daisy had admitted. "I think I should send word to Annabelle and Evie."

"They'll find out soon enough from Westcliff," Lillian said. "And they won't be one bit surprised."

"Why do you say that?"

"With your fondness for stories with dramatic twists and characters with mysterious pasts, it's a foregone conclusion you wouldn't have a quiet, ordinary courtship."

"Be that as it may," Daisy had replied wryly, "a quiet, ordinary courtship sounds *very* appealing at the moment."

After a restless sleep, Daisy awakened in the morning as someone entered the room. At first she assumed it was the maid come to light the grate, but it was too early. Daybreak had not yet arrived, and the rain had slowed to a sullen drizzle.

It was her sister.

"Good morning," Daisy croaked, sitting up and stretching. "Why are you up so early? Is the baby fretful?"

"No, she's resting." Lillian's voice was husky. Wearing a heavy velvet robe, her hair in a loose braid, she came to the bed with a steaming cup of tea in hand. "Here, take this."

Daisy frowned and obeyed, watching as Lillian levered herself onto the edge of the mattress. This was not the usual pattern of things.

Something had happened.

"What is it?" she asked, a feeling of dread crawling down her spine.

Lillian nodded toward the tea cup. "It can wait until you're a bit more awake."

It was too soon for any news to have come from London, Daisy reflected. This couldn't have anything to do with Matthew. Maybe their mother had taken ill. Maybe something dreadful had happened in the village.

After downing a few swallows of tea, Daisy leaned over to set the cup on the bedside table. She returned her attention to her sister. "This is as awake as I'm going to get today," she said. "Tell me now."

Clearing her throat roughly, Lillian spoke in a thick voice. "Westcliff and Father are back."

"What?" Daisy stared at her in bewilderment. "Why aren't they in London with Matthew?"

"He's not in London either."

"Then they're all back?"

Lillian gave a stiff little shake of her head. "No. I'm sorry. I'm explaining badly. I . . . I'll just be blunt. Not long after Westcliff and Father left Stony Cross, their carriage had to stop because of an accident ahead at the bridge. You know that creaky old bridge you have to cross to stay on the main road?"

"The one that spans the little creek?"

"Yes. Well, the creek isn't little right now. Thanks to the storm, it's a big rushing river. And apparently the bridge was weakened by the current, and when Mr. Waring's carriage tried to cross, it collapsed."

Daisy froze in confusion. *The bridge collapsed.* She repeated the words to herself, but they seemed as impossible to interpret as some ancient forgotten language. With an effort, she gathered her wits. "Was everyone saved?" she heard herself ask.

"Everyone but Matthew." Lillian's voice shook. "He was trapped in the carriage as it was swept downstream."

"He's all right," Daisy said automatically, her heart beginning to thrash like a caged wild animal. "He can swim. He probably ended up downstream on one of the banks—someone has to look for him—"

"They're searching everywhere," Lillian said. "Westcliff is organizing a full-scale effort. He spent most of the night searching and returned a little while ago. The carriage broke into pieces as it went downstream. No sign of Matthew. But Daisy, one of the constables admitted to Westcliff . . ." She stopped and her brown eyes sparkled with furious tears. ". . . admitted . . ." She continued with effort. ". . . that Matthew's hands were tied."

Daisy's legs moved beneath the bedclothes, her knees bending, drawing up tight. Her body wanted to occupy as little physical space as possible, shrinking away from this new revelation.

"But why?" she whispered. "There was no reason."

Lillian's determined jaw quivered as she tried to

regain control over her emotions. "Given Matthew's history, they said there was a risk of escape. But I think Waring insisted on it out of spite."

Daisy felt lightheaded from the thunder of her own pulse. She was frightened, and yet at the same time part of her had become bizarrely detached. Briefly she summoned an image of Matthew, struggling in dark water, his hands bound and thrashing—

"*No,*" she said, pressing her palms against the violent throb of her temples. It felt as if nails were being driven into her skull. She couldn't breathe well. "He had no chance, did he?"

Lillian shook her head and looked away. Drops of water fell from her face to the counterpane.

How strange, Daisy thought, that she wasn't crying too. Hot pressure built behind her eyes, deep in her head, making her skull ache. But it seemed her tears were waiting for some thought or word that would trigger their release.

Daisy continued to hold her pounding temples, nearly blind from the pain in her head as she asked, "Are you crying for Matthew?"

"Yes." Lillian pulled a handkerchief from the sleeve of her robe and blew her nose roughly. "But mostly for you." She leaned close enough to wrap her arms around Daisy, as if she could protect her from all harm. "I love you, Daisy."

"I love you, too," Daisy said in a muffled voice, hurting and dry-eyed, and gasping for breath.

* * *

The search continued all that day and the next night, but all the ordinary rituals, the times for sleeping and working and eating, had lost their meaning. Only one incident managed to reach through the numb weight that pressed at Daisy from all sides, and that was when Westcliff had refused to let her come help in the search.

"You'll be of no use to anyone," Westcliff had told her, too exhausted and bedeviled to exercise his usual tact. "It's dangerous and difficult out there with the water so high. At best you'll be a distraction. At worst, you'll get hurt."

Daisy had known he was right, but that didn't stop a flare of outrage. The feeling, startling in its force, threatened to disintegrate her control, and so she had hurriedly withdrawn back into herself.

Matthew's body might never be found. That was too cruel to bear, the fate of having to reconcile herself to that. Somehow a disappearance was even worse than a death—it was as if he had never existed at all, leaving nothing to mourn over. She had never understood before why some people needed to see the body of a loved one after they had died. Now she did. It was the only way to end this waking nightmare and perhaps find the release of tears and pain.

"I keep thinking I should know if he were dead," she told Lillian as she sat on the floor next to the parlor hearth. An old shawl was wrapped around her, comforting in its time-worn softness. Despite the heat of the fire, the layers of her clothing, the mug of brandied tea in her hands, Daisy couldn't seem to get warm. "I should feel it. But I can't feel anything, it's as if I've been frozen alive. I want to hide somewhere. I don't want to bear this. I don't want to strong."

"You don't have to be," Lillian said quietly.

"Yes I do. Because the only other choice is to let myself break into a million pieces."

"I'll hold you together. Every single piece."

A paper-thin smile touched Daisy's lips as she stared into her sister's concerned face. "Lillian," she whispered. "What would I do without you?"

"You'll never have to find out."

It was only the prodding of her mother and sister that induced Daisy to take a few bites of supper. She drank a full glass of wine, hoping it would distract her from the endless circling of her mind.

"Westcliff and Father should be back soon," Lillian said tensely. "They've had no rest and likely nothing to eat."

"Let's go to the parlor," Mercedes suggested. "We can distract ourselves with cards, or perhaps you might read aloud from one of Daisy's favorite books."

Daisy gave her an apologetic glance. "I'm sorry, I can't. If you wouldn't mind, I'd like to be alone upstairs."

After she had washed and changed into her nightclothes, Daisy glanced at the bed. Even though she was tipsy and weary, her mind rejected the notion of sleep.

The house was quiet as she went to the Marsden parlor, her bare feet touching shadows that crossed the carpeted floor like dark vines. A single lamp sent a yellow glow through the parlor, light catching in faceted crystals that hung from the shade and sending scattered dots of white over the flower-papered walls. A pile of printed flotsam and jetsam had been left by the settee: periodicals, novels, a thin volume of humorous poetry she had read aloud to Matthew, watching for the elusive smiles on his face.

How was it that everything had changed so quickly? How could life so cavalierly pick someone up and set them on a new and violently unwanted path?

Daisy sat on the carpet beside the pile and began to sort through it slowly . . . one pile to be brought to the library, another to be taken to the villagers on visiting day. But perhaps it wasn't wise to attempt this after so much wine. Instead of forming two neat piles, the reading materials ended up scattered around her like so many abandoned dreams.

Crossing her legs, Daisy leaned against the side of the settee and rested her head on the upholstered edge. Her fingers encountered the cloth covering on one of the books. She glanced at it with half-closed eyes. A book had always been a door to another world . . . a world much more interesting and fantastical than reality. But she had finally discovered that life could be even more wonderful than a fantasy.

And that love could fill the real world with magic.

Matthew was everything she had ever wanted. And she'd had so little time with him.

The mantel clock rationed quiet little *ticks* with miserly slowness. As Daisy leaned against the settee half-drowsing, she heard the door creak. Her sluggish gaze followed the sound.

A man had entered the room.

He paused just inside the doorway, contemplating the sight of her on the floor with all the discarded books around her.

Daisy's eyes lifted jerkily to his face. She froze with longing and fear and terrible yearning.

It was Matthew, dressed in rough, unfamiliar clothing, his vital presence seeming to fill the room.

Afraid the vision would disappear, Daisy was as still as death. Her eyes stung and watered but she kept them open, willing him to stay.

He approached her with great care. Sinking to his haunches, he contemplated her with immeasurable tenderness and concern. One of his big hands moved, shoving aside some of the books until the space between their bodies was clear. "It's me, love," he said softly. "Everything's all right."

Daisy managed to whisper through dry lips. "If you're a ghost . . . I hope you haunt me forever."

Matthew sat on the floor and reached for her cold hands. "Would a ghost use the door?" he asked gently, bringing her fingers to his scratched, battered face.

The touch of his skin against her palms sent a dance of painful awareness through her. With relief Daisy finally felt the numbness thaw, her emotions unlocking, and she tried to cover her eyes. Her chest seemed to break open with sobs, the sounds raw and unrestrained.

Matthew took her hand away and pulled her firmly against him, murmuring quietly. As Daisy continued to cry he held her more tightly, seeming to understand that she needed the hard, almost hurtful pressure of his body.

"Please be real," she gasped. "Please don't be a dream."

"I'm real," Matthew said huskily. "Don't cry so hard, there's no—oh, Daisy, love—" He gripped her head in his hands and pressed comforting words against her lips while she struggled to get even closer to him. He eased her to the floor, using the reassuring weight of his body to subdue her.

His hands clasped with hers, fingers interlaced. Panting, Daisy turned her head to stare at his exposed wrist, where the flesh was red and welted. "Your hands were tied," she said in a rough voice that didn't sound at all like ers. "How did you free them?"

Matthew bent his head to kiss the tear-slicked surface of her cheek. "Pen-knife," he said succinctly.

Daisy's eyes widened as she continued to stare at his wrist. "You managed to get a pen-knife out of your pocket and cut the ropes while floating down the creek in a s-sinking carriage?"

"It was a damn sight easier than goose-wrestling, let me tell you."

A watery chuckle escaped her, but it quickly turned into another broken sob. Matthew caught the sound with his mouth, his lips caressing hers.

"I started to cut through the ties at the first sign of trouble," he continued. "And I had a few minutes before the carriage rolled into the water."

"Why didn't the others help you?" Daisy asked angrily, scrubbing the sleeve of her gown over her dripping face.

"They were busy saving their own skins. Although," Matthew added ruefully, "I would have thought I merited a little more importance than the horses. But by the time the carriage started moving down the current, my hands were free. Debris was knocking the vehicle into matchsticks. I jumped into the current and made it to the shore, but I was bit pummeled in the process. I was found by an old man who was out searching for his dog— he brought me to his cottage, where he and his wife took care of me. I lost consciousness and woke up a day and a half later. By that time they had heard of Westcliff's search, and they went out to tell him where I was."

"I thought you were gone," Daisy said, her voice cracking. "I thought I would never see you again."

"No, no . . ." Matthew smoothed her hair and

kissed her cheeks, her eyes, her trembling lips. "I'll always come back to you. I'm dependable, remember?"

"Yes. Except for the—" Daisy had to take an extra breath as she felt his mouth move down to her throat. "—the twenty years of your life before I met you, I'd say you're so dependable you're almost pre—" His tongue had dipped into the pulsing hollow at the base of her neck. "—predictable."

"You probably have a few complaints about that little matter of my assumed identity and grand larceny conviction." His exploring kisses moved up to the delicate line of her jaw, absorbing the vagrant tear.

"Oh, no," Daisy said breathlessly. "I f-forgave you before I even knew what it was."

"Sweet darling," Matthew whispered, nuzzling the side of her face, caressing her with his mouth and hands. She held onto him blindly, unable to get close enough. His head drew back and he looked down at her with a searching gaze. "Now that the whole business has reared its ugly head, I'm going to have to clear my name. Will you wait for me, Daisy?"

"No."

Still sniffling, she applied herself to unfastening the wooden buttons of his borrowed clothes.

"No?" Matthew half-smiled and looked down at her quizzically. "Have you decided I'm too much trouble?"

"I've decided life is too short—" Daisy grunted

as she tugged at the coarse cloth of his shirt. "—to waste a single day of it. Blast these buttons—"

His hands covered hers, stilling their feverish plucking. "I don't think your family is going to be enthusiastic about letting you marry a fugitive from justice."

"My father would forgive you anything. Besides, you won't be a fugitive forever. Your case will be overturned once the facts are made known." Daisy pulled her hands free and clutched at him tightly. "Take me to Gretna Green," she begged. "Tonight. It's how my sister got married. And Evie too. Elopement is practically a wallflower tradition. Take me—"

"Shhh . . ." Matthew wrapped his arms around her, cradling her against his sturdy frame. "No more running," he whispered. "I'm finally going to face my past. Although it would be a hell of a lot easier to solve my problems if that bastard Harry Waring hadn't died."

"There are still people who know what really happened," Daisy said anxiously. "His friends. And the servant you mentioned. And—"

"Yes, I know. Let's not talk about all of that right now. God knows we'll have time aplenty in the coming days."

"I want to marry you," Daisy persisted. "Not later. Now. After what I've gone through . . . thinking you were gone forever . . . nothing else is important." A little hiccup disrupted the last word.

Matthew smoothed her hair and smudged a

drying tear-track with his thumb. "All right. All right. I'll talk to your father. Don't cry again. Daisy, don't."

But she couldn't stop the fresh tears of relief that leaked from the outward corners of her eyes. A new trembling came from the marrow of her bones. The more she stiffened against it, the worse it became.

"Sweetheart, what is it?" He ran his hands over her shaking limbs.

"I'm so afraid."

He made a low, involuntary sound and cradled her tightly, his lips moving over her cheeks with impassioned pressure. "Why, dearest love?"

"I'm afraid this is a dream. I'm afraid I'll wake up and—" Another hiccup. "—and I'll be alone again and I'll find out you were never here and—"

"No, I'm here. I won't leave." He moved down to her throat, pulling the sides of her nightgown apart with slow deliberation. "Let me make you feel better, love, let me . . ." His hands were gentle on her body, soothing and distracting. As his palm slid over her limbs, his touch sent darts of heat through her, and a low moan broke from her lips.

Hearing the sound, Matthew drew a ragged breath and searched for self-control. He found none. There was only need. Lost in the desire to fill her with pleasure, he undressed her right there on the floor, his palms stroking her chilled skin until the pale surface was steeped in a severe blush.

Trembling wildly, Daisy watched the candlelight

shimmer over his dark head as he bent over her body, scattering kisses in unhurried paths . . . her legs, her bare stomach, her quivering breasts.

Everywhere he kissed her, the cold shaking dissolved into warmth. She sighed and relaxed into the assuaging rhythms of his hands and mouth. As she fumbled to open his shirt, he reached to help her. The rough-woven cloth dropped away to reveal satiny male skin. Somehow it reassured Daisy to see the the shadows of bruises on him, they were proof that she couldn't be dreaming. She pressed her open mouth to one of the dark marks, touching it with her tongue.

Matthew drew her carefully against him, his hand riding over the curve of her waist and hip with a sensuality that caused gooseflesh to rise on her thighs. Daisy squirmed in mingled pleasure and discomfort as the wool pile of the carpet abraded her oversensitive skin, causing speckles of pain on her bare bottom.

Comprehending the problem, Matthew laughed quietly and pulled her up against him, into his lap. Perspiring and dry-mouthed, Daisy urged her breasts against his chest. "Don't stop," she whispered.

His hand cupped over her tingling backside. "You'll be rubbed raw on the floor."

"I don't care, I just want . . . I want . . ."

"This?" He rearranged her in his lap until she straddled him, the fabric of his trousers taut beneath her thighs.

Embarrassed and excited, Daisy closed her eyes

as she felt him caress the intricate folds of her body, gently layering moisture and sensation over her burning flesh.

Daisy's arms felt weak as she slid them around his neck and wrapped the fingers of one hand around the wrist of the other. If it weren't for the support of his hard arm across her back, she wouldn't have been able to stay upright. All awareness was focused on the place where he touched her, the slide of his knuckle around the tiny silky-wet cusp . . . "Don't stop," she heard herself whisper again.

Her eyes snapped open as Matthew eased two fingers inside her, and then three, while desire writhed inside her like flames feeding on burning honey.

"Still afraid it's a dream?" Matthew whispered.

She swallowed convulsively and shook her head. "I . . . I never have dreams like this."

The corners of his eyes crinkled with amusement, and he withdrew his fingers, leaving her shuddering with emptiness. She whimpered and dropped her head on his flexing shoulder, and he hugged her securely against his naked chest.

Daisy clung to him, her vision misting until the room was a mosaic of yellow light and black shadow. She felt herself being lifted, turned, her knees pressing into the carpet as he helped her to kneel before the settee. The side of her face pressed against the smooth upholstery, while her lips parted to accomodate her hard-rushing breaths. He covered her, his big, solid body fitting behind and around her, and then he was pushing inside, and the fit between them was tight and slippery and exquisite.

Daisy stiffened in surprise, but his hands came to her hips, stroking in reassurance, encouraging her to trust him. She went still, her eyes closing while pleasure rose with each slow thrust he made. One of his hands swept down her front, and his fingertips found the plump rise of her sex and caressed her until she reached a bright blinding summit, overtaken with shudders of sharp relief.

Much later, Matthew dressed Daisy in her nightgown and carried her through the dark hallway until they reached her room. As he lay her in bed, she whispered for him to stay with her.

"No, love." He leaned over her prone body in the darkness. "Much as I'd like to, we can't go *that* far beyond propriety."

"I don't want to sleep without you." Daisy stared into the shadowed face just above her own. "And I don't want to wake without you."

"Someday." He bent to press a firm kiss on her mouth. "Someday I'll be able to come to you any time, night or day, and hold you as long as you want." His voice deepened with emotion as he added, "You can depend on that."

Downstairs, the exhausted earl of Westcliff lay on a sofa, his head pillowed in his wife's lap. After two days of relentless searching and precious little sleep, Marcus was weary down to his bones. However, he was grateful that tragedy had been avoided and that Daisy's fiance had been safely returned.

Marcus was a bit surprised by the way his wife had fussed over him. As soon as he had arrived at the manor, Lillian had plied him with sandwiches and hot brandy, wiped the dirt smudges from his face with a damp towel, applied salve on his scrapes and bandages to a few cut fingers, and even pulled his muddy boots off.

"You look far worse than Mr. Swift," Lillian had retorted when he had protested that he was fine. "From what I understand he's been lying abed in a cottage for the past two days, whereas you've been foraging through the woods in the mud and rain."

"He wasn't exactly lounging about," Marcus had pointed out. "He was wounded."

"That doesn't change the fact that *you've* had no rest and practically nothing to eat while you were looking for him."

Marcus had submitted to her attentions, secretly enjoying the way she hovered over him. When she was satisfied that he was fed and bandaged properly, she cradled his head in her lap. Marcus sighed in contentment, staring into the blazing hearth-fire.

Lillian's slender fingers played absently in his hair as she commented, "It's been a long time since Mr. Swift went to find Daisy. And it's too quiet. Aren't you going to go up there and check on them?"

"Not for all the hemp in China," Marcus said,

repeating one of Daisy's new favorite phrases. "God knows what I might be interrupting."

"Good God." Lillian sounded appalled. "You don't think they're . . ."

"I wouldn't be surprised." Marcus paused deliberately before adding, "Remember how we used to be."

As he had intended, the remark diverted her instantly.

"We're still that way," Lillian protested.

"We haven't made love since before the baby was born." Marcus sat up, filling his gaze with the sight of his dark-haired young wife in the firelight. She was, and would always be, the most tempting woman he had ever known. Unspent passion roughened his voice as he asked, "How much longer must I wait?"

Propping her elbow on the back of the sofa, Lillian leaned her head on her hand and smiled apologetically. "The doctor said at least another fortnight. I'm sorry." She laughed as she saw his expression. "*Very* sorry. Let's go upstairs."

"If we're not going to bed together, I fail to see the point," Marcus grumbled.

"I'll help you with your bath. I'll even scrub your back."

He was sufficiently intrigued by the offer to ask, "Only my back?"

"I'm open to negotiation," Lillian said provocatively. "As always."

Marcus reached out to gather her against his

chest and sighed. "At this point I'll take whatever I can get."

"You poor man." Still smiling, Lillian turned her face to kiss him. "Just remember . . . some things are worth waiting for."

Epilogue

As it turned out, Matthew and Daisy were not wed until late autumn. Hampshire was dressed in scarlet and brilliant orange, the hounds were out four mornings a week, and the last baskets of fruit had been harvested from heavy-laden trees. Now that the hay had been cut, the raucous corn-crakes had left the fields, their clamor replaced by the liquid notes of song-thrushes and the chatter of yellow buntings.

For the entire summer and a good part of autumn, Daisy had endured many separations from Matthew, including the frequent trips to London to manage his legal affairs. With Westcliff's help the extradition requests from the American government were firmly blocked, allowing Matthew to remain in England. After settling on a pair of skillful barristers and acquainting them with the particulars of his case, Matthew had dispatched them to Boston to file with the appeals court.

In the meantime Matthew traveled and worked ceaselessly, overseeing the construction of the Bristol manufactory, hiring employees and setting up distribution channels throughout the country. It seemed to Daisy that Matthew had changed somewhat since the secrets of his past had been revealed . . . he was freer somehow, even more self-assured and charismatic.

Witnessing Matthew's limitless energy and his growing list of accomplishments, Simon Hunt had informed him decisively that any time he tired of working for Bowman's, he was welcome to come to Consolidated Locomotive. That had prompted Thomas Bowman to offer Matthew a higher percentage of the soap company's future profits.

"I'll be a millionaire by the time I'm thirty," Matthew had told Daisy dryly, "if I can just manage to stay out of jail."

It had surprised and touched Daisy that everyone in her family, even her mother, had rallied to Matthew's defense. Whether this was for Daisy's sake or her father's was unclear. Thomas Bowman, who had always been so severe on people, had immediately forgiven Matthew for deceiving him. In fact, Bowman seemed to regard him more than ever before as a de facto son.

"One suspects," Lillian had told Daisy, "that if

Matthew Swift were to commit cold-blooded murder, Father would say on the spot, 'Well, the boy must have had an excellent reason.'"

Discovering that keeping busy helped the time to pass more quickly, Daisy occupied herself with finding a home in Bristol. She decided on a large gabled seaside house that had once belonged to a shipyard owner and his family. Accompanied by her mother and sister, who both liked shopping far more than she did, Daisy purchased large, comfortable pieces of furniture and richly colored window hangings and fabrics. And of course she made certain there were tables and shelves for books in as many rooms as possible.

It helped that Matthew sped to Daisy whenever he could steal away for a few days. There were no constraints between them now, no secrets or fears. As they shared long conversations and walked through the sleepy summer landscape, they found endless delight in each other's company. And on the nights when Matthew came to Daisy in the darkness and made love to her, he filled her senses with infinite pleasure and her heart with joy.

"I've tried so hard to stay away from you," he whispered one night, cuddling her while the moonlight made stripes across the shadowed hills of the bedclothes.

"Why?" Daisy whispered back, crawling over him until she was draped over the muscled surface of his chest.

He played with the dark cascade of her hair. "Because I shouldn't come to you like this until we're married. There's a risk—"

Daisy silenced him with her mouth, not stopping until his breath had hastened and his bare skin was as hot as a stove-plate beneath her. She lifted her head to smile down into his gleaming eyes. "All or nothing," she murmured. "That's how I want you."

Finally word came from Matthew's lawyers that a panel of three Boston judges had examined the trial court records, overturned the conviction, and dismissed the case. They had also ruled that it could not be refiled, thereby defeating any hopes of the Waring family prolonging the ordeal.

Matthew had received the news with a remarkably calm demeanor, accepting everyone's congratulations and earnestly thanking the Bowmans and Westcliffs for their support. It was only in private with Daisy that Matthew's composure had broken, his relief too great to endure stoically. She had given him all the comfort she could, in an exchange so raw and intimate that it would forever remain just between the two of them.

And now it was their wedding day.

The ceremony in the Stony Cross chapel had been unmercifully long, with the vicar determined to impress the crowd of wealthy and important visitors, many of them from London and some from New

York. The service included an interminable sermon, an unheard-of number of hymns and three seat-numbing scripture readings.

Daisy waited patiently in her heavy champagne satin dress, her feet tingling uncomfortably in her beaded heeled slippers. She was half-blinded by the elaborate Valenciennes lace veil sewn with pearls. The wedding had become an exercise in endurance. She did her best to look solemn, but she sneaked a glance at Matthew, tall and handsome in a crisp black morning-coat and a starched white cravat . . . and she felt her heart skip with sudden happiness.

At the conclusion of the vows, despite Mercedes's previous stern admonitions that the groom was *not* to kiss the bride, as the custom was never followed by people in the best society . . . Matthew tugged Daisy up to him and crushed a hard kiss on her lips in full view of everyone. There was a gasp or two, and a ripple of friendly laughter through the crowd.

Daisy glanced up into her husband's sparkling eyes. "You're being scandalous, Mr. Swift," she whispered.

"This is nothing," Matthew replied in an undertone, his expression soft with love. "I'm saving my worst behavior for tonight."

The guests proceeded into the manor. After receiving what seemed like thousands of people, and smiling until her cheeks were sore, Daisy let out a long sigh. Next would come a wedding breakfast that could feed half of England, and then hours of toasts and lingering farewells. And all she wanted was to be alone with her husband.

"Oh, don't complain," came her sister's amused voice from nearby. "One of us had to have a proper wedding. It might as well be you."

Daisy turned to see Lillian and Annabelle and Evie standing behind her. "I wasn't going to complain," she said. "I was only thinking how much easier it would have been to elope to Gretna Green."

"That would have been quite unimaginative, dear, considering that Evie and I both did it before you."

"It was a lovely ceremony," Annabelle said warmly.

"And a long one," came Daisy's rueful rejoinder. "I feel as if I've been standing and talking for hours."

"You have been," Evie told her. "Come with us—we're going to have a wallflower meeting."

"Now?" Daisy asked bemusedly, glancing at her friends' animated countenances. "We can't. They'll be waiting for us at breakfast."

"Oh, let them wait," Lillian said cheerfully. She took Daisy's arm and pulled her out of the main entrance hall.

As the four young women proceeded to a hallway leading toward the morning room, they encountered Lord St. Vincent, who was strolling in the opposite direction. Elegant and dazzling in his formal clothes, he paused and regarded Evie with a caressing smile.

"You appear to be escaping from something," he remarked.

"We are," Evie told her husband.

St. Vincent slid his arm around Evie's waist and asked in a conspiratorial whisper, "Where are you going?"

Evie thought for a moment. "Somewhere to powder Daisy's nose."

The viscount gave Daisy a dubious glance. "It takes all four of you? But it's such a little nose."

"We'll only be a few minutes, my lord," Evie said. "Will you make excuses for us?"

St. Vincent laughed gently. "I have an endless supply, my love," he assured her. Before he let go of his wife, he turned her to face him and kissed her forehead. For the briefest of moments, his graceful hand touched low on her midriff. The subtle gesture went unnoticed by the others.

But Daisy saw, and she knew at once what it meant. *Evie has a secret*, she thought, and smiled.

They took Daisy to the orangery, where warm autumn light glittered through the windows, and the scents of citrus and bay hung thick in the air. Removing Daisy's heavy orange-blossom wreath and veil, Lillian set them aside on a chair.

There was a silver tray on a nearby table, laden with a bottle of chilled champagne and four tall crystal glasses.

"This is a special toast for you, dear," Lillian

said, while Annabelle poured the sparkling liquid and handed the glasses out. "To your happy ending. Since you've had to wait for it longer than the rest of us, I'd say you deserve the entire bottle." She grinned. "But we're going to share it with you anyway."

Daisy curved her fingers around the crystal stem. "It should be a toast for all of us," she said. "After all, three years ago we had the worst marriage prospects imaginable. We couldn't even get an invitation to dance. And look how well things turned out."

"All it t-took was some devious behavior and a few scandals here and there," Evie said with a smile.

"And friendship," Annabelle added.

"To friendship," Lillian said, her voice suddenly husky.

And their four glasses clicked in one perfect moment.

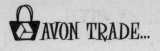